Riding the Rails

Locomotive Lust
and Carnal Cabooses

Visit us at www.boldstrokesbooks.com

RIDING THE RAILS

LOCOMOTIVE LUST
AND CARNAL CABOOSES

edited by

Jerry L. Wheeler

A Division of Bold Strokes Books

2011

RIDING THE RAILS: LOCOMOTIVE LUST AND CARNAL CABOOSES
© 2011 BY BOLD STROKES BOOKS. ALL RIGHTS RESERVED.

ISBN 13: 978-1-60282-586-4

THIS TRADE PAPERBACK ORIGINAL IS PUBLISHED BY
BOLD STROKES BOOKS, INC.
P.O. BOX 249
VALLEY FALLS, NY 12185

FIRST EDITION: DECEMBER 2011

CREDITS
EDITOR: JERRY L. WHEELER
PRODUCTION DESIGN: STACIA SEAMAN
COVER DESIGN BY SHERI (GRAPHICARTIST2020@HOTMAIL.COM)

CONTENTS

INTRODUCTION (OR, THE WOLFMAN THAT ATE ME NEAR CHICAGO)

Okay, I don't *know* that he was a wolfman, but in the darkness of the train at midnight I saw a figure more hair than skin, dressed in a tan trench coat, scarf, slacks, and black boots. His slouch hat was pulled low over his ears and he carried a thick walking stick in his gloved hands— yes, he wore a scarf and gloves on an eighty-seven-degree August night, the air so muggy and thick you could spoon it into your nostrils.

My perceptions might have been skewed, however, by two days of sleep-deprived drunken debauchery aboard the California Zephyr from Denver to Chicago—roomy, air-conditioned coaches full of napping men with unconscious boners and a bar car chock full of horny, half-drunk studs taking progressively unsteadier trips downstairs to the restrooms.

I bagged three down there the first day, let alone the gay couple who took me to their sleeper after we dined together and the scruffy-bearded college kid across the aisle who hauled his cock out of his baggy gray shorts and watched me watching him jack his morning wood while the rest of the car was asleep and his girlfriend was gone in search of coffee. Who needed sleep?

After forty-eight hours, I did—that's who. But when I changed trains at Chicago, the cars were no longer roomy or air-conditioned. They were hot and crowded, even in the middle of the night, with sprung seats and thin, vibrating walls suited more for concussion than comfort should your head happen to loll against them. Determined to try a catnap, I balled up my sweater, leaned against the window, and closed my eyes in futile effort.

We squealed to a stop a half hour out of Chicago, embarking passengers noisily shuffling in the aisle trying to find seats and places to put their bags. That's when the wolfman came aboard. Naturally, he headed for the empty seat next to mine. I watched him through squinched eyes, feigning sleep for fear he'd want to talk to me. I was in no mood for chitchat with a shape-shifter.

Every visible part of his body was covered with hair. His face was obscured by a full beard that seemed to reach up to his eyes, and his bushy eyebrows beetled down the side of his head to meet it. He took off his gloves and put them in his pocket, the backs of his hands thick with fur. That's when his smell hit me—pungent and feral with a topnote of panic, like an animal running through the woods to escape its pursuers.

It almost gagged me at first but the more I smelled it, the more intriguing it became—and, unbelievably, the hornier it made me. My cock was not only stirring, it was well on its way to raging hard. The wolfman sitting beside me seemed to sense his effect, too. I peeked out, not daring to open my eyes further. He was smiling at me.

At least it *looked* like a smile beneath all that fur.

The realization gave me a start, then I felt the pressure of his leg against my shin. He moved over slowly, entwining his leg with mine until I was suffused with his scent, trapped between the wolfman and the wall of the train. My cock strained at the fabric of my jeans, but I kept my head on my sweater and my eyes closed. From my ragged breathing, we both knew I was awake, but I had a feeling whatever was going to happen next would be best experienced unseen.

His scent was really working on me. Loamy, primal, and base, it touched me in places that had never been probed. And then I felt his paw-hand steal over my crotch, exploring the bulge between my legs. I swore I heard a low, growling chuckle as my zipper went down and he gingerly pried my dick out of my jeans. Once it was exposed to the night air and the roughness of his skin as he gently pumped the shaft, it got even harder, if that was humanly possible.

He bent his head over my lap and took me into his mouth, sheathing me with his warm wetness while his heady aroma pervaded my senses. As my orgasm built, I felt I was rushing through the woods by his side, consumed by the pump of our sleek haunches as we galloped past trees and leapt over branches—it didn't matter whether in pursuit or retreat. The run was all that counted.

And suddenly, I exploded. I don't know if I cried out or if anyone was listening or if we were still on the train anymore. I must have shot a gallon of cum into his mouth, but his steady, sucking pressure never wavered. Spent and weary beyond belief, I opened my eyes once, saw I was still in my seat, then fell into the deepest sleep I'd had in two days.

In the morning, he was gone. One of the advantages of supernatural one-night stands is that they never sleep over. They're always done by dawn. My dick was tucked safely inside my jeans once again, but my zipper was at half-mast and my hand was crusted with dried cum. And the seat beside me was covered with a mat of dark brown fur, as if someone had melted a cat there. No one else sat in it for the rest of the trip.

It was probably the smell…

❖

This wolfman is the only shape-shifter aboard our train, but there are plenty of other wild rides to exotic places. Jeff Mann's trip on the "Highland Sleeper" binds and gags an Irish jewel thief for a private investigator's pleasure while Jeffrey Ricker takes us on a Martian train trip to ancient Rome in "Mount Olympus." 'Nathan Burgoine travels back in time for a bittersweet romantic ride in "Elsewhen," and Joseph Baneth Allen also pushes the temporal envelope for very different purposes in "Geronimo's Laughter." You want present-day stories? Rob Rosen scrubs up a hot hobo in "No Mincing Words" while Hank Edwards uses a wedding for a "Reunion on the Rails" and Daniel M. Jaffe explores the lighter (and darker) side of sexual attractiveness in "Resist Me, Please!"

But we haven't forgotten the historical rides. Dusty Taylor saves us a seat at the locomotive races circa 1925 in "The Roundhouse Men," Dale Chase shows us how Victorians did it in "Royal Service," and Jay Neal takes us back for oral sex and murder "One Night on the Twentieth Century."

Erastes and Rick R. Reed give us love stories with a twist in "The

Blue Train" and "The Train Home," respectively, newcomer J.D. Barton sends chills down our spines with his "Shadow Mapping," and Gavin Atlas serves up the strangest trip of all with a psychiatrist, a dream of pirates on a train, and government-sanctioned rape in his beautifully warped "Engine of Repression." Finally, William Holden burrows deep into the subways of Boston for the return of Nate the Midnight Barker and "The Last Train."

So climb aboard, let the conductor punch your ticket, and settle back for some of the hottest, most intriguing rides you'll ever take. Have lunch in the dining car, watch the scenery from the observation deck, and even cruise the restrooms downstairs—but keep a sharp eye out for handsome strangers.

Or wolfmen.

HIGHLAND SLEEPER
JEFF MANN

And "Levorcham," said Deirdre, "that man only will I love, who hath the three colours that I see here, his hair as black as the raven, his cheeks red like the blood, and his body as white as the snow."

—The Exile of the Sons of Usnach

Irish charm, dark good looks—no wonder the girls in the lounge car cluster about him. The train rattles and thrums on its way north; his admirers giggle, arranging their bodies as provocatively as possible. He stretches, spreads his legs, tells bawdy tales in his deep brogue. Every now and then his long-lashed brown eyes catch mine. Tonight, he's just across the aisle; come dawn, if all goes as planned, he will be far closer.

I watch his adept flirtations while I savor my meal. This is the Caledonian Sleeper, en route from London to the Scottish Highlands, so I've chosen the traditional Scots combination of haggis, neeps and tatties, washed down with a couple of pints of ale. Plate emptied, I sit back on the leather couch, sipping a dram of Glenfiddich. As I study him, his thick black eyebrows, the cocky gleam of his smiles, I give silent thanks that the duke chose this boy for my last job. It's a fine way to end a career.

It's very late by the time the vixens depart. Now, other than the barman, who's busy washing glasses, my quarry and I are the only ones left in the car. We both sit back, sipping Scotch. He gazes at me, I gaze at him. What a beauty, with his trimmed black beard, his long black hair pulled back in a ponytail. He's thirty years old, five foot eight—younger than me by fifteen years, shorter than me by half a foot. His jaw's square, his cheekbones prominent, his lips red, full, almost delicate. The gray slacks and maroon silk shirt are just tight enough to reveal his thighs' lithe lines, the wiry muscles of his arms. The shirt's unbuttoned one button past modest, giving me a glimpse of his pale chest. The boy's obviously more than aware of his charms. He will add quite a bit of pulchritude to my new home.

"Cheers," he says, lifting his glass. "Where ye be heading to?"

"Fort William," I say. "Just bought a nice piece of retirement property in the Hebrides."

"Ah. Lovely country, mate, though I'm thinking you're looking too young to retire."

I chuckle, running my fingers through my salt-and-pepper beard. "Kind of you to say. And you? What's your destination?"

"Uh, just…on holiday." He cocks a bushy eyebrow and grins. He takes a long sip of the amber glinting in his glass. "Came upon a bit of windfall."

Indeed. A windfall I've been tracking for weeks. "Are you in coach?" I ask.

"Aye. Trying to save some pounds."

"I have a sleeper. Single berth, first class. Small but comfortable. I recommend them."

"'Tis a space I'd like to see," says my handsome target, giving me a bold wink.

"The Hebrides make some fine whiskies," I say, taking a sip. "Better than this. Have you had Tobermory? I have some in my flask. Back in my cabin." I reach across the narrow aisle and offer my hand. "I'm Bruno. From America originally. Virginia."

"James," he says. "Grew up in Dublin." He squeezes my hand hard; I squeeze back. First touch, and we're already fighting for top. Little does he know this is not a contest he can win.

❖

I flip on a dim lamp, pour us Tobermory, and sit on the bed. My visitor takes the window seat, only inches away. Our chat's inconsequential, since both of us are lying. Behind him, the English landscape rushes by in autumn dark. Every now and then, the lights of towns glint, church steeples flash past, there's the incandescent twining of traffic, then we're back to the flow of black fields.

He wastes little time, which is fine by me, since we'll be getting to Fort William tomorrow morning and I'll need to have him prepared by then. Only a few minutes have passed before he decisively gulps his Scotch and unbuttons his shirt.

"So, Mr. Bruno, is this what you're wanting to see?" He shrugs the shirt off, spreads his legs, and cups the bulge of his crotch.

The boy's very lean, his torso snow white. His chest's curved, his belly flat, his shoulders and arms sinewy, well defined. A bit of black hair rings his soft, prominent nipples; there's a sparse dusting of hair between his pecs, around his navel, a thicker coat on his arms. Celtic knots and spirals tattoo his shoulders; a cross is inked inside his left forearm. His body's a revelation, one I've been awaiting a long time.

"You're as delicious as I expected," I say. "Yes, this is what I want to see. I'm disease-free, by the way. You too, I hope." As if I don't already know. My employer's money has already gotten me access to any number of files.

"Oh, yes. Tested just a few weeks ago." He unbinds his hair, letting it fall about his face. He stretches, showing off the thick hair of his armpits, which exude an intoxicating musk. The boy clearly hasn't bathed in a while. "So what are you wanting tonight?"

"Ah, I'm pretty perverse. And I'm a Top. I think I'd like to tie you up and fuck you."

"Aye, well, I'm the one does the fucking. I don't get fucked, and I don't swallow, but I can give you a superlative knob job. This Scotch is very fine, Mr. Bruno, and you're built like a bull and bloody handsome, but still 'tis five hundred pounds I'm requiring. Six hundred for kink."

"That's a good bit." I lean toward him, elbows on my knees. I touch the smooth skin of his chest. "Are you worth all that?"

"Indeed." He unzips, pulling out his cock. It's half-hard, long and thick, uncut. He peels up the foreskin. He spits in his hand, wetting the heart-shaped head. He strokes himself. For a good minute we sit in silence save for the train's soothing, incessant roar and watch his cock lengthen.

"What think ye of this, Mr. Bruno? 'Tis yours to handle all night for a modest fee." Taking my hand, he wraps it around his penis. I jack him; he closes his eyes and hums.

"Beauty does tend to come with a high price." Sighing, I give his cock a squeeze and stand. I pull down the window blind. Turning to the door, I lock it, and then I pull the pistol from my shoulder holster. "Your real name's Colin, isn't it? Colin, you're quite the greedy brat. Isn't the ruby you stole enough?"

The boy's very fast, up off the seat and grabbing for my gun. I'm faster, giving him an elbow to the mouth. He spins and crumples, slumping over the window seat. Before he can resist me further, I'm on top of him, one arm wrapped around his neck, the gun's muzzle pressed against his right ear.

"Keep still and shut up. I'm not a cop. But if you give me any trouble, the cops will be here posthaste."

"Fuck all," Colin pants. "Fuck all." He's rigid beneath me, his butt hard beneath my crotch.

"I promise you, you're fair and squarely caught, you little bastard. I've been on your trail for weeks. Now are you going to do what I tell you to? Or shall I call security? Or just break your neck?" I tighten my arm around his windpipe and prod his head with the gun. "You going to behave?"

Colin's answer is a snarl and a nod.

"Keep quiet, or I'll gag you sooner rather than later. Don't want to wake the nice people." From my pocket I pull handcuffs. I lock my captive's hands behind him, lug him up, and throw him roughly onto the bed. He lies there, on his back, bare chest swelling, hair falling across his face, fear and hate mingling in his beautiful brown eyes, blood welling from his split lips.

"Let's see the rest of that sweet little body," I say. "And if you kick me, I'll break your jaw." Colin gives me no fight as I pull off his shoes, socks, and pants, then his skimpy black briefs. His hips are slender, with that combination of curves grading into the groin that compose what I've always called Apollo's lyre, a bodily poetry reserved for the young and the fit. Inside its dense black bush, his cock's a tiny bud of fear. His legs are long and muscular, coated with dark hair. The cabin's suddenly heady with the aroma of his unwashed crotch and ass. "Mmm, you're ripe," I say, licking my lips.

"Goddamn you," he whispers. "Who the fuck are you?"

"You should have figured that out by now. Nice disguise, by the way. Very fetching, the long hair and beard. If I weren't a connoisseur of handsome men, I might not have recognized you in London."

"The duke? He sent you?" There's a quaver in his voice.

I chuckle. "Afraid? You ought to be. Yes, I've been retained by the duke over many years, for many delicate cases. This one perhaps the most delicate of all."

"Why you? Why not the cops? What was delicate? 'Twas only a jewelry heist, you ball of shite."

"Manners." I slap the side of his head, then drag him to his feet by his hair and shake him. "You have no idea what went on after you left. The duke's son tried to hang himself. I guess he really was in love with you."

"William? He—?" Colin sways in my grasp. His black eyebrows angle, his forehead creases, an expression very much resembling honest concern. "Oh, no. Oh, no. I never meant— Oh, I'm fucked. I'm screwed."

"Screwed indeed. The maid interrupted his attempt and called for help. He's institutionalized now, thanks to you. The duke didn't want the scandal-hungry tabloids to get wind of the fact that his only son's a poof who fell in love with a fencing coach who turned out to be a jewel thief. The duke very much preferred discretion, to keep the mess you made a private affair. So instead of involving the authorities, he called me. I'm here instead. And we have big plans for you."

I shove Colin down onto the bed, into a sitting position. From my travel bag I fetch coils of rope.

"What, what plans?" He's entirely terrified by now, and the sound of that terror is sweet, the baritone brogue of a strong, cocky man shifting into a shaky tenor.

"Don't worry, pretty boy. No prison for you, and no grave in the woods either, if you do as you're told."

I unroll the first coil, a good ten feet worth. With it I bind Colin's ankles together. I unroll more rope, with which I lace his elbows and upper arms together behind him. I circle his torso and arms with another five or six yards, securing him further. He groans as I pull the rope tighter, then tighter still, before finishing off the knots. The cord furrows the white skin of his chest and inked biceps.

"Where's the ruby, boy?"

"Ah, I've sold it, you ball-bag. You're too late."

"You're wasting my time. I followed you all over London, and you never met with a fence." From my suitcase, I fetch a rag and hunting knife. I hold the blade to Colin's windpipe. "Open up." When he obeys,

I cram the cloth in his bloodied mouth. "Keep quiet," I say, "or I'll cut your throat." I give him a sharp fist jab to the belly. He doubles over, making a stifled squeal. I punch his torso. His muscles are hard hills beneath my knuckles. The squeals move into ragged grunts.

I pull out the bloodstained cloth. "Where's the ruby, boy?"

"Fuck you, you can of piss."

I stuff the rag back in. I continue pummeling him, vacillating between his chest and belly. Already his pale skin is bruising, puddling with purple.

After a lengthy round, I pull the rag out. This time Colin gasps, "In, in my t-trousers, you fucker, you bloody arsehole."

I shove him onto the floor. Pressing my boot sole to his face, I apply pressure.

"You're telling me the truth?"

"Damn ye, yes," Colin snarls. Kneeling, I rummage through his pants. My fingers close on something hard. I pull it out. Scarlet facets glimmer in the dim light. "Good boy," I say, pocketing it. "The duke will be pleased. Now for my reward."

"What's that?" Colin groans. In the wake of my elbow's blow, his pretty lips are already swelling. "How much did the old git pay you to find me?"

"My own private island, actually. But my real reward is you."

"What?" Colin gasps. "Me? What d'you mean?"

"I'm a little besotted with you, Colin. I've wanted to own you ever since the duke first showed me your photograph."

"Own me? What the fuck?"

"Don't be stupid. You've surely heard of Master/slave relationships. I'll use your body when I please. You'll keep up my house, serve me, and obey me in all things. In turn, I'll care for you, protect you, and provide for you."

"And why would I want to tolerate that, mate, as handsome as y'are?"

"Because, from what I can tell, your only ambitions are comfort, good food and drink, lots of sex, and money, all of which I can provide. Because you're sure to have a far better life with me than you would in prison—how many years would you get?—or hustling and conning the way you have for years. Aren't you tired of living like that?"

I hoist Colin to his knees. He stares up at me, his panic shading into wonder.

"Yes, fuck all, it's knackered I am," he blurts, face crumpling like a tearful child's. "Wrecked. Weary of running. Weary of lies. Weary of the shabby streets. All turned to shite, it has. Shite, shite, shite…"

"Well, here's your chance for a new life. You prove an eager slave, submissive in all things, and you not only survive, you thrive. You fight me, you fail to please me, and I turn you over to the authorities, and you're off to prison."

"No, don't do that."

"Or I could turn you over to the duke."

"No, Jesus, please! You know how he is. It's in the Thames I'll end up, or buried beneath the sod."

"Or you could serve me. Are those options clear?"

When Colin nods, I pull out my very hard penis. "So you decide. Now. Do we have a deal?"

Colin stares at my cock for a long moment. Then he groans, closes his eyes, and takes me on his tongue.

❖

Split lip or not, Colin's a skillful cocksucker. As my tightly bound prisoner kneels between my legs, slurping and gulping, I sit back on the bed, stroke his long hair, and run my fingers through his beard, face-fucking him slowly. Now that I've found what I was sent to find, I can afford to be tender.

When he pulls off to catch his breath, I wipe saliva from his beard. "Taste good?"

"Yes. It's a grand one, it is. Must admit I'm always starving for dick."

"Good." I shove my cock back in his mouth. "Where we're going, you'll be getting more than enough. Now get to it. I need to come, and you need to swallow. Don't worry, I'm healthy."

I ride Colin's face for a long time. When I reach between his hairy thighs, I find his cock stiff and dripping. Part of his fellating eagerness is probably due to my threat, what will happen if he doesn't satisfy me. Part of his dick's excitement might be the predicament in which he finds himself. Odd how the presence of danger sometimes makes men's lusts rage wilder. Or perhaps he's naturally submissive. I hope so. That would make his future much easier.

When I come in Colin's mouth, he gulps down my load with palpable enthusiasm, suckling my spent cock as it grows limp. When I pull out, he greedily laps the post-cum ooze.

"Damn, a fine big knob." He licks his lips. "That was, I'm hoping, good enough a sucking for you to…" Trailing off, he swallows hard and hangs his head.

"To keep you around, yes," I say, wiping a bead of spilt semen from his beard. "Time for bed." I pat his head. "We're due into Fort William around ten a.m."

The bed's very narrow, so I arrange Colin on the floor. I ball up the rag and press it against his lips. "I need to gag you now."

Colin shakes his head. "No need, mate. I'll keep quiet, I promise."

"Sorry, friend, you're a trickster. I don't trust you yet. Open up."

Sighing, he obeys. I push the rag in, tying it in place with rope threaded between his lips and knotted around his head. Tenderly I cover him with a blanket, as if he were my son.

Snug beneath my duvet, surrounded by the soporific rocking of the train, I'm asleep in minutes, hugging a pillow. I wake to the racket of cars uncoupling. Four thirty. Standing, I peer around the window blind. At my feet, Colin gives a muted moan. He's lying on his side, half-exposed, the blanket fallen to his waist. I hunker beside him, brushing black locks from his face. His eyes are wide with pleading.

"We're in Edinburgh. They're splitting the cars. You all right?"

Colin moans again, shaking his head. I lay a palm on his bare chest. He's trembling. "Cold?" Lightly I brush his hard nipples with the back of my hand. "You want up here with me?"

When he nods, my heart melts. As we've moved north, the air in the cabin has indeed dropped in degrees. Despite all the damage he's done, the trouble he's caused, suddenly I pity him: so vulnerable, powerless, and frightened.

"Come on." I lift him to his feet, then pull him beneath the duvet. The bed's just wide enough for the two of us if I wrap my arms around him. "God damn, you're a tasty haul." I suck on his nipples for a while and knead his buttocks. Then I roll him over and pull his back tightly against my chest. "Warmer?"

Colin nods. I hold him close, stroking his hair till he falls asleep.

❖

Knocking. The steward. Must be the steward with breakfast.

Colin barely manages to take a breath before my hand's over his mouth and my arm's wrapped around his throat. He gives a muffled yelp, straining against me, trying to kick. I pin his legs with mine and roll on top of him, forcing him to the bed with my greater weight. "You keep real quiet, okay?" I hiss. "Otherwise, you'll be going straight from the train station to the Fort William jail."

"Mmm-mmm," Colin mumbles, immediately limp and compliant. Rolling out of bed, I hide my captive beneath the duvet, unlock and crack the door, fetch the sausage roll and tea. I put the tray on the window seat and tug the duvet off. Colin's still on his belly, face pressed into the pillow, the tight globes of his ass white in the morning light. Climbing back into bed, I roll us onto our sides and cover us, snuggling up against Colin's back.

"You like getting fucked?" I ask, fingering his ass crack.

Colin shudders. He shakes his head. "Uh-uh."

"Oh, right. You always do the fucking, huh? Not this time. Those days are over. You have been fucked before, surely?"

Another shake of the head, more emphatic.

"Really? A virgin? How fucking delicious. I'm about to be your first." I rub my cockhead against his cheeks, nudge it against his hole.

"Mmm-mmm!" Colin grunts, as strenuous an objection as his rag-and-rope gag will allow. *"Mmm-mmm!"* More forceful shaking of his head, more pent-up struggles.

"Stop fighting me!" Fetching the knife from the floor, I scrape the edge against his throat. "You stupid kid, I told you to keep quiet! You do remember what I said about your life depending on how well you please me?"

Colin ceases his resistance. Nodding, he falls silent.

"I'm going to rape you now, Colin." I unbind his feet, roll him onto his belly, and prop his lean hips atop a pillow. "I've been wanting to take you this way for a good while. This will be the first of many, many times. This is something you're going to have to get used to. So spread your legs and shut up. If you make a lot of noise, someone will complain, and then I may have to give you up to the security officer. You don't want that, do you?"

Colin shakes his head, then takes a deep breath. What he exhales is not just air but independence, fight, the hope of freedom.

"Christ, you've got a lovely butt. It's about to get the reverence it deserves." I caress his ass cheeks, bend to kiss each one. His buttocks are smooth, snow white, very round and tight, with curly black hair in the cleft. I force his cheeks apart; I push my face into the fur mist there and lengthily feast on his hole. He trembles, spreading his thighs wider, making tiny moans.

"You like that, huh?" I ask, triumphant. "Want more?"

When he nods, I continue, pushing my tongue inside him, lapping his fuzzy crack from top to bottom, nibbling his taint and gently biting his buttocks. Finally, after lubing us up, I push my cockhead against his tiny opening. He sobs softly, flinching as I enter him, clearly in pain.

"Relax, kid. You need to relax. Open up for me. I'm not going to go any further until you say you're ready."

We lie there for a while, only the tip of my cock inside him. He's a marvel, so warm and strong, so young and helpless. It's rapture to have him bound beneath me. I nuzzle his beard, stroking him and soothing him till he grows less tense.

"Ready? Can you take more now?"

When he nods, I slide into him, as slowly and tenderly as my lust will allow, until at last I'm all the way inside. "Oh, Christ, you're so hot and tight," I groan. I ride him on his belly for a long time, and his sobs and whimpers are sheer bliss. Then I pull out, roll him onto his back, hoist his legs over my shoulders, and thrust into him again. I gaze down at my captive in the dim light, his black hair tousled, spread across the pillow. His cock's hard now, bobbing between us.

"God, you're beautiful," I gasp, thrusting deeper. He winces, his eyebrows knitting with pain, his white teeth gritting the rope. "Just like the Irish triad. Hair black as a raven, lips red as blood, skin white as snow." His deep brown eyes blink up at me, wet at the edges. I jack him, pound his ass harder, wipe tears off his cheek. He comes just before I do, a great jet of cream spouting over my hand like a wave slamming into the western cliffs of Ireland.

❖

I've split my cold tea with him, fed him half my sausage roll before gagging him again. Now I pull out rubbing alcohol and syringe.

Colin whines, looking up at me with obvious anxiety. "Just to knock you out," I say, swabbing his biceps. "Since you've put up a struggle at every opportunity, since you obviously haven't yet learned it's stupid to keep fighting your fate, you need to be drugged for the remainder of the trip. Now hold still."

Colin obeys, leaning against me as I administer the drug. "There you go," I say, putting the bottle and hypodermic away, then helping Colin curl up on the bed. I sit beside him, watching his eyes grow glazed and unfocused. "Just give in, kid. Just surrender. When you wake up, we'll be home."

Colin gives a drunken nod. He's nearly out.

"Don't worry, boy. As fine a possession as you are, I plan to take immaculate care of you." I play with moist curls in his ass crack till his breathing slows and he passes out. Then I remove his bonds and dress his limp body.

❖

"Poor bloke," says the train attendant, draping Colin's left arm over his shoulder.

"Yes," I say, taking Colin's right. "He gets these fainting spells. We're driving straight to the hospital."

We drag my drugged boy along the train's narrow corridor and down the steps to the platform. It's a gray day, with light drizzle. Above the grimy town, Ben Nevis looms, its crown swathed in cloud. There's Angus, the driver, waiting in the parking lot as prearranged. He helps us load Colin into the backseat. I thank the attendant, then climb in beside my prisoner. He slumps against me, dead weight, as Angus drives us out of the lot and onto the road that leads toward Arisaig, where our private ferry to the island waits. As soon as we're safely out of Fort

William, I cuff Colin's hands behind him and plaster strips of duct tape over his eyes and mouth. No reason to take chances, in case the drug wears off prematurely.

Curled up in the seat, covered with a blanket, his head on my lap, Colin sleeps soundly as Angus maneuvers the winding roads. I study my prize, stroking his bearded cheeks, the outline of his lips creasing the silver-gray tape. So innocent he looks asleep, his helplessness as arousing as his beauty. Retrieving my cell phone, I give the duke a quick call, then with difficulty pull my attention from Colin's handsome face to take in the Highland landscape. We pass browning pastures, herds of sheep, rock walls, forests of white birch turning gold. The road grows narrower still, so much so that we must pull into turn-offs to allow the few oncoming cars to pass. We ascend slopes, cross wind-savage passes, descend toward the rocky coast. The rain comes and goes, slowing our progress. We're still ten tortuous miles from the ferry when Colin begins moaning. When he tries to rise, I hold him down.

"Still more resistance?" I pull the syringe from my travel bag. "Don't you know better by now?" Feebly, Colin writhes against me, kicking the car door, shaking his head, pleading against the tape, but I slip the needle into his arm and soon he's out again. He gives me no further trouble during the drive's remaining miles.

The harbor at last. I drag him from the car. The ferry's already here. I shake Angus's hand, heave my priceless plunder over my shoulder—there's many an advantage to being a strong man, but this is the first time the benefit's been the ease with which I carry a drugged captive—and tote Colin through heavy rain to the boat.

It's a long crossing to Siantan, and rough, the sea slapping the ship, smashing whitely across the stern, wind spinning spume off the wave-tops. On the island, the wind's wilder still. I load Colin into my car's trunk. Since Siantan's tiny—so small and so remote it's left off most maps—the drive to the farmhouse is brief, up from the stony beach through heath-coated hills. The house is snug and solid, built of native stone and wood, what I've been dreaming of for years, my reward for so many decades in the duke's service.

Depositing Colin on the big bed, I cover him with a quilt, one my great-aunt made for me when I was still a poor kid in the Virginia mountains. Already it's dusk—the autumn sun sets early this far north. Pouring out Scotch, I light a peat fire, then sit in the armchair by the wide window overlooking the sea. In the farthest distance, the hills of Skye hump, purple-gray against pearl-gray sky. Gusty rain slams and streams the glass.

Finishing my dram, I rise. I light a candle by the bed and pull the blanket off my captive. I strip him, using my knife to cut off his pants, his shirt, his briefs; the kid will have little need for clothing here. I sit by him then, admiring his nakedness, running my hands along his hips, his ass, the swirls and knots of his tattoos. When I check his cuffed hands, I find them warm, evincing no circulation problems. I lock the slave collar on him. It's thick steel chain, with a five-pound padlock.

Eager to be inside him again, unwilling to wait for him to wake, I strip, then roll him onto his belly. I eat his butt for a long time, and the taste of his hole is an earthy, musky joy. I work my lubed cock up inside him, and I fuck his ass, slowly at first, then deep and hard. He rocks and bounces beneath me, insensible. So hot, his hairy tunnel, what a treasure, so hot, moist, and tight, like a fist of flame. When I feel myself coming close, I pull out, wanting to prolong ecstasy. I stand by the window, sipping Scotch, watching the heave of sea, the claw of rain. Then I apply more lube, lie on top of him, and slip inside him again.

After a good thirty minutes of such on-and-off ravishing, my prisoner begins moaning. He's finally coming to. I pause in my thrusts to peel the tape off his eyes and mouth.

"Where...?" he mutters, licking his lips and swallowing hard.

"Welcome to Siantan. We're home." I rub my bearded cheek against his. I pull all the way out, slam in again. Colin gasps.

"This collar around your neck means you belong to me. It also means, if you pass the rim of the island, you'll receive savage shocks strong enough to knock you out. You'll never find the key—it's locked inside a hidden safe—so don't even think about breaking something over my head and trying to escape. Get it?"

Colin nods. I embed myself deeper. He gasps again, then grits his teeth.

"Does it hurt?" I wrap an arm around his chest and prod him harder.

"Umm. Uhh! A, a bit, mate. Ow. Uhh! Uhhhh! B-burning some. Not as bad as, as before. Uhf. Uhf."

"Not going to fight me?"

"N-no, mate, no. Uhh. Now that I'm here, uhf, you got me. N-no reason—Ow!—to keep fighting. Umm! I'm tired of fighting."

"Good to hear. I'm going to fuck you till you learn to love it." Grinning, I start a steady rhythm. Now there are no words, only the crackle of the fireplace, the slap of storm against the house, my soft growls, and Colin's groans, moving from discomfort to pleasure and then back again. I ring the changes, screwing him on his belly, then bent over the bed's edge, then with his legs in the air. It's on his side that I find that place inside him that makes his groans grow deeper.

"Oh, God!" Colin gasps, bucking back against me.

"Found your sweet spot, huh?" I chuckle.

"Harder, mate. Uhf, yeah. Yeah. God, that's good. Fuck me. Fuck me harder," Colin begs, squirming against me. "Please. Uhf, oh yeah. Uhf, fuck, yeah." His hole ripples, clenching my cock. I give his butt cheeks a few open-handed slaps and then pound him, rougher than I've ever pounded any man.

"*Oh!* Oh, Jesus!" Colin, shaking, gives a great shout, and now his ass ring's pulsing around my shaft and he's coming hugely onto the mattress. I'm right behind him, spurting my own load inside him.

We lie there panting. Then Colin laughs, and I do too. I pull him close and we guffaw like fools. It takes a good while for our laughter to taper off.

"So that's what it's all about. Hell, mate, never came like that before," Colin says. "It's a wonder. No hands!"

"Better than prison, I'm assuming? So being ridden agrees with you?"

"You're correct in that, I'm thinking. 'Tis a bloody surprise, but a welcome one. Would you leave your prick up in me? It feels powerful and fine lodged up there."

The boy seems so acquiescent, so resigned to his fate. I believe I'll save the bad news for the morning.

❖

The evening passes quickly. "I could eat a baby's arse through the bars of a cot!" Colin exclaims—a particularly colorful Irish way of expressing hunger—and soon he's sitting, entirely docile, at the kitchen table, hands cuffed comfortably before him, sipping ale, a woolen shawl wrapped about his bare shoulders while I throw together bangers and mash for supper.

"Going to keep you cuffed till I'm sure you'll behave. Once I think I can trust you, you can do most of the cooking," I say. "Meanwhile, well, I love to eat and drink, and I'm a pretty good cook, so that lean body of yours is likely to grow meatier."

Colin shakes his head in amazement, looking around the farmhouse, then out the water-stippled windows and over the sea. "I'm a good cook too. Learned from my ma, God rest her, though, for most of my youth, we were so poor we half starved." Colin takes a big swig of ale. "Meaning I'm always ready for food. You can trust me to stay, Bruno. Never have I seen such a place. It's fucking paradise. And a paradise of fucking. Though I am a tad sore." Grinning ruefully, he rubs his ass. "Small price to pay, though. In prison it's far sorer I'd be, I'm guessing."

"Pretty as you are, yes. You'd be the bitch of every brute in sight." I heap the plates with food and fetch a bottle of brown sauce.

"And it's your bitch I am now?" Colin says, sipping ale. I sit across from him; we look into one another's eyes.

"In a manner of speaking, yes. We'll live well here, I swear."

Colin stares out over the waves, tugs at the chain locked around his neck, then looks back at me. He gives me a thin grin and lifts his pint glass. We clink glasses, then fall to. We eat with abandon, having had nothing since the paltry train breakfast. When we're done, I serve up a treacle pudding with custard. Afterward, I push Colin to his knees, pull out my dick, shove it into his mouth, and fuck his face till he's choking on my cum.

❖

Our first night together. The rain's become a downpour streaking the windows. Gusts batter the house. I chain Colin's cuffed hands to the headboard, loosely, so he'll be comfortable enough to sleep. We cuddle together in my big bed, Colin's head resting on my chest, listening to the low roar of waves and the hammer of storm, watching the fire slowly fade. We talk about his early years in the Dublin slums, his jail time for petty theft and brawling, my profitable but lonely years working for the duke.

Midnight, and we're both yawning. When I reach for the roll of duct tape by the bed, Colin says, "What's the point of that?"

"I'm going to tape your mouth for the night. There's a bucket here by the bed, so if you need to piss, wake me and I'll help."

"Why gag me, bloke? No one here but us. And I won't make any noise. Why keep me cuffed and chained, for that matter, since this collar won't let me leave the island?"

"Because I don't trust you yet. Because you're damned pretty silenced and restrained. Because controlling your movement and your speech makes me feel powerful. Your helplessness makes me feel powerful. And feeling powerful turns me on. Eventually, if you're a good boy, some days I'll allow you to cook and clean and work on the grounds or in the garden. Other days you'll spend in shackles, or bound to a chair with a bit strapped in your mouth, or in the closet, hogtied and plugged at both ends. Every night you'll spend beside me, chained and gagged. Because it pleases me. That's reason enough. Understand?"

Colin bites his lip. "Yes."

I pull off a strip of tape. "Kiss me," I say, leaning forward. He does so, tentatively at first, then deeply, wetly. Our tongues slide together. I nibble his swollen lips, then I pull away. "Hold still." Our eyes meet and lock as I press the tape over his mouth and smooth it over his lips and beard. "Come here," I say, embracing him. "I want to hold you in my arms all night."

We sleep long and hard. Near morning, Colin's nudges and mumbles rouse me; his hang-dog humiliation as I help him piss is downright precious. We slumber longer; we wake late, to drizzly gray, both of us hard again. I unchain my captive long enough to drag him to the toilet and clean out his ass. Back in bed, I chain him up again, haul him onto his elbows and knees, lube us up, and fuck him doggy-style. He's hurting, I can tell. I'm plowing him too fast, too hard, too deep, but I can't help myself. Beneath the tape, he makes a lot of pained noise, but dutifully he keeps his head down and his butt up, enduring another ass pounding without complaint. After I come, we drowse together, listening to the rain. Leaving him still chained and taped, snoring and snuggled deep in heaped blankets, I head to the kitchen to prepare good behavior's reward: a big Irish breakfast of tea, bacon, eggs, white and black puddings, and fried potato bread, a meal I serve to him in bed. It's only after breakfast's done that I break the news: the duke's due in for afternoon tea.

❖

The morning's cozy, caloric comforts are very far from Colin's mind now. I have him prepared for the duke's visit: naked, hands bound together, arms stretched above him and tied to a rafter in the living room. A tarp's spread beneath him to protect the floor.

"Bite down on this when it really starts to hurt," I say, pushing a thick rope between his teeth and knotting it behind his head. Colin sways on his toes. His brown eyes are so wild with panic I blindfold him with a bandana, because the looks he gives me make me nauseous with guilt.

"Just suffer this, get through this, and he'll leave us alone. He's promised."

My noble guest arrives at four, as planned, just as it's getting dark. He's a short, portly man in his fifties, with prematurely white hair and a bit of a shuffle. We exchange pleasantries. I ask after his son, am told he's recuperating slowly. He admires the house, the view out to sea. He studies my strung-up slave. "Very good. Very good," he says, taking a seat at the table. "Though I would have preferred him crucified." I serve the duke a plate of sandwiches—cucumber, watercress, ham and pour him Darjeeling tea in a china cup.

"I want to see his eyes," the duke says, so I remove the blindfold. Colin shakes the hair away from his face, looks up at the duke, whimpers, and drops his gaze.

"Begin," says the duke. I lift the bullwhip.

I beat Colin, steadily, methodically, for a long time, moving around him in a slow circle. The duke keeps his eyes on the spectacle he's ordered as he sips tea and takes little bites of food. The lash slices into Colin's muscled back, then cuts across his chest, already bruised from my blows. It opens up the skin of his sculpted belly and his hairy thighs. It cuts crimson welts into his beautiful ass. He screams, he sobs, he thrashes. Face contorted, he tosses his head, gnawing the rope till he's drooling. Blood unscrolls down his back and torso like liquefying poppies; it dribbles into his pubic hair, dripping off his shrunken cock. I beat him till the duke's finished the last sandwich, the very last sip of tea.

The duke folds his napkin and puts it beside his emptied plate. "Done," he says.

I drop the whip. Colin hangs there, head bowed, chest heaving, sobs slowly receding.

"My ruby," says the duke.

I retrieve it from a desk drawer and ceremoniously place it in his palm. He holds it up in the dusky light, smiles, and slips it into his pocket. Then he shuffles over to Colin. Gripping his long hair, he pulls his head back. They stare at one another for a good minute before the duke gives him a sharp slap across the face. Colin whines; his swollen lips begin bleeding anew.

The duke releases Colin's head and takes a step back. He looks Colin up and down. "He does resemble Our Lord, does he not, with the long hair and beard? After the flagellation at the post? At Pilate's palace. The Caravaggio painting. No wonder my son was smitten. No wonder you're smitten. Black, red, and white. The boy could be Deirdre's lover. What was his name? Noisiu? Conchobar? Cúchulainn? Ah, can't remember. No matter."

Cupping Colin's saliva-streaked chin in his hand, the duke again lifts his head. "I wanted you shot through the brain, boy, but this man pleaded for your life, simply because he thinks you're beautiful. You owe him everything. If ever you leave this island, it will be your death. Do you understand?"

Colin nods. He groans once, slumps in his bonds, and passes out.

The duke gives Colin's cheek a brisk pat and wipes his spit-smeared palm on his pants. Turning, he shakes my hand. "All yours, Bruno. I'll miss you. Enjoy your island. It's lovely." With that, he's gone.

I undress. I circle my unconscious prisoner—beauty bound, bruised, and bleeding. Painfully hard, I stroke myself. I embrace him then; his welted nakedness smears mine with scarlet. I lick salty tears off his face, viscous drool off his chin. I lap blood from his breast, his muscled back, the hard curves of his ass, the tip of his limp cock.

Untying Colin from the rafter, I carry him to the bathroom to wash, salve, and bandage his wounds. Then I cuff his hands before him and carry him to bed.

Wind batters the house; fresh rain spatters the windows. After starting a new fire, I sit on the bed's edge and watch my captive sleep. Colin moans. He rolls over. "Oh, Lord God, Bruno." His eyes go wide, then clench shut. His lips quiver. "Jesus, oh, Jesus, oh Christ Jesus, it hurts."

"I'm sorry, Colin." Wrapping one arm beneath his shoulders and one beneath his knees, I lift his wincing body onto my lap. He sobs for a while, quaking against me. I rock him like a child.

"The duke's gone," I say. "And if you do as you're told, no one will hurt you again."

Colin wipes his eyes. He clasps my hands, snuggles against me, and presses his face into the hair on my breast. "Aye, so you promise? For in terrible hurt I am, and would not want to suffer so again."

"I promise. You've suffered, and now you're clean. We're both clean."

"Thank you," Colin whispers. "I know he badly wants me dead, and I don't blame him. Thanks for it. Deliverance, as the holy fathers would say."

"Purely selfish," I say, tugging on his steel collar. "You're too handsome to kill. And I'm tired of being lonely. Siantan is your second chance."

"Redemption," he murmurs against my skin.

"In a manner of speaking. You're going to bear a welter of scars, but on you they'll look grand." I kiss his bloody lips, his brow. "Tomorrow I'm going to teach you how to bake scones. A slave should know how to bake. All right?"

No response. Colin's passed out again. I cradle him, the ferrous taste of his blood in my mouth, remembering those long years alone, wanting men I could not have. I prayed a lot then. I prayed for a beautiful man I could possess entirely, a man as maimed and as hungry as I. After long years, that treasure's huddled in my arms. Tonight's prayer is new. *Lord,* I mutter, *give us mutual salvation, mutual healing. For long years, Lord, may your dark-eyed blessing remain.* There's no answer, of course. And so I rock my snoring savior and watch the fire glow, while the wind's talons rake the farmhouse roof and the Atlantic breaks on rough rocks below.

No Mincing Words
Rob Rosen

W as early still, sun barely poking its bright orange head above the horizon we were chugging along into. Baggage handler knocked on my thin slice of door. "What?" I grumbled, rubbing the sleep from my eyes.

He paused, answering me through the wood. "Think I spotted a tramp at the previous stop. Last baggage car. Train'll be pulling into Newark in twenty."

I coughed, shot up. "Fine," I replied, slipping on my overshirt, pants over my long johns. No rest for the weary. Not like I could complain, though. Bulls, as they called us, didn't work regular hours. If'n the train was running, so was I. Find 'em and chuck 'em off. That's what they paid me to do. Not well, but enough. I coughed again, opening the door. Handler was gone. "Smart handler."

I hotfooted it to the kitchen car and grabbed me a tepid cup of coffee. Needed me some steam as much as that old engine of ours did. Whistle blew a few minutes later, the train slowing down. We were pulling in. Time for work.

I waited for the passengers to get off, their baggage quick to follow, cars loaded and unloaded, new passengers boarding. I tapped my foot, shoulder leaning against the hot wood, watching them all scurry around like rats. Then I walked the length of the train, stopping at the last baggage car. Door was still open, so I hopped inside.

"Make it easy on me and I won't toss you off *after* the train starts running," I hollered, my voice bouncing around the small enclosure. Then I waited. "I'll give you to three, then I'm coming to look for you. And, trust me, you don't want me to get to three." Again I paused, ear held up, listening, waiting. "One," I started.

"Wait!" came the shouted reply, the sound coming from deep within a stack of burlap sacks. An arm poked up, then two, a head quick to follow.

"Off," I told him. "Now. No tramps."

He shook his dirty mane of hair from side to side. "Not a tramp. Looking for work down in Atlanta."

I pointed to the doors. "Off. Now. No hoboes allowed, neither."

He pushed the bags aside and stood in front of me. Young guy, mid-twenties, tattered clothes, covered in grime from head to beaten shoe. Only thing that stood out were eyes the color of a summer sky, twinkling big and blue and bright, causing my cock to pulse. "Please," he pled, voice gravelly. "Ain't no work 'round these parts."

"Ain't no work no place, buddy," I told him. "Now off with ya. That's the rules. If you ain't working here or paying to ride, then you don't have no business aboard this here train."

He paused, clearly weighing his options, which seemed slim to none to me. "Then give me some work, just until Atlanta."

I sighed. It was those eyes of his. Like magnets. Drawing me the fuck on in. "Can you shovel coal?" I asked.

"Suppose so," he replied. "Just need the shovel." He smiled, those eyes of his crinkling, my cock thickening in double time all of a sudden.

"Fine," I relented, hopping off. "We's short a man, I hear. Follow me and let's see if they can use you in the engine car."

His smile ignited like a keg of dynamite. He hopped down and followed close behind. "Thanks," he said. "Name's Joe."

"Bert," I told him. "And don't thank me yet."

Anyway, long and the short of it, one of the shovelers was down with something. Team was working up a sweat to keep up. Took that Joe kid and put him right to work, they did. He shot me a wicked grin and a thumbs up as I took off. Popped me a load a few minutes later, thinking 'bout them eyes of his, then made my rounds. See, where there's one hobo, there's bound to be more of 'em, times being what they were, so us bulls were kept busy enough. That day wasn't no exception.

Ten hours later, we was out somewhere where the grass was high and the sky full of stars, probably just past Maryland, if I figured correctly. The sound of the train as she blew off steam made my eyes heavy. Was just about asleep, too, when the knock came, low and rumbling.

"Bert," came the whisper. "It's me, Joe."

Suddenly, I was wide awake. I jumped out of bed and slid my door open. Had to laugh, too. "Boy, you's black as tar and twice as foul smelling."

He looked at me, tired as all get-out, but smiled just the same. "Shoveling coal. Messy work," he said, by way of an explanation. "They told me you'd show me where I could get cleaned up."

I snickered, straightening out my long johns. "Lazy fucks." Then I led him to the kitchen car. I knew it would be closed for the night, empty, no wait to get cleaned up like back in the workmen's cars. I pulled out a washbasin, big enough for him, if just. "Hop in. I'll get the water boiling for you."

He looked from it to me. "Tight fit." He shrugged. "Guess it beats waitin' for the next good rain, though."

I started pumping the water, getting the stove hot. "That it does." I watched as he undressed, sort of out of the corner of my eye. Kicked off his shoes first, peeled off two layers of socks, enough holes in them to make a brick of Swiss cheese jealous. Feet were about the cleanest things on him, too, which wasn't saying much. Shirt got unbuttoned next, filthy thing dropped to the ground. Undershirt next, also dropped. Boy was dirty all over, black around the neck and hands, only slightly lighter as my eyes worked their way inward. Had to stifle me a moan at the sight of him, though. All dense muscle, wiry, thin, curly black hair that trailed down his chest and etched belly. Had to look away for a second before my long johns gave way at the midsection.

Still, I looked back quick enough when he unhooked his belt, popping open the buttons of his measly pants, which came sliding down before they were kicked off. Joe had thick thighs, boulder-shaped calves, hairy as all hell. Slight up top, dense down below. Must've done a lot of walking, I figured. Ratty boxers came off next, ass pointed my way, that moan of mine stifled again. Finest ass this side of the Mississippi. Maybe the other side, too. Then he turned, locked eyes with me before I could stare down at his dangling willy. He winked and hopped in. "Hope you got yourself a mess of soap," he said with a good-hearted chuckle.

I found him a bar and tossed it his way. "You're a mess, boy," I told him. "Gonna take a flood of water to get you all clean."

He laughed and shrugged. "I'd settle for mostly clean, by this point. Been a long while since I had me a proper bath."

I lugged over a heated pot of water and ladled out a pan-full. I dumped it over his head as he sighed. "Not exactly a *proper* one," I said. "But it'll do."

He smiled and started scrubbing, layers of black soot and grime sloshing down the length of him, the suds foaming just as black. Took a while, too, to get it all out. Had to keep emptying out the basin. Still, he was turning pink soon enough. Boy was mighty fine-looking, too. A right stunner, he was. Though his backside wasn't getting much better. The water could only do so much, you see. Meaning, he soon handed me the soap, which I took with just the slightest tremble to my hand. "Hate to ask a favor, Bert," he said, eyes shining out from between the wet hair that fell over his face. "But might as well get it all done, right? Mama always said that a job half-done ain't worth doing."

"Smart woman," I replied, taking my arms out of my sleeves and sliding down my long johns to the waist, so as not to get them all wet. He stared at me in silence, big blue eyes like saucers now, a telltale gulp that made his Adam's apple bob. Then I moved behind him as he ladled the water over his shoulder. He bounced in place as I scrubbed, a river of black waterfalling down him.

I followed its direction. My hands went from his shoulders to the backside of his arms, working through the muck and grime that caked his lower back, that tangled the mound of hair above his fine ass. But still he kept pouring, and so still I eagerly kept cleaning. Like his mama said, this wasn't a job worth half-doing. Still, I stopped at his rump.

"You want to take it from here, Joe?" I asked, voice raspy, thick as molasses.

He turned his head my way and winked. "Nah, Bert. You're doing just fine. Might as well keep on going." He spread his legs as wide as they'd go inside the tub and leaned over, ass jutting out, hairy crack parting. "Unless I'm keeping you, I mean."

I cleared my throat and doused his ass with a pot-full of water. "Nope. Might as well finish." I crouched down, butt to face, and commenced to scrubbing, kneading his mounds of flesh, prying them apart until his hole came into view, balls dangling and bouncing in between his meaty thighs. Was enough to make a grown man crazy. And hard as granite.

Me and him both, I was soon to discover.

I slid my soapy hands inside, scrubbing his tender hole out, his legs suddenly buckling, swaying in time with the train, his moans swirling around my head like a swarm of bees. Louder when my hand kept going, reaching past his heavy balls, my fist grabbing onto his cock, thick as a tree limb and twice as hard. "Keep scrubbing, Bert," he groaned. "That there's the dirtiest part of me."

I laughed and kept right on stroking. "I can see that, Joe." Then I laughed some more. "So tell me, what's the real reason you came back to my cabin and not to the other workers'?"

He groaned again. "You're holding it, Bert." He leaned forward, ass jutting out all the more. "And if you want to fuck that bunghole of mine, have at it."

I let go off his pole and stood up, walking around to his front side. Those killer eyes of his locked on to mine, vise-tight. "You don't mince words, do ya, boy?"

He reached out and tweaked one of my nipples, then the other, my eyelids fluttering in response. "Mama hated mincing, too, Bert." He smiled, head tilted in, lips perched just a hair's breadth above mine. I closed the gap, mouths pressed up so snug it was hard to tell where he ended and I began. Then he pulled back, breathing hard, puffing like the train beneath our two sets of planted feet. "Those britches of yours come off, Bert?"

I smirked and shoved them down and off, my cock pointing up at him like a divining rod, the wide head already leaking. "Better?" I asked, lips again connected, tongues swirling, swapping some heavy spit.

He answered by hopping out of the tub and getting on all fours, legs wide, cock hovering, balls hanging low. Prettiest sight I'd seen in a long while; better than any view that old train ever afforded me, for sure. Downright delectable it was. Which is why I couldn't help but have me a taste, especially now that he was so clean and all.

I dove in head-first, lapping and licking at him, while he bucked his ass into my face, purring all the while. Boy tasted just as good as he looked. I leaned back and spat at his ring, then shoved my index finger up and in and back. He howled and rocked, as did the train, huffing and puffing right along with us. I joined a second finger to the mix, shoving them deep inside while I bit his ass and stroked my hefty prick. After one more finger up and in, he was ready for the real thing.

I flipped him over, his cock swaying, those eyes of his lit like a Christmas tree, smile so wide and beautiful as to take your very breath away. He stared down hungrily at my cock as it butted up against his chute. "Now I see why they call you a bull."

I teased it in, gently, body tingling from the top of my head to the end of my toes. "And I fuck like a jackrabbit." I slid it all the way in, his head tilted back, mouth in a pant.

"Show me," he moaned, stroking his thick prick now, glorious eyes once again open, locked and loaded.

Well now, didn't have to tell me twice. Especially since the train was slowing down some. Meaning I'd have to be back at work soon enough. So I let him have it with both guns, ramming and cramming my cock inside him, sweat pouring down my forehead, my chest, my back. His body shook as I fucked him, his ass meeting me with each thrust, with each slam.

"Close, Bert," he growled, jacking his cock fast as lightning now, giant balls bouncing.

"Closer, Joe," I gasped, one final shove inside him as me and the train blew, the whistle screaming as I filled up his tight hole with my heavy load, until it dripped and dribbled out of his asshole. He came right along with me, too, cock spewing thick ropes of man-sap that flew up and splattered his chest and belly in a dense coating of white.

I fell on top of him just after that, lips again together, urgent, eyes still open, rapture spreading through me like wildfire. But the train was stopping, a new station fast approaching. I pulled away. "Gotta get back to work, Joe," I whispered.

He laughed. "More tramps and hoboes like me to catch?"

I kissed him, soft as a breeze. "Ain't no one like you, Joe. No sir, no how." Then I grew silent, my smile flickering. "When we reach Atlanta, you still getting off?"

He shook his head from side to side. "Hell no," he said, all gleeful-like. "Got me a job here now. That feller I replaced ain't never gonna be good to shovel again." Then he laughed again, shooting me that wicked-ass grin of his. "Though he still has his bunk until we make it to Chattanooga."

I jumped up and got back into my long johns before helping him to his feet. "So you ain't got nowhere to sleep for a couple of days?"

He grinned, eyes twinkling again. "You offering, Bert?"

I grabbed him and pulled him in tight, just as the train came to a screeching halt. "You acceptin', Joe?"

Then the eager nod. "I'm accepting, Bert," he whispered, biting down on my earlobe, a swarm of butterflies set loose in my belly. "Only, I bet *sleep* ain't what we're in for."

"Nope. On account of that would be a job half-done, Joe." I kissed him long and deep and hard.

"Ain't nothing worse than that, Bert," he replied, kissing me back, just as long, just as deep, just as hard. "Ain't nothing worse than that, no mincing about it."

ELSEWHEN
'NATHAN BURGOINE

It's late on a Thursday night, and I'm watching Parliament burn down again. The heat is intense, the smoke makes my eyes water, and I have to struggle not to cough.

I can't get close enough. I'd like to figure out which wayward soul is stuck—what need or wrong has kept this echo repeating all these years—but the same quirk that lets me see these ghostly reenactments makes it too real for my flesh. I have enough scars from other souls. I don't want to burn.

I long ago stopped being angry about it. Like anything else, sometimes it is beautiful, sometimes not. Sometimes I have to ask questions of a spirit to learn who they were, and return when they echo again with the right answers. I love helping children—so often they just want to know their parents lived good lives. Sometimes I cannot learn anything, and so I lie and hope to find the right words to help them to their next place—a lie for a good cause. The angry are harder. And there are wrongs I cannot right. Those continue to echo without solution, a tug on the back of my mind that I know will never go away.

Watching the old Parliament buildings burn is like that. Ghostly men in thick jackets spray water into the smoke. It was February when they caught fire—no one knows what sparked it. Many perished. In the flames and smoke of the past, someone needs help, but I can't figure out how to do it. These kinds of haunting make me wish there was someone to go home to. Someone to whom I could tell these stories of the dead. Someone who isn't my dog, as wonderful as she is.

"Sorry I'm late. There was a dead woman at the market who kept me later than I thought. How about pasta for dinner?"

Not likely.

I turn my back to the heat, frustrated that I am no closer to solving this problem. Ottawa's downtown—the real downtown, not the icy echo of the night Parliament burned down in 1916—spreads out before me. The early spring breeze is cool, and by the time I reach the War Memorial, the only heat I can feel is from the sun sinking low amongst the buildings behind me.

I'm about to start walking home when the air around the federal Conference Centre ripples. I feel the tug, and I turn before I can help myself. The bridge over the canal starts to shimmer like the air over hot concrete. The flags lose their colour. The entirety of the Nicholas Expressway warps and blurs. Everything shifts slightly out of focus, and I feel my hands clench into fists as I hold on to the now.

Tracks appear, snaking up to the Conference Centre.

It used to be a train station, but it's been closed since the centennial. I vaguely remember a tour guide telling me the Conference Centre was once a major hub of the massive railways that ran through Ottawa. The Grand Trunk, I suddenly recall.

I cross the street, squinting to make sure I still catch view of the living world. It would be easy to see the echoes of past streetcars and miss the reality of an SUV on my literal and figurative cross over to the other side. I hear the beat of an engine on a railroad. The Conference Centre is already shedding its current façade and returning to the station it once was. Pillars stained with gray smoke stretch out above me. Archways and spherical lamps form out of the whitish mists of the past. My feet touch the opposite pavement, and a train coalesces further down the translucent tracks that have completely replaced the traffic on Nicholas. It grows louder and more solid as it approaches—passing through buildings and lamps and flagpoles as though they weren't there.

A train is pulling into the Grand Trunk station, which has been closed since 1966.

This is new.

❖

I find a bench—a real bench—and sit. With three deep breaths, I rise with only half of who I am, feeling the tenuous shiver run through my body. The now fades into the barest of shadows, and all around me, the echo of an older Ottawa sharpens.

I walk into the station as the train hisses and whistles its arrival. I can't help but look around—the Conference Centre isn't open to the public. It's beautiful. Wooden benches with glass-shaded lamps are arranged in rows across from the tracks, and the pillars reach the ceiling in flared arcs that form arches and curves of carved stone. All around me, echoes of the dead are walking. The train is the sharpest image, holds the most colour, and I direct my attention to it. The third cab is nearly shining, so I move toward it.

I shouldn't do this. It's one thing to stand at the edge of an echo and find out what went wrong, or to call to a spirit and speak with it. It's enough to try to help a soul realize it is time to move on. It's another thing entirely to walk into the false past. But I've been seeing Parliament burn down for weeks. The desire to help is a constant itch. I'm tired of watching.

The train stops, and shifting shapes that are more or less people drift from the cabs. It's easy to skim the crowd when they are barely a part of this echo, so it doesn't take me long to see him. He stands at the opening of the car. He keeps one hand on the threshold while he faces out into the station. I think he would be scanning the crowd for someone were it not for the cloth running across his eyes. His uniform is plain simple khaki, simple buttons, two front pockets—his pants clean and pressed even after a train ride. His boots are shined. He has short fair hair and is so clean-shaven I think he might not need to shave often at all.

I watch, torn. He doesn't move. Soon, I think, the train will move on. Soon, whatever—or whoever—he is waiting for will not have appeared, and the echo will move on until it replays again. And again.

I start walking through the crowd of half-remembered people. I'm at the bottom of the steps before long, and I reach out with one hand, not quite sure that even this vibrant echo can be real enough to support me.

I take the bar and tug myself up onto the train. The soldier's head tilts toward me, and I hesitate a moment before I touch his shoulder. Speaking to an echo casts me in the role they need the most, and they see who they want to see—but his eyes are bandaged. I steel myself.

"Julian?" he asks. His voice is uncertain. "Is that you?"

The coincidence is shocking. I shiver. Whoever this dead soldier waited for shared my name. I clear my throat, and say, "Yes." It is refreshing to play a part without lying from the first breath.

❖

With a hand tracing the walls of the car, he leads me further into the train. It's old-fashioned, with narrow wooden doorways and curtained windows. Close behind him, I can smell the faintest trace of talcum powder. He isn't tall, coming only to my chin, and the cloth wraps around the back of his head, where it is clipped with a single silver pin. We reach the third door from the steps. He opens it, steps through, and sits on one of the two benches that face each other.

I come in after him and close the door.

The train whistle blows. I sit. Moments later, there's a lurch as the train begins to move. My stomach clenches.

"I didn't know if you'd come," he says, finally.

This is dangerous. I have to play a part, but I don't know my role. We're inside a train that isn't, moving across tracks that aren't, and I'm sitting across from someone who shouldn't be, but is.

"I had to," I say. Oddly, it feels true.

His lips quirk. It's handsome and natural. I get the feeling that before, he was someone who often smiled, and the habit isn't one he's having luck breaking.

"Julian," he says, and again the coincidence of names makes me shiver. "I…" He swallows. He's sitting so still on the bench seat. He breathes out.

I wait. I don't know my lines.

"You pity me," he says.

"No," I reply, and it comes out quickly and firmly because it is the truth. I have scars myself, and I have never wanted pity.

Another quirk of his lips. "I suppose it does mean I won't have to see that ugly mug of yours."

I laugh. I like this dead man. The train picks up speed, turns a corner. We rock to the left. The view out the window is indistinct and colourless. The unfinished business is not about out there.

"Remember the blackout?" he asks. I know enough history to know how cities turned off their lights to avoid giving bombers targets.

But there's a specificity to his tone that tells me he means a particular blackout.

A particular night.

"Yes," I say. My first lie.

He nods. "All night in the dark. You and me. The noise…" He swallows. "You remember how you said it was easy to talk in the dark because you didn't have to look me in the eyes? The dark is for truth-telling, you said." He offers another almost-smile and with one slender hand, he touches the cloth across his eyes. "Well, here's a truth: it'll always be dark for me now, and I love you." He breathes. "I love you, Julian."

Oh God.

I'm frozen. I can't think or speak. I don't know what to do. Some reflex makes me reach out and take his hand. He squeezes.

"I know it's harder for you," he says. "I have money. My father's money, but it will be mine. I'll never lack. And I know you have Lindsay and Laurel and Audrey to look after, and the farm, but…" He squeezes my hand. "I could…We could…Somehow…" Each aborted sentence makes his hand shake a little more.

I move from my bench to kneel in front of him, and I put my other hand to his cheek. He stops talking and I kiss him. His free hand takes the back of my neck.

The kiss breaks.

"The door," he says.

We break apart long enough for me to find the latch and snap it shut. I draw the curtains over the small glass window above the handle. I press my forehead against the wood that isn't there and feel the sway of the train that doesn't exist. Then I turn and take his shoulders in my hands and kiss him again.

❖

He doesn't let me remove the bandage, pulling my hands away when I touch it, but everything else is soon shed beneath us, between the benches. His body is lean, with sinewy muscle and fair skin and a strength belied by his frame. He is quick with his fingers and mouth, tugging my clothes off and kissing my throat and chest—here pausing to call me a "hairy beast"– and then my nipple. His fingertips find my scars; shoulder, forearm, the left side of my stomach—and he kisses each place without comment.

I go for his neck, which is soft, and his thighs, which are hard. When I take him into my mouth, he makes a noise somewhere between a gasp and a whimper, and I tease his length with my tongue.

I can taste him.

Before long, his hands are tight in my hair, and he is breathing in short bursts.

"Julian…wait…" he gasps.

I release him and slide awkwardly along his body, crammed between the two benches, finding his mouth for another kiss. We grind, his hardness against mine, and his touch, his mouth, and his soft swallowed cries have me so hard I can barely breathe.

We move, the rocking of the train a delicious counterpoint, sweat building as we rub against each other and tease each other further and further. He twists in my grasp until I am lying on top of him, and he is on his stomach beneath me.

"Please," he says.

"I don't want to hurt you."

"You won't."

I try everything I can think of to make that true. My tongue, my finger, so much saliva and sweat, but when I enter him, I'm sure it hurts him. He breathes sharply, and I hesitate, arms straining.

"Please," he says again.

I push into him, and he surrenders to it. We shift into a new rhythm, each clack of the track beneath us another thrust opposite to my own. We breathe, then gasp, then move to more base noises before a release that leaves us both collapsed on the floor of the compartment.

"I love you," he says again.

This time, he doesn't fight my fingers when I remove the cloth around his eyes. They are ruined. Scarred, burned and sightless. I kiss one, then the other.

"I love you," I say.

The train shimmers. I feel a sob in the depth of my chest.

"I love you," I say again.

I mean it.

Between the start of his smile and the touch of his hand to my cheek, the world comes apart. I am sitting on a bench in front of the

Conference Centre that was once the Grand Trunk station, and a brown-eyed police officer is shaking my shoulder and asking me if I need a hand.

I tell him of my "seizures." He's patient, and assumes my tears are born of embarrassment. He tells me not to worry, that he doesn't think anyone else noticed. I don't bother to contradict him. He lets me leave after I convince him I am fine.

I go home.

❖

Julian is not an incredibly common name. With time, finding a Julian with relatives named Lindsay, Laurel, and Audrey doesn't prove impossible. Speaking to him does. Julian Mitchell has been in a long-term care facility for a number of years, no longer brought out in a wheelchair even for Remembrance Day, since he cannot speak and doesn't react to voices any more. He has a nose that was obviously broken more than once, and in pictures I find online of his younger self, I can nevertheless see a rugged—if somewhat brutish— handsomeness to him.

The train pulls into Grand Trunk two weeks later. And again the week after that. Sometimes I watch, sometimes I climb aboard again. The same police officer finds me there twice more, and I switch to a different bench along the canal after that, when his kindness starts to make me think of pity. For nearly four months this is the routine. I tell the fair-haired soldier I love him, and sometimes for as long as two weeks, his echo abates. But it always returns. I wonder what I'm missing, but a part of me isn't sure I want to know.

I haven't even tried to learn the soldier's name.

When Julian Mitchell's death notice appears in the paper, I almost miss it, but my eye is drawn to my name. I wait at the Conference Centre for four nights for the train to appear. When I step into the Grand Trunk station this time, I look through the crowd carefully.

Julian Mitchell is there. Young, strong and afraid. His uniform is the mirror of the young soldier's on the train. I move to his side.

"Laurel will marry well, and the farm won't need you," I say.

Julian turns, surprised at my voice. "What?" he says. "Who are you?"

The train has stopped. Indistinct passengers are disembarking.

"It doesn't matter," I say. I wonder who he sees.

There is some fear in his eyes, but more than that there is a kind of recognition. I think about his time. How hard it must have been.

The passengers have all stepped out of the train. The soldier appears at the opening of the car. I hear Julian's shallow gasp.

"His eyes," he says.

"Yes," I say. Then, unable to help myself, I ask. "What's his name?"

Julian's jaw tightens. He looks at me again. "Stephen."

"Stephen," I repeat. "For the rest of your life, you'll wish you got on that train with him."

"What can I do?" Julian says. His voice is low, pitched for privacy from people who can no longer hear us talk. "His father can take care of him. I can't."

Stephen stands there still. I want to go to him. I look at Julian again.

"Close your eyes."

"What?"

"Just do it!" This is louder than I intend, and he flinches. But he closes his eyes.

"It's dark," I say, and touch his shoulder. "So tell the truth. Do you want to go get on that train?"

There is a long pause. I look at this strong young man, who spent the rest of his life on a small farm, even after his sister's husband took it over. Julian Mitchell never married. Julian Mitchell was—the obituary said—a brother, an uncle, and a veteran. No one's beloved.

"Yes," he says, and opens his eyes.

I watch him walk to the train. He climbs aboard and touches Stephen's shoulder. I watch their lips move, unable to hear them. They walk deeper into the train.

I wait for the whistle. Then I wait until the train leaves. I wait until the walls of Grand Trunk fade into clouds of nothing. I wait until I cannot even see the ground at my feet. When there is nothing but white mist as far as the eye can see, I let go and come back to myself on the bench by the Canal.

I'm crying. I won't see the train again, I know. Nor Stephen. The train will take them to a place and time that never was. They'll be happy, I tell myself, not caring that I don't know any of this for sure. A lie for a good cause.

I shift, and I realize that someone has draped a heavy jacket over my shoulders. Beside me, sitting quietly, the same brown-eyed police officer looks out over the water. He's not in uniform. When he hears me move, he looks at me.

"Thought you might like some company," he says.

I nod.

"My father had seizures," he says. "Bad ones. Not like yours. Cracked his skull once."

I clear my throat. "It's not a seizure exactly."

"Oh?" He looks at me. He has kind eyes, but there's no pity in them.

"I'm Julian," I say, and offer a hand.

He takes it. "David." Our handshake lingers just a little. He smiles.

I pause. "Did you know there used to be a train station here?"

He shakes his head.

I start to tell him.

MOUNT OLYMPUS
JEFFREY RICKER

If his grandmother hadn't died and left him everything, Dan would never have come to Mars. He wouldn't have been on a train racing at five hundred kilometers per hour across the Tharsis Planitia from the spaceport toward New Lisbon. He stared out the window at the rust-colored landscape and wondered why his grandmother ever moved here.

His memory of her was indistinct, like an out-of-focus picture. She left Earth when he was ten, and what he remembered most were his parents' protests at her departure: It was too dangerous. Too far, too insane. They'd never see her again. Dan wanted to say *take me with you*, but that would never have happened. So he forgot about it— forgot about *her*, really, apart from her occasional e-mails, which they sometimes read to him, sometimes not. Twenty years passed like this, and then, six months ago, the letter from the lawyer arrived.

"Why do you have to go there?" his mother asked.

"Stipulation of the will," Dan said. "It needs to be read in New Lisbon."

"That's not what I meant," she said, "and you know it. Why are you going at all? Isn't the farm enough?"

His grandmother had also left Dan her Terran assets: a farm in upstate New York and all its contents, including a lot of old science textbooks on terraforming.

"It's not about anything being enough," Dan said. His mother came to his apartment while he packed—ostensibly to get instructions on looking after his cat while he was away—but she had spent little time since her arrival on the finer points of Darwin's care and feeding.

"Would you mind telling me what the point is?" she asked. She had mourned her mother earlier, when she left for Mars—as far as she was concerned, that was Catherine Graves's original date of death.

Dan smiled. "As soon as I figure that out, I'll let you know. But I don't think I'll find the answer here."

His mother shook her head. "I wish your gran had never heard the word 'terraforming.'"

Regardless, she had, and here he was.

Dan was prepared to be disappointed by Olympus Mons. He'd read about it, along with the other notable landmarks on Mars. It was so big that the curvature of the planet made it impossible to get a sense of the sheer scale of the peak. He hadn't read about the five-mile-high cliff faces skirting the base of the long-dormant volcano, though, and the sight of the walls of rock blocking out the sun as the train hurtled toward them was awe-inspiring. It was hard to imagine that there was still a mountain on the top of that plateau.

There were few people on the train. New Lisbon wasn't a large city, only a few thousand, mostly terraformers or support providers. Train service was limited to one run per day.

"Train?" Dan asked the desk attendant at the spaceport. "Wouldn't flying there be faster?"

The man in line behind him all but sneered at Dan. "No flights. The maglev doesn't use even a tenth of the power a flight would use. And it moves faster than this line does."

The train was six cars long, including the main control car and two cargo cars. Of the other three passenger cars, one was empty, one was somewhat crowded, and the only passenger in the third car was the grumpy man from the line. Dan was about to head for the empty car when the man, who was reading a tablet, said without looking up, "They'll be uncoupling that car before we leave."

They were in the back of the train. If Dan backtracked toward the other, more crowded car, the man would know Dan was deliberately choosing to sit as far away as possible. He slid into a seat a couple rows behind the man. About the same time, he heard a clanging noise and the end car started rolling away from the train. A low hum ran through the floor and, as Dan watched, the platform receded into the darkness of the tunnel.

"You'll want to look out the windows on your side in about thirty seconds," the man said, still without looking up.

Sure enough, in less than half a minute, the tunnel walls dropped away and the train appeared to soar through the air. In reality, it was elevated about a hundred meters off the ground, magnets suspending it above the track as it leisurely descended toward the planet's surface. Really, it *was* kind of like flying. The city fell behind them rapidly, and the vast, high desert-looking terrain of Tharsis stretched out in front of Dan.

"Wow," Dan said, all but pressing his face against the glass.

The man laughed. "That's pretty much what everyone says the first time they see it."

"What gave it away that this is my first time here?" Dan asked, trying not to bristle at the suggestion that he was a greenhorn. Mainly because that's what he was.

Finally, the man set his tablet on the seat next to him and turned to look at Dan. "This train only makes one stop, and New Lisbon's pretty small. Everyone knows everyone else. Newcomers tend to stand out."

"And what made you think this is my first time on Mars? Not that it isn't; it is. My first time on Mars, I mean."

"The thing at the spaceport about flying to New Lisbon. Takes too much fuel. The train hardly has to do anything to get us there at about the same speed a light flyer would. It's the sort of thing that gets in your head when you live here, conserving everything you possibly can. You never know when you're going to need it."

"How long have you lived here?"

The man smiled. "My whole life. Born in Cydonia City, been in New Lisbon ever since I finished school. And before you ask, no, I've never been to Earth."

"Wasn't going to be my next question, actually," Dan said. Actually, it *was* what he'd been thinking of asking. "But since you brought it up, how come?"

He shrugged, and Dan realized he didn't even know the man's name yet. "What's the hurry? Earth's been there for billions of years. It's not like it's going to vanish any time soon. Besides, how many Earthers have been to Mars?"

"Point taken," Dan said. "My name's Dan, by the way."

The man's handshake was brief but strong, the skin of his fingers and palm rough. "Nathan. Pleased to meet you. What brings you to New Lisbon?"

"My grandmother. She died a few months back."

"You're Catherine Graves's grandson?" Nathan's eyes lit up at that. Dan noticed for the first time that they were pale green, a stark contrast to his jet-black hair. Why did he usually not notice the color of people's eyes? He couldn't have said what color his gran's eyes were.

"That's me," Dan said. "Did you know her?"

"Everyone knew her. Small town, like I said. Everyone knows everyone else. She was our best horticulturist. She could make anything grow."

"It's been a long time since I last saw her. Twenty years, I guess." Where had the time gone? His grandmother worked to transform the face of a planet. What did he have to show for the years?

A sudden burst of laughter and shouting from the car ahead of them interrupted his momentary introspection. Dan looked up, startled, and Nathan smiled. "The main car is also the ad hoc bar car. That's why I'm sitting back here. They'll all be shitfaced before we're halfway to New Lisbon."

"Nice."

"Will you be staying long?"

Dan shrugged. "I guess that depends on the terms of her will. I've only been here a day."

At that, Nathan picked up his tablet and began to read again. "Well, enjoy your time here. You might want to head up to the observation deck. You'll get a good view from up there."

Dan stared at the back of Nathan's head for a short time, wondering why he'd been given the brush-off so abruptly. Had he missed something? He waited a moment longer before heading toward the spiral staircase at the back of the car.

The upper deck was a dome of glass with low seats running along each wall. In every direction the rusted landscape met the dusty yellow sky. No one else was on the deck. Nathan settled into one of the seats and let the reality of being on another planet sink into him. He knew no one here, except the lawyer in New Lisbon (probably the only lawyer in town, if Dan had to guess). It would take him six months to get home. Practically speaking, he'd never been this alone.

Staring at the landscape lulled Dan into a trance, so he wasn't sure how much time passed before Nathan came up the stairs and sat across from him.

"So, my ex-husband is from Earth," Nathan said without preamble. "He was here with the university. We hit it off almost right away, and when it came time for him to leave, I asked him to stay and marry me. He was happy for about another year, then he decided that he missed things like blue skies, grass, oceans. I still loved him as much as I did the day I married him, but I can't compete with a whole planet. I've been a little jaded when it comes to Earthers since then."

"So why are you telling me this?" Dan asked, though he had a feeling he knew why. "I'm just a stranger on a train."

Nathan opened his mouth to respond, but a thought seemed to cross his mind before he could actually speak. He closed his mouth, looking puzzled, then smiled. "I have no idea, to be honest. Have you ever been married?"

Dan shook his head. "Never met the right guy, I guess." This was true and not quite true at the same time. He'd met the right guy, but unfortunately, he was the only one who thought so. Reese had claimed he was trying to let Dan down easy, but too often that can seem like stringing someone along. When the end finally came, Dan was so crushed he quit his job, left New York—where he'd lived ever since he graduated from college—and moved back to St. Louis. That was a year ago. Since he'd moved back, the journey to Mars was the first time he'd left the city, much less the planet.

"You know," Nathan said, interrupting Dan's reverie, "for some reason I'm not quite convinced you've never met the right guy."

"Oh? Why's that?"

"Because you've been staring out the window and not saying a word for almost a full minute. If I had to guess, I'd say you're thinking about him right now. What's his name?"

Dan smiled. "My mom always tells me you can read everything I'm thinking on my face. Reese was his name. He just wasn't as into me as I was into him."

"Is that why you're here? To get away from him?"

"Not exactly. Let's just say the letter from my grandmother's lawyer was serendipitous." He turned back to the window. "You know, I can't figure for the life of me why she decided to move here." Dan suddenly realized what he'd said and added, "No offense."

"None taken. You mean why did someone whose life revolved around making green things grow decide to go somewhere nothing grows?" When Dan nodded, Nathan continued. "From what I can tell, the only thing Catherine enjoyed more than gardening was a gardening challenge. Believe me, this place is a challenge."

"Was she able to make anything grow?"

"She could make a seed sprout in the dark with no dirt and almost no water. Which is not far from what she actually did. Our hydroponics grove is amazing. You have to see it to understand just how much of a miracle it is. Thirty thousand square meters of unbroken vegetation pumping out food and oxygen. If we can replicate this worldwide, we can turn Mars into a living, breathing planet just as sustaining as Earth. More, even."

"How would you know if you've never been there?"

"Your grandmother believed it would happen. She said we were better off here. She thinks we're on the right track."

"*Thought* you were on the right track."

Nathan started to say something else but sat back in his seat instead. "She never wanted to go back to Earth. Maybe if you stick around for a while, you'll come to see in this world what she did."

Dan shrugged and looked out the window again.

"Catherine loved it here, she really did," Nathan continued. "She always said this place has a way of getting inside you, manages to creep under your skin and won't let you go until you're part of it. It's always been part of me, but she didn't want to leave any more than I did. Who knows, maybe it'll get inside you too."

"Maybe," Dan said. "I know I just got here, but I'm already looking forward to going home." Four months of slow sleep on the transport sandwiched between a mind-numbing month of near total boredom on each end. He wanted to settle his grandmother's estate and get on his way home so he could start putting the unpleasantness of the return journey behind him.

Nathan looked out the window too. "She accomplished a lot here. You can be proud of that. I just hope we can keep it going now that she's gone."

Their conversation trailed out after that. Nathan went back to reading his tablet while Dan fell into an uncomfortable, restless sleep. He dreamed of standing outside on the flat volcanic plain, only this time it was no longer dormant, and he was no longer himself. A fierce, hot wind lashed at him, whipping his hair into a blond halo around his face—only it wasn't his hair, any more than the slender bare arms he crossed below his chest were his.

Two men stood in front of him. One had long, dark hair and a beard. He was dressed in bronze armor and held a sword. The other wore a blacksmith's apron and held a glowing pair of tongs and a massive hammer.

"Why must you make me choose?" Dan cried. He spoke in the voice of an anguished woman, but…somehow more than a woman. He fell to his knees, folds of diaphanous lavender cloth billowing around him. He raised his slender, bejeweled hands to his face to cover his tears before they could fall to the dusty ground. "Must it always be like this?"

"You can't have us both, even if you are a goddess," the armored man said.

"Decide," said the man with the hammer. "Will you forsake your husband?"

"Will you forsake true love?" the armored man asked, saying it to the other man as much as to her. They didn't bother to conceal their disdain for each other.

She pressed her hands to the sides of her head. "Then I choose neither of you! And no other man shall have me!"

With a sweep of her arms, the ground exploded in a swirling fury of dust, sending both men staggering back. Whispering "Hermes, help me," she fled, her feet barely touching the ground, the dust storm roiling in her wake. Hermes heard her call, and she moved faster than sound. The storm behind her grew higher and more ferocious with every step.

In the distance she saw a train.

Dan awoke. The train pitched left, sharp. Metal ground against metal, the maglev cut out, and the train slammed into the track. The cars accordioned and bashed sideways into each other before plunging into the ground. He landed flat on the floor, the breath forced out of him by the impact. He stayed there until the train at last came to a halt. The cacophony died down, and all that remained was a hiss.

Nathan leapt to his feet, yanking the cushions off the seats. From the storage bins beneath, he pulled out two environment suits, helmets, and oxygen canisters. He knelt by Dan and helped him up roughly.

"Put this on. Hurry."

Still dazed, Dan began to unfold the coveralls and struggle with the zipper. Nathan took it out of his hands and jerked the zipper open. When Dan was finally able to work the rest of his way into the suit, Nathan headed across the deck, which was tilted at a seasick angle, for the stairs.

The respirator covered Dan's nose and mouth. He stepped into the environment suit, then clamped the helmet down. As he screwed the oxygen canister into place, he looked up and saw the hiss was coming from a thin crack in the supposedly unbreakable clear canopy. He cranked open the oxygen valve and stood back, momentarily relieved. Then, stepping carefully along the crazily tilting floor, he went in search of Nathan.

On the main level, the windows along the left side were covered in dirt. It took Dan a moment to realize the train had landed on the surface and half buried itself in the soil. Dan held on to the backs of seats as he headed toward the other car.

The hatch between the cars didn't open automatically when Dan approached. He pulled the manual release. Nothing. He grabbed the handle and tugged harder, trying to ignore the sense of panic—*I'm not trapped, it's just the helmet's got me feeling claustrophobic, that's it.* Before long, though, he was yanking at the release and kicking the door, then wedging his shoulder and foot in opposite sides of the shallow recess in hopes of getting more leverage.

The hatch finally screeched open, and on the other side lay a tangle of bodies. Kneeling amid them was the armor-clad form he'd seen in his dream, but when the form looked up at Dan, he was only Nathan, the armor gone. The pile of bodies was other passengers starting to sit up and get to their feet.

Nathan helped him shut the hatch again. "The oxygen generators are still running in here. If we can keep this shut, we may have a chance."

"Is anyone hurt?" Dan asked, looking around at the passengers.

"Not badly. Maybe all the alcohol relaxed them beyond the point of feeling pain."

"What happened?"

"Biggest dust storm I've ever seen. The sand and grit was so thick you could have walked on it. Even so, I don't know how anything could push this train off the track. I swear, it was like it came out of nowhere."

Dan headed toward the front of the train, hoping he wouldn't have another hallucination. He remembered enough of his Greek mythology class to know the men in his dream were Ares and Hephaestus, lover and husband, respectively, of Aphrodite, the goddess of love. Why had he dreamed he was Aphrodite? What did the gods have to do with the red planet anyway?

"The back car is shot," Dan said to Nathan. "If this one and the control car are still serviceable, we might be able to restart."

A glance through the window in the hatch dashed any hope of that. They could see only one person alive on the other side. He wore an environment suit and sat at one of the control seats, wires sprouting out like weeds from the open panel in front of him. Three bodies lay on the floor, their skin blue-gray.

The one live crewman noticed them and got up. He pressed the intercom by the door.

"We're screwed," he said. "The controls are fried and the track below your car is mangled. We'd have to push the whole train onto unbroken track before we could move. I've radioed ahead and New Lisbon's sending a rescue team."

"What if we disconnected the cars and all squeezed into the control car?" Nathan asked.

They decided to try. While everyone started the cumbersome process of suiting up (even more clumsy when most of them were half-drunk), Nathan started outside to work on disconnecting the car from the engine.

"Here's your chance to walk on the surface for real," Nathan said to Dan. "Want to come?"

The first thing that struck Dan was the wind. He'd expected it to be as quiet as the void, but Mars was not the moon. A breeze whistled over the dome of his helmet, background music for the slow percussion of his breathing. His boots scratched in the sand.

"Welcome to Mars," Nathan said.

Dan turned to him, puzzled. "What?"

"The real Mars. Not the artificial environment under a manmade sky." He kicked up a dusty plume. "This is where the decisions you make every hour can be life-or-death ones. You'd be amazed how many

Earthers come here and never set foot on the actual surface, never feel the ground beneath them. You haven't even been here a day and already you've experienced more than most."

Including hallucinatory dreams and a near-death experience. Dan followed Nathan to the end of the second train car. "Sounds like you've never let your familiarity with Mars get to the point where you take it for granted," Dan said.

"Mars won't let you." Nathan knelt by the coupling between the second and last cars. "The minute you take him for granted, he kills you."

The coupling still held together, but the metal was so badly twisted, the cars would have to be cut apart. Nathan set to work with a laser torch. Dan turned to the sheer rock face north of them. It went straight up for miles, like the world ended at its edge. Once the sun passed the midday point, the cliff would cast nightlike darkness on the plain. Whenever midday arrived. Dan couldn't remember how long a Martian day was. Did it even matter? Listening to the wind, he closed his eyes.

Come to me, my love, someone said.

Dan knew he hadn't imagined that voice. It was the woman in his dream.

"Did you hear that?" When Nathan didn't answer, Dan turned to ask again—only now, Nathan wore Hephaestus's leather apron, and he swung at the train coupling with the god's hammer.

The sight of Nathan's transformation (*there's no such thing as gods*) wasn't what made him start running the half mile toward the rock face. He was running toward the source of that voice.

I am here, she said. *I am waiting for you.*

He knew the cave opening would be there, a small black dot at first that grew to almost four meters in height. He passed through it, his helmet lamp switching on automatically. The cave sloped gently downward, gradually narrowing.

Come to me, my love.

Through several twists and turns he followed the tunnel's route until it abruptly opened into a massive cavern. The walls glowed brightly with phosphorescent mineral veins. Spent from running, Dan stopped and bent over, hands resting on his knees as he tried to catch his breath. His helmet soon fogged up—*Great, how am I supposed to clear that off?*

He lifted a gloved hand to his helmet and realized the condensation was on the outside. The oxygen meter on his wrist had gone from red to green.

Malfunction. It has to be. When he lowered his hand from his helmet, though, he noticed the lawn and the grove.

Ahead, the cavern floor dropped abruptly. A carpet of grass began a short distance beyond, the long blades gently bowing over. The lawn ran maybe twenty meters up to about fifteen or twenty rows of trees, some of them reaching nearly to the cavern roof and extending into the distance farther than he could see.

"Where is she?" said Nathan.

At the sound of his voice, Dan turned. But Nathan had become Ares, the god from his dreams, standing at the mouth of the tunnel. Dan now held Hephaestus's hammer—*where did that come from?*—and wore his apron.

Dan, burning with rage, rose at the sight of Ares and flung the hammer. Ares used his shield to bat it away. When it landed in the gravel, Dan saw that the hammer was his helmet.

"She's gone," Hephaestus said. "It's as if she were never here."

"And what about that?" Ares asked, gesturing with his sword at the grove beyond.

"How is it even possible?" Dan whispered. Hephaestus once more, he turned toward Nathan, anger rising like flame. "That was my wife you were seducing."

Ares lowered his sword. "I think you have that the wrong way around."

Hephaestus sneered. "Small consolation to the one you cuckolded."

Ares dropped his shield. Walking up to Hephaestus, he put his free hand on the other god's neck. "Forgive me. I thought you didn't love her."

Hephaestus shook his head. "As if she could ever love one like me."

He looked down, but Ares lifted his chin to look him in the eyes. "Of course she could. You're a god."

Dan felt as if he were peering through fog, trying to see Nathan. "I'm not sure what's happening."

"Neither am I," Nathan said, pulling at Dan's sleeves.

"This isn't real, is it?"

"The hell it's not," Nathan said. He kissed him.

Dan closed his eyes and let himself get lost in the sensation. When he opened his eyes again, Ares dropped his sword and used both hands to untie the leather apron. Dan closed them again, opening them once more to see Nathan grasping at the clasps sealing Dan's gloves to his suit. Nathan's own gloves were already off. Dan reached behind Nathan's back and unbuckled the belts holding Ares's armor in place. The armor clattered to the ground. Dan ran his hands across the hair and muscles of Nathan's chest, descending to his waist. One moment, his fists were grasping Nathan's environment suit and pulling it lower; the next, Hephaestus was undoing Ares's kilt. Dan stopped trying to tell one vision from the other when Nathan at last stood naked before him and there were fewer differences to confuse him.

"Is this how the god of war declares victory?" Hephaestus asked between kisses.

"This is how the god of war surrenders," Ares replied.

As Nathan pulled him to the ground, Dan felt his own personality sinking below the surface, weighed down with carrying a heavier presence. It was like possession, and yet he felt no sense of coercion— not a victim, but rather a vessel. Nathan's mouth traced a trail down his chest to his abdomen, and when his chin grazed Dan's cock, it felt like electricity coursing through him and he arched his back, his body practically begging Nathan to do what he did next.

It was only when Dan gasped that Nathan stopped. "Are you okay?"

Dan kept his eyes shut. He didn't want his vision to confound everything he was feeling. "More than okay. Dear gods, don't stop."

Nathan only paused long enough to slide back up Dan's body and kiss him as he guided Dan's erection into him. The sensation of heat made Dan gasp again, his eyes opening wide to see Ares straddling him, head tilted back, the veins in his throat standing out as he grasped his own erection. All around them, the phosphorescence in the walls was glowing brighter, bringing daytime to even the farthest corner of the cavern.

Still keeping the rhythm of their bodies working together, Ares looked down at him and smirked.

"Is the light show your work?"

"I like to see what I'm doing," Hephaestus replied.

"I should have known you had that in you."

"And a few more tricks." Grasping Nathan's waist, Dan flipped the two of them over, staying inside Nathan, who now lay on the ground. Dan slid his hands down Nathan's thighs, lifting his legs until his calves rested on Dan's shoulders. Nathan grinned wickedly, strained upward to lock Dan in a kiss, and gave a moan that was all the encouragement Dan needed. Nathan came with a bellow that sounded beyond human, echoing off the cavern walls. Accompanying Dan's release was a blinding flare of the glowing minerals embedded in the rocks.

Exhausted, Dan collapsed on top of Nathan. Slowly, as they caught their breath, Dan looked at Nathan's face and found he couldn't remember exactly the face he'd seen earlier.

Dan sat back on his heels. "What the hell just happened?"

"If I had the answer to that, I'd probably say I was losing my mind," Nathan answered. He winced as he sat up, and Dan felt a pang of guilt for having been so rough.

"Did I hurt you—"

"I'll be fine," Nathan said, grinning again. It was a look that Dan would have taken for Ares and not Nathan. "It's not every day I get banged in the dirt by the god of fire."

Dan stood up and, suddenly feeling self-conscious about his nakedness, began gathering up his clothing and the environment suit. "Even so, I feel like I should apologize."

Nathan stood and put his hand on Dan's arm, stilling him. When Dan finally looked up at him, Nathan stroked his cheek. "If you apologized, I'd think you didn't mean it. I hope you meant it."

Dan dropped the tangle of clothes and pulled Nathan closer, settling against him as they kissed. His fading erection stirred against Nathan's belly.

"Down, boy," Nathan said. He laughed.

Finally, they both suited up again, Dan feeling a little sadder as more of Nathan's flesh was covered up. He felt like a spell had been broken. Dan stared once again down the rows of trees. "What *is* this place?"

"This looks like what your grandmother was working on before she died," Nathan said. "All of New Lisbon's oxygen supply is produced by underground greenhouses similar to this, only much smaller. They get all the CO_2 they need from the atmosphere, and we use minerals extracted from the soil for fertilizer. Catherine hoped to create enough of these worldwide that they might be able to play a part in converting the atmosphere to a breathable mix."

"It's beautiful," Dan said.

"They also supply a lot of our food." Nathan stepped to the edge of the overlook. He had put on everything except his helmet. "I wish she could have lived long enough to see this," he said.

Dan tucked his helmet under his arm and stood next to Nathan. He put his other arm around Nathan's waist. Nathan leaned into him. Dan didn't say it, but he wondered if his grandmother might have had a similar vision to his. She must have traveled the same train route at least once.

Nathan stepped away from the edge and put his helmet on. As he snapped the latches shut, another thought set off alarms in Dan's head.

"The train," he said, eyes wide. "What if they left—"

Nathan shook his head. "I told them you had wandered off and I was going to look for you. You're an Earther, so they didn't even bother to doubt me."

Dan grinned. "You're enjoying my status as an outsider far too much."

"I have to until you decide to stay."

They fell into silence as, side by side, they walked back out through the tunnel. The dew clinging to their helmets dried long before they reached the surface. Dan could barely see the train in the distance once they emerged, but as they walked closer it gradually came into view, along with a second train on the tracks in front of it.

"There's our ride from New Lisbon," Nathan said.

Dan looked behind them at the dwindling sight of the cave opening. "I'm not in all that much of a hurry to get back, honestly."

"Really? I can't wait to take this helmet off and kiss you again."

Dan looked over at him, caught him grinning again, or maybe still, and couldn't help but smile. "So it wasn't just a one-time thing?"

"I suspect the part where we were possessed by the spirits of ancient gods was likely a one-time thing, but as for the rest of it? That barely scratches the surface of all the things I'd like to do with you. And I'm not just talking about sex, though that was pretty damn divine."

Nathan took Dan's gloved hand and held it close to this thigh reassuringly.

"What do you think happened?" Dan asked. "Really?"

"No idea." Nathan shook his head. "I'm not much of a spiritual person to begin with, much less of a pantheon that hasn't been actively worshipped in at least three thousand years."

He stopped and looked behind them, at the cliff face rising above the flatlands, the mountain peak beyond that too vast to see from the ground. "But this *is* Olympus Mons."

Dan looked at him questioningly.

"Mount Olympus. The home of the gods."

Dan gazed up, wishing he could see the peak, but once you got far enough away from the mountain to see anything that high, the curve of the world had already obscured it from view. Fitting, perhaps, that the home of the gods should be impossible to see.

"I'm still not sure I believe it," he said.

Nathan took his hand once more. "Believe this, then."

Dan smiled. It was more than enough.

REUNION ON THE RAILS
HANK EDWARDS

A wicked thunderstorm raged above the city the day the invitation arrived in the mail. I was expecting it, but as I stood there in the lobby of my apartment building, the rain dripping off my nose and smearing my name etched in careful calligraphy, a cold seed of loneliness took root in my chest. I had seen the Facebook posts, followed the Twitter feeds, even read through Amy's lengthy e-mails and responded with advice throughout her courtship with Noah. I felt more than a little responsible, of course, because Stu and I had introduced them four years ago.

Stu. The thought of him watered the seed of loneliness and helped its roots dig in deeper. A collage of memories whipped through my mind as thunder grumbled outside and a taxi horn blared in frustration. I saw the whole span of our five-year relationship in a matter of moments: the day we met in IKEA, both of us trying to decide which bookshelves would take less effort to assemble and helping each other load the bastard things into our respective cars; a string of dates to various bars and restaurants; my habit of choosing bad movies that, on a second glance, never looked promising; winter afternoons spent in bed, my lips chapped from so much kissing on Monday morning as I rushed to work.

We eventually moved in together, and it had been good for a few years, but then things changed; Stu changed. And maybe I had, too. Either way, we grew apart, and as Amy and Noah were falling in love, I was looking for a new apartment uptown and surreptitiously separating my CDs from his, making my own shelf on my set of IKEA bookshelves.

"You just gunna stand dere all day?"

I jumped and let out a startled squeak. Turning, I found Angelo Freedom standing half inside the small lobby. Rain ran down his long, flat face, and his small, dark eyes were narrowed.

I cleared my throat and fumbled with my keys to open the interior door. "Sorry, Angelo."

"Don't be sorry, Tyler," he grumbled as lightning flared inside the small lobby. "Just open the mother-lovin' door."

I grinned as I spun the key in the lock. Angelo had a two-year-old son and had been told by his wife in loud, forceful words to tone down his swearing or spend the rest of the year on the sofa. "Working on it. You know it sticks in the rain."

"That's what she said," Angelo muttered and we both chuckled.

The lock finally relented, and we stomped into the long, dark hallway. Angelo shook the rain off like a big, shaggy dog and stopped to peer at me curiously, as though I were an oddity in a tank.

"Never heard that it's impolite to stare?" I asked, my tone more defensive than I had intended.

Angelo pulled his head back, then grinned. "You got some bite to you." He paused as he looked at me some more. "I like that."

I grinned without meaning to. "Thanks."

"You okay? You looked a little lost there in the entrance."

I nodded and looked away from his gaze. Nobody looked at me too closely these days, and his stare was making me uncomfortable. "Yeah. I'm good. Just got a wedding invitation."

His eyes brightened and he smiled. "Yeah? A gay wedding?"

My lifestyle was a constant source of interest to Angelo, who had never known a gay man until he had moved out of his old neighborhood. He liked to ask me specific questions, like how two men decided who would be the man and who did the dishes.

I shook my head. "Sorry. A friend who's a girl and the guy I helped introduce her to four years ago."

That made him smile even wider. "Yeah? Look at you, helping us breeders out."

"Yeah, look at me." I lifted my hand and started off down the hall to my apartment. "Give Angelo Junior a hug for me."

"I will. Have a good night, Tyler."

I listened to him stomp off to the stairway and then to his heavy steps as he ascended to his apartment. My apartment was at the end of the hall and I let myself into the small, one-bedroom space and closed the door. The invitation felt like lead in my hand and I let it and my keys drop onto the small table Stu had given me one year for my birthday. I shrugged out of my wet overcoat and scrubbed my hair dry with a dish towel. Switching on the burner beneath the kettle, I stripped off my work clothes as I walked into the bedroom and slipped on pajama pants and a long-sleeved T-shirt.

I brought the mail to the small galley counter and, with a cup of tea at my elbow, I opened the invitation. The script was clear and concise, and a warm, sad feeling of regret bloomed from the roots of my loneliness.

"A train," I muttered to the steaming teacup with a sad smile. "They're actually getting married on a fucking train."

❖

The engine was a big brute of shiny black steel with hard angles and an honest-to-God cowcatcher on the front. A round light, big as my head, sat in the center of the engine's face, staring belligerently ahead as steam hissed around it.

Ten passenger cars plus two dining cars trailed behind the engine like the wives and children from Bible stories. I pulled my rolling bag along the station platform, swerving around groups of people babbling excitedly. I recognized a few from various functions with Amy and Noah, and I smiled but didn't stop to talk. I would be on a train with these people for two days, traveling from New York to Chicago. Three of the travel cars and one of the dining cars were reserved for the wedding. All in all, according to Amy, it had been cheaper to rent cars on a train instead of a church in New York City.

"Tyler! Ty!"

I turned at the shrieking to find Amy rushing toward me. Her blond hair was pulled back, and her shining face was nearly split in half by the width of her smile. She grabbed me in a bone-grinding hug, and I laughed, then inhaled the light scent of her perfume, her signature scent, and hugged her back. It had been a long time since someone had hugged me so ferociously, and I found that I missed it.

Too soon Amy released me and stepped back. Her blue eyes searched my face and then she scowled, that familiar, tiny crease digging in between her expertly shaped brows. "You look thin, sad, and lonely."

I laughed; it was impossible not to. "And it's good to see you, too, my dear."

She hugged me again, just as tight, then folded my arm in hers and pulled herself close to my side as we walked along the platform. "I was so glad when I got your RSVP and saw you were coming. I was worried you wouldn't."

"How could I miss your wedding?" I looked along the train. "Quite a unique way to get married. Are you going to explain the significance of getting married on a train to the other guests during a toast?"

A delicate pink blush warmed her cheeks and she squeezed my arm. "You're incorrigible."

I laughed. "Do people still use that word?"

"Polite people do."

I leaned closer and whispered, "Do polite people also have sex with their boyfriend for the first time on a train to Boston?"

Her clear, surprised laugh attracted several looks, which she smiled at in return. She squeezed my arm again and put her head on my shoulder. "God, I've missed you."

I kissed the top of her head, breathed in the exotic scent of her shampoo, and whispered, "Me too, Ames. Me too."

"Promise you won't stay away so long, please?"

I smiled in a non-committing way. "I promise to work on it."

She sighed and pouted, but kept my arm in her grip. "Well, it's a start. Same old Tyler, stubborn as ever."

"Same old Amy," I replied, "beautiful and bubbly as ever."

That smoothed away her pout and we continued on to the cars reserved for her wedding.

❖

I had decided to go on the cheap and reserved two business-class seats. I figured I would be up most of the night drinking and talking with people so a private sleeper room, in my opinion, would have been a waste of money.

As I arranged my carry-on items in my assigned row, people filed by in the aisle. Some stopped to say hello, but then kept on moving, swept along by the tide of arrivals. I had just pulled out my Kindle when I sensed someone standing over my shoulder. A light, clean scent, like the ocean at night, slipped around me and I felt the sad tug of memory. I steeled myself and turned, trying not to let the melancholy I was already feeling show in my eyes.

It was Stu, of course. He looked handsome and fit, his dark, wavy hair worn a little longer than usual, his brown eyes warm and inviting.

"Stuart," I said and extended my hand. "Hi. Good to see you."

Stu frowned at my hand and stepped into my row of seats. He opened his arms and pulled me against him. The heat of his body soaked into me, throwing sunlight on the fallow fields of my soul. I breathed in the smell of him, soap and that ocean-at-night scent, and hugged him back. At last, Stu stepped back, but not too far, staying out of the flow of people looking for their seats.

"It's good to see you, Ty," he said. "You look good."

I grinned and turned away. "Liar."

Stu chuckled. "No, really. You look good."

"Well, thanks." I glanced back at him, then away. I could only take looking at him in small doses, it seemed. "Were you in on any of this wedding-on-a-train idea?"

He laughed outright, and the sound of it soothed and hurt all at the same time; God, how I missed his laugh. He shook his head and shrugged. "Not even a little. I was just as surprised as everyone else when I got the invite."

I cocked my head. "You haven't seen Amy and Noah that much?"

His smile dimmed a little and his gaze shifted away. "Not lately. It just…wasn't the same somehow."

"Oh." I looked down into my carry-on bag, but all that was left was underwear and socks. I zipped it shut and left it on the seat next to the window, then looked back at him. "Sorry. I thought you still saw them on a regular basis."

He shrugged. "It's okay. I did see them a lot right after... Well, once you moved out. But I think we all found it difficult." He sighed and looked away. "It happens, right? When one couple breaks up, sometimes their friends don't see either of them that much anymore."

"Well, I'm sorry."

Stu grinned. "You've said that."

I grinned and it was my turn to shrug. "Maybe I have a lot to apologize for."

The touch of his hand on my arm seared like a brand. My cock took notice and stirred inside the cotton confines of my Jockeys. I thought about all the nights we had spent together, the intimate invasions, and the sweaty, sometimes-desperate couplings that always ended in such sweet release.

"Let's forget all that, okay? Just enjoy the train, the wedding, and the company." He smiled. "Even each other."

I nodded and smiled back. "Deal."

❖

The train rocked beneath me as I sat and tried to focus on my Kindle. The motion of the car, however, put me in a different mindset from the Civil War historical novel I had thought looked interesting from the reviews. Convenient as it was to carry five thousand books with me, I sometimes missed touching a book and looking at the back cover before I bought it.

I lowered the ebook reader and turned to gaze out the window at the hills rolling past. The rocking of the car and the rhythm of the wheels riding the rails sent me into a tailspin of flashbacks. Memories of Stu flicked by with the landscape and I caught fleeting glimpses of our relationship, most glazed with sweat and semen.

I recalled the first night we had had sex, how awkward and lovely it had been. Stu's toned body, covered with dark, trimmed hair, had shone in the glow of a streetlight through the window. We had kissed with no rhythm, yet to learn the tilt of each other's heads and shape of our mouths. Stu's cock rubbed against mine, both weeping precum that smeared across our hips. At one point his knee connected with my balls and left me gasping, but he made up for it with a long, gentle blow job and, when it was time, held my cock beside his cheek and stroked me to climax, turning his face into the spray of my cum. I returned the favor by stretching out beneath him and holding his balls tight in my mouth as he pumped his fist along his cock. The hot splash of his semen felt like baptism, and I knew right then I was lost to him.

A groan of springs as the train rounded a bend brought me back and I shifted in my seat, making room for my erection. Maybe I should have spent the money on a sleeper room. I lifted up in my seat and peered up and down the aisle. Other frugal wedding guests were talking quietly, playing video games or reading. My hard-on throbbed with needy intentions and I decided now was as good a time as any to see to it. We had a few hours before the wedding. I could lock myself in the bathroom between cars and take care of myself in no time.

I pushed up from my seat and stepped into the aisle. At that moment, Amy and Noah came through the door from the dining car, holding hands. People greeted them with cheers, whistles, and applause, and I joined in as well. My smile started to feel forced, however, when Amy set her gaze on me. She excused herself from the couple they were talking to and, pulling Noah along behind, made a beeline in my direction.

Oh damn.

"Tyler," Amy said with a spark in her eye that made me uneasy. "Do you have a moment to come to the dining car with us?"

"Uh, sure." I bid farewell to my moments alone and followed them back along the aisle, smiling at the curious eyes that tracked our passage.

In the dining car, I stopped in surprise at the sight of Stu waiting at a table for four set with china, crystal, and linens. Two candles flickered in the middle of the table, and a waiter in a white coat stood nearby holding a bottle of wine.

"What's all this?" I asked, erection long gone and replaced by a trembling flutter in the pit of my stomach.

Amy explained as she led the way to the table. "If it hadn't been for you and Stu introducing us at your Just for the Hell of It Party all those years ago, Noah and I would never have met." She sat across from Stu and Noah sat beside her, leaving me no other option than to sit next to Stu.

"In honor of that," Amy continued, "we wanted to spend some quality time with you both, just the four of us."

Her genuine thoughtfulness sparked a hot prick of tears that shut down my usual sarcasm. Instead, I simply nodded and smiled at Stu as I took the seat beside him. I was nervous. Hell, I was terrified. It was like a blind date with someone who knew all of my habits and quirks. He knew every button to push, every pet peeve, every annoying habit. This was the man who had straddled me in every imaginable position, pushed his cock deep inside my body, and taken my cock inside his. I had swallowed his semen and sucked on his toes. We had held one another on the anniversary of 9/11, sobbing as we thought about those friends we had lost. This was a man I had wanted to spend my life with, and here I was more nervous than I had been on our first date.

I smiled at Stu and he smiled back, then reached over to squeeze my hand reassuringly. I let out a breath and forced my stomach muscles to relax. Things were going to be all right.

And they were. It was surprisingly easy to have dinner as a foursome again. I had forgotten about Noah's quick wit always punctuated by Amy's sweet laugh. I had also forgotten how handsome Stu looked in profile and couldn't seem to take my eyes off him. Why had we let things slip away so fast?

The food and two bottles of wine were gone before I realized it and we all stood up and hugged in the aisle.

"Thank you," I whispered to Amy. "You don't know what this meant to me."

"I do," she whispered back and hugged me tighter. "Because it meant even more to me."

Stu and I made our way back to the passenger car while Amy and Noah went in the other direction to get ready for the ceremony. At my row, Stu slid in after me and sat in the aisle seat.

"Don't you have a sleeper compartment?" I asked.

Stu nodded. "I do. But I wanted to talk with you a bit."

We talked about our jobs and families and mutual friends, catching up with each other's lives. All the while I focused on the heat of his leg pressed against mine and tried to keep my erection at bay.

Finally, Stu leaned in and said, "Ty, I have to ask you something."

I swallowed past a sudden, dry clod of nervousness in my throat. "Sure."

"Did we get along this well when we lived together?"

I smiled, a little sadly, and said, "No. But we were a lot younger then."

Stu let out a breath. "I'm glad you agreed, because if we got along this well back then, I'd really be kicking myself for letting it end."

There was nothing to say to that, so I simply nodded.

Leaning closer, Stu lowered his voice and asked, "Want to get changed in my room?"

"More than anything," I said.

Stu shot out of his seat as if he had been ejected. He helped me gather my belongings and stuff them in my large carry-on bag, then led the way up the aisle toward the sleeper car. I avoided looking at the other frugal wedding attendees as I walked quickly after Stu, keeping my gaze on his round, delicious ass beneath the smooth lines of his khakis. How did he manage to find pants that looked so good on him?

The sleeper compartment was ridiculously small and, after I had shut the door behind me and leaned back against it, Stu turned to face me. He stood about three feet away, leaning back against the small table bolted to the outer wall beneath the window, and we both burst into laughter.

"Did you specifically request the hobbit-sized sleeper?" I asked.

"I know!" Stu agreed, and we laughed some more.

The tension eased from my shoulders until he stepped forward. A soft, warm brush of his lips against mine sent my equilibrium spinning. It wasn't a deep or demanding kiss, but it was intimate and filled with our shared history. He pulled his head back but remained standing right in front of me, a grin on those full, soft lips.

"Hi, Tyler," he said.

"Hi, Stuart," I replied, grinning back. "It's good to see you."

Stu leaned in and kissed me again, more firmly. His tongue pressed against my lips until I opened to him. Our tongues pushed and rolled together, a familiar waltz learned long ago.

I tugged at the buttons on his shirt until I had them all open and pulled the end of his undershirt out of his pants. His torso was just as I remembered: toned and warm, covered with silky hair. His nipples ripened into pebbles of arousal at the touch of my fingers and I pinched them, hard, just like he enjoyed.

"Oh, Ty," Stu breathed into my mouth. "God, I've missed you."

Our lips met again, our tongues more urgent. He fumbled with the buttons of my shirt as I unbuckled his belt and opened his pants. The khakis slid down his legs to puddle around his feet and I pressed my palm against the fattening bulge within his briefs.

Stu managed to get my buttons undone and we broke our kiss to peel off our undershirts. He got my pants open and pushed them down my legs, then pulled me against him, our bare chests pressed together as our cocks strained within our underwear. I reached around him and slipped my hands beneath the waistband of his briefs to squeeze the furry mounds of his ass and press his cock more firmly against mine.

He pulled his lips from mine to lean down and suck my nipples. I ran my hands up and down the soft skin of his back, sighing and groaning as he nipped and sucked. The world sped by outside the window, and I watched the blur of small houses and cars waiting behind crossing gates flash past.

Stu dipped his head lower, and I leaned back against the door as he slowly, so slowly, ran his tongue down the quivering skin of my torso. He knelt before me, pressed his open mouth over the bulge of my erection, and I moaned. It had been months since I had been with anyone, and years since I had been with someone I truly cared about.

Looking down, I watched Stu close his eyes and run his tongue over the rounded white cotton mound of my sex, and it felt as though we had never been apart. The depth of my emotions spun inside my chest like a miniature galaxy, filled with the light and energy of a small sun and all the ordered chaos of the revolving debris. Memories, happy and painful, flashed past like the scenery outside the window, swirling in the endless chasm of my relationship with Stu that seemed rooted somewhere near the middle of my chest.

He eased the waistband of my underwear down, allowing my cock to spring out at him like a spring-loaded toy. Nimble as ever, Stu caught it on his tongue. Pausing with his lips pursed around the head, he raised his gaze to look up at me. Our eyes locked for an intense moment and then his closed and he proceeded to suck me.

Stu had always been good at oral sex; suspiciously good. I wondered at times in our relationship if he didn't have a bevy of lovers around the city that he visited for practice. Even if he had, I might have forgiven him for the skill it provided.

His expertise was even more honed now. He swallowed my cock to the root, huffing a breath into the sweat-damp bush at the base before backing off. I groaned as quietly as possible against the thin metal door, resting a hand on the back of his head and closing my eyes as he worked my cock. I was close to the edge of orgasm, so very close, and was about to warn him to slow down when Stu released me and slowly stroked the spit-slick shaft as he smiled up at me with swollen lips.

"You still taste so good," Stu said.

"My skin brings all the mosquitoes to the yard," I replied, singing to "Milkshake," one of our old favorite songs, and we both laughed.

He stood up, planted a kiss on my mouth, and turned us so he leaned back against the door. I took my turn kneeling before him but wasn't as smooth as Stu had been; I immediately pulled his underwear down and gobbled up the arching length of his cock. The taste of his precum burst across my tongue, a sweet-and-sour nectar. I smelled the damp musk of his sweat mingled with his ocean-at-night scent. His thighs trembled beneath my touch and I worked the tight, corded muscles before moving up to pull taut his balls.

"I don't want to come yet," Stu said. "I want to fuck you, Ty. Can I fuck you, please?"

I didn't reply. Instead, I stood up and kissed him, our cocks crossing. I reached down to take hold of his cock, then stepped backward until the backs of my thighs bumped against the edge of the table. He set his feet between mine and, still kissing me, eased me back on the table. I lifted my legs and he slid his arms under them as if we had been doing this all along and never been apart. His touch felt good, familiar, and a small, pinched-up cyst of loneliness inside my chest seemed to burst, the cold contents evaporating beneath his touch.

Stu's cock poked against my hole, and I felt the muscle tremble at the impending invasion. He leaned away a moment, cool air rushing in to replace the touch of his body. I heard the rustle of fabric as he searched in his luggage and a moment later he was back, his sweat-tacky skin pressed against mine. I opened my eyes, watched him tear open a condom and apply a squirt of slick to his covered dick.

He leaned in over me, his expression intense as his dark eyes searched mine.

"Ready?"

"Yeah."

With a kiss, he slid slowly into me, parting muscle that seemed to adjust for him as if from memory. We had always fit together well, and I hadn't realized just how much I had missed having him inside me until that moment. It felt so good, so very right, to have his cock in my ass and his tongue in my mouth, that I thought nothing could ever again keep us apart.

He paused only a moment once he was fully inside, his tongue wrapping mine in an intimate spiral, then he pulled his hips back and started to fuck me. I gripped the edges of the table, feeling it shift and shudder as he pounded his length into me. Tipping my head back, I watched the world speed by, wondering idly if those watching us pass were able to catch a glimpse of my legs upraised in a V and Stu standing between them. The rocking motion of the train seemed to intensify the depth and position of Stu's hips as he plowed me, his cock stroking and spanking the tender nut of my prostate. I felt Stu's fingers tighten around my ankles, heard his breath quicken, and knew he was just as close to orgasm as I was myself.

"I'm close," he alerted me in his familiar breathy hiss.

The sound of his voice and the force of his fucking took me to that magic pinnacle and pushed me off the edge. I gasped as I stroked myself to a splattering climax, my muscles clenching around him. Stu pressed himself deep into me and I felt the pulse of his body as he came into the condom, a grunt punctuating each wave.

After, he leaned over me and we kissed for what felt like hours. Stu eased out of me and we kissed some more, the table creaking and groaning beneath us, as another small town zipped past, looking like all the others before it.

Finally, Stu helped me up from the table and held me against him as the sweat and my semen dried on our skin.

"That was amazing," he said.

"It was," I agreed, still a little stunned.

"Thank God I got a sleeper," he whispered in my ear and we both giggled.

We cleaned up as best we could at the tiny sink, using a sweaty T-shirt Stu had worn to the train to wipe ourselves clean. We kissed and touched as we danced around each other in the small space, getting dressed and laughing as we caught each other's gaze.

A question lingered in my chest, an obstruction that felt like heartburn after a favored meal. I wanted to ask what our next steps would be, what this afternoon tryst meant to him, but I was scared. I had felt the intensity of his emotion during the act of sex itself. And afterward, we were comfortable with each other, laughing and touching. But what did it mean beyond this train ride and Amy and Noah's wedding? What happened when we returned to New York and our day-to-day lives?

I had almost worked up the nerve to ask him how he felt now as a precursor to further questions when Stu took my hands and smiled at me with a mix of emotions. We had both managed to dress in our suit pants, white shirts, and ties and had twenty minutes before the ceremony was to begin.

And all at once I knew what to expect, and how blind I had been. Typical Stu, leaving the bad news for the very last when I would not have time to add my own opinion or a rebuttal. Aggravation, frustration, and a quiet sense of grief welled up in me at the sight of his sad brown eyes.

"Ty," he said, his voice quiet and an embarrassed shame on his face.

I squeezed his hands and smiled as bravely as I could. "It's okay."

"No, it's not," Stu said. "I didn't mean for this to happen."

"It's okay, Stu."

He blew out a breath and widened his eyes. "Will you just let me talk, please?"

I pressed my lips together and tried my best to keep the sadness rooting once again in my chest from showing in my eyes.

"I was nervous about seeing you again. Really nervous. I didn't know how you would react, how I would feel, all of it." He raised his eyes and smiled. "It was so much better than I expected. Obviously." He blushed. "And worse. I really do feel that we wasted so many years, and I wish we could get those years back and try again, you know?"

I nodded, unable to say anything, if there had been anything to say.

"But we can't go back. And, well, I've been trying to move on." He sighed and looked away out the window at the rest of the world passing by. "I'm meeting someone in Chicago for the weekend."

His words struck an ice-cold nail into my chest and, for a moment, I was unable to find my breath. I wanted to shout at him, throw my hands in the air and stomp around his tiny sleeper compartment, but, really, what good would that do? And hadn't we already played that scene out dozens of times before?

"Who is he?" I heard myself ask, and the words and tone of my voice sounded so casual, so unaffected, I wondered who had taken over control of my body.

Stu pursed his lips, glanced at me, then released my hands as if holding me while talking about him would be even worse to this new man than fucking me on the table in his train compartment. "His name is Tony. We met at a conference."

I swallowed past the regret and caught his eye. "I'm glad for you."

He gave me a miserable look and tried to smile. "I'm sorry, Ty. I didn't mean to lead you on or anything."

I shook my head and reached out to touch his knee, needing to feel a connection with him one last time. "You didn't." I tipped my head to see his watch and then looked up at him again. "Come on, we're going to be late."

❖

The wedding was held in the dining car. Stu and I slipped in the back, ducking our way through the tittering bridesmaids as the train bucked and swayed beneath our feet. We found a couple of chairs in the back of the car, and I tried to keep from being distracted by Stu's presence beside me as the wedding party made the walk down the aisle. I could still feel the dried patch of semen on my chest and the lube around my asshole. The sensations, Stu's proximity, and the wedding itself sank me into a swamp of memories of Stu and I together: shopping at Bloomingdale's; cooking together in our tiny kitchen; the one New Year's Eve we decided to brave the crowds and cold of Times Square; the sweaty nights spent fucking followed by days at work exhausted and chugging coffee as my sphincter pulsed with the memory of his repeated invasions.

Then I thought about this faceless Tony taking my place alongside Stu in my memories. Tony replaced me at Stu's side, laughing, kissing and loving him. A bottomless pit of desolation opened within me, and I could feel my heart dangling over the abyss on a dangerous thread.

I was pulled from my misery by the light touch of Amy's hand as she walked past and I focused once again on the ceremony before me. Amy and Noah stood swaying back and forth with the rhythm of the train as the pastor recited the sacred words to bind their lives together. A wellspring of anguish rose up within me, and I stood up the moment the vows were over. Without a word or a glance at Stu, I pushed through the doors connecting the cars and fled to my seats. I had hauled my luggage back to my reserved spot after my tryst with Stu, and now I sank into the seat and stared out the window at the countryside flowing past, tinged with shadow as the sun set on my heartache and Amy and Noah's blessed day.

After a time, I heard music from the dining car and the enticing smells of food forced me from my seat. I joined a group of older people at a table near the back of the car, introduced myself, and dug into the chicken dinner set before me. I turned away from my cares by asking questions of the people around me and offering few details about myself in return. All the while I was aware of Stu sitting up front, surrounded by couples himself. Our eyes met once, but I turned away before he could try to communicate.

By the time I followed a group of drunken revelers back to the passenger car and stretched out in my seat, it was after one a.m. Stu had left the reception earlier, and I had watched him go with an ache in my chest as if he were going off to war. I closed my eyes, my head spinning a bit from the drinks I had tossed down after dinner and the motion of the train car. I recalled the sensation of Stu kissing me, holding me, pushing into me, and I had to stifle a moan.

It was going to be a long night.

We arrived in Chicago early in the morning. The group of us frugal travelers sat up, blinking and hungover, too tired and miserable to argue about who got to use the tiny bathroom first.

After we pulled into the station, I gathered my belongings and made my way off the train. I didn't see Amy, Noah, or Stu, and I felt relieved and disappointed. Unlike most attendees who had elected to fly home, I had booked two seats on the train returning to New York. I stopped at the ticket counter and upgraded my seats to a sleeper compartment. There was no way I wanted to spend another day and night sitting among strangers. I wanted to wallow in my broken heart in solitude.

I ate a greasy breakfast at a small diner while I waited through the several-hour delay for the call to board the train back to New York. People hurried through the station, and I wondered about their lives. Were they happy with their partners? Were they on their way to cheat with a new lover or perhaps one from their past?

At last my train was called, and I made my way to the platform. I boarded and, dragging my luggage behind me, sidled through the other passengers to the numbered sleeper compartment I had been assigned. It was identical to Stu's compartment on the trip to Chicago, and I avoided looking too long at the table bolted beneath the window as I got settled.

I pulled out my Kindle and settled in to lose myself in reading, looking up and out the window as the train gave a mournful whistle, then pulled out of the station. I watched the rail yards of Chicago creep past and tried not to think of Stu in some Chicago apartment embracing his new love.

A knock on the door drew me out of my dark thoughts, and I got up to pull the door open, expecting to find a porter asking to see my ticket. Instead, I found Stu standing there, beads of sweat dotting his forehead as he tried to catch his breath.

"Stu?" I said as a startled tremor fluttered through my belly. "What are you doing here?"

He grinned, and I felt my legs go weak. "Can I come in?" Stu asked.

"Um, sure. Yeah." I stepped aside, and he walked past me.

I shut the door, and we settled in the small booth seats across the table from each other.

"I thought you were staying in Chicago for the weekend?" I said, and couldn't help adding, "With Tony."

"That was the plan," Stu said. "But I couldn't do it. After we…got back together, I couldn't stop thinking about you."

I opened my mouth, but no words were waiting there to come out.

Stu continued: "I went to see Tony and broke it off with him." He reached out and took my hands. "I had to run to make the train. And then it took me a while to find out which compartment on the train was yours. I had to tell you, Tyler: I don't want to lose you again."

His hands tightened on mine, and I squeezed back before turning away to look out the window and collect my thoughts. When I was ready, I looked back at him and said, "Are you sure?"

"I've never been more sure of anything," Stu said. He got up and came around the table to slide in beside me. "I think we can do it this time. We can make it work. Tell me you feel the same way. Didn't last night feel good to you, too?"

We kissed, and I felt my resolve melting beneath his lips. He pressed a palm against my crotch, and I groaned into his mouth.

"I love you, Ty," he said.

"I love you, too," I replied.

The train rocked beneath us as we kissed and peeled away clothing. We got up and pulled the scratchy blankets off the lower berth, then fell nude on the thin mattress. I felt Stu's cock, hard and persistent as it poked into my belly. Stu rolled me onto my back, and I started to lift my legs to allow him between them, but he pushed them back down and straddled me.

"I've missed having you inside me," he said between kisses, and my cock jumped at the thought of fucking him.

He rolled a condom on me and slicked it up with lube. With one bare foot on the floor, he positioned himself over my hips and slowly sat on my cock. The smooth, wet heat of his ass grasped my length, and he moaned as he impaled himself. His cock bobbed and swayed over my belly, drooling a long, glistening line of precum onto my belly.

Fully seated on me, Stu leaned down for a kiss before lifting himself up and sitting back down again. He fucked himself hard, tightening his muscles around me and adjusting his stance to allow me to pierce him deep. With a shuddering growl, he stroked himself to a gushing climax that covered my belly with his hot, slick cum.

I closed my eyes and lifted my hips, driving myself deeper into him as I lost myself to the rhythm of orgasm. My muscles pulsed with release, and when I had finished, he eased off my softening length and nuzzled my neck.

"Let's make it work this time," Stu said.

"I want to," I replied.

We lay together on the single berth, arms and legs entwined, and drifted off to sleep as the world outside rolled past and the sun made its way across the sky.

THE BLUE TRAIN
ERASTES

*P*ermettez-moi, monsieur."
    "Allez, allez…"
"Cordon!"
"Laissez la porte ouverte, s'il vous plait."

The jumble of phrases grated on Edmund's sensitive ears and acid roiled in his gut. There was something so sickly about a champagne hangover that made Edmund wonder what all the fuss was about drinking the stuff in the first place. Seemed stupid to spend all that money just to make yourself feel like death. Staggering behind his employer as he crossed the concourse to the Blue Train's platform, Edmund felt like a massive sabre was stuck between his eyes, and the threat of physical nausea was very real. Stupid to get that drunk just to ease Jimmy's rejection. He could have easily have drowned his sorrows in beer, but the great Obermeyer had—in a rare spirit of republicanism—decided that he wanted his secretary at his embarkation party, and with the promise of free champagne, who was Edmund to refuse? He'd found that champagne quelled the heartache a lot faster than beer, but good Lord he was paying for it now.

Somewhere on the ferry from Dover, he was sure he was going to die, and he'd felt it as something of a relief. It was ghastly to be tottering down into the bright, sunny cold of Calais only to find he was still alive.

"Go and find my compartment, Dawson." Mr. Obermeyer sank onto one of the benches on the train's platform, no doubt feeling as bad as Edmund himself, but losing none of his authority. "Come and find me."

Edmund forced one foot in front of the other and walked as quickly as he dared—without causing his head to actually fall off—toward the blue and gold train.

He found himself dizzied and disoriented by the bustle. Although he had rudimentary French, enough to get by, the staccato chatter of the porters was less comprehensible than birdsong. After the stolid and slightly plebeian transfer from the English boat train to the ferry, stepping onto French soil was like being buffeted by a fresh, southerly breeze that spun you around and felt sorry for you that you were not French. "We are Europeans. Not like you poor souls!"

At Victoria station, the porters had been reluctant and sullen, scruffy and inattentive, even those assigned to the first-class passengers. Clearly they did not consider the tips they received were worth earning and few of them bothered to work hard. To Edmund's eyes, and to his experience, this seemed odd. Did these men, in their dusty uniforms and dull boots, earn so much that they did not need to supplement it with the biggest tips they could? It seemed unlikely. And to Edmund, who knew how tips could keep you away from destitution—even if it was only one step—their disinterest appeared the pinnacle of stupidity, when for a smile one could earn an extra shilling.

Perhaps they were not as easily cajoled into selling themselves.

However, twenty short miles across a choppy grey-green sea brought a different attitude entirely. The French porters seemed to have a snap to them which the British lacked. They stood more upright, wore more smiles, and were quick to seize Mr Obermeyer's baggage, manhandle it expertly onto trucks, and speed off down the platform, leaving Edmund to follow as best he could. Even through his alcohol-soaked daze, Edmund couldn't help but notice that some of the porters were slender and whipcord strong. Lithe in tight dark blue pants which left little for the imagination and everything for the brain and the cock to admire.

A small residue of guilt washed over him—strongly diluted by secondhand champagne—that he was eyeing up porters' behinds just a day after leaving Jimmy's behind…behind. It was almost ironic. All he wanted was to collapse in his compartment and wallow in his misery. To remember their last night together, remembering every bittersweet taste and sound and memory of their final, frantic fuck. But he'd a couple of hours of work to do before that was possible. At least.

With a weak smile for the conductor, Edmund gave the man their tickets. For a fraction of a second—no doubt when he saw the name Obermeyer—the conductor seemed almost as if he were about to be polite. But with one searing Gallic sweep of his eyes, he took in Edmund's functional suit, off-the-peg shoes, and badly tied necktie and realised Edmund's status in a heartbeat. He seemed then to blame Edmund in some way for attempting to fool him, and as he demanded, *"Où est Monsieur Obermeyer?"* Edmund had the distinct feeling that the man was accusing him of murdering Obermeyer on the way over La Manche, dropping his body into the water and pretending to be the great man himself.

"La bas." Edmund gestured back up the platform. *"Il est resté."* When reassured that Monsieur Obermeyer was not drowned but simply waiting at the top of the platform, the conductor strode away, obviously wishing to deal with the millionaire himself. Edmund watched him go with jaundiced eyes. It was not concern for Obermeyer's comfort the conductor was after, but the privileged position he had to become the sole attendee upon such a rich man. Edmund had seen it all over New York, and in England too. Money, money, money. And as sly as Obermeyer was reputed to be, he could be parted with his money easier by good service and compliments than he could by sharp businessmen. Obermeyer loved to be toadied to, that was sure, and as Edmund watched the conductor return at a slightly slower pace, speaking volubly with Obermeyer at his side, he could see that Obermeyer would get all the toadying he required this journey.

Strange, Edmund thought with a sour twist to his mouth that echoed the bile in his stomach, the conductor had no problem speaking English to a millionaire when he couldn't be bothered to do so to his flunky.

Edmund trailed behind with Obermeyer's briefcases. The conductor was obsequious enough for two Uriah Heeps as he escorted the two of them onto the train. He accompanied Mr Obermeyer to his cabin personally, earning himself a fat tip and a wide smile in the process, but merely pointed Edmund down the corridor. "Your room is down there," was all the attention Edmund was granted.

Obermeyer's compartment was a roomy single, the best money could buy—all honeyed wood panelling, peacock veneers, and gold furnishings complete with two armchairs on either side of a small round table. "I'll lay out your dinner things, sir," Edmund said as Obermeyer did no more than peer in, then left him alone to find the bar and smoking room.

Edmund arranged his employer's possessions so they were easy to access: the clothes he hung under a paper wrapper on the door, his watch on the train's fob holder, and shoes, shined to perfection, placed in a box on the bed. As he finished and looked around the stunning compartment, the train lurched forward and began the slow crawl around the outskirts of Paris on its overnight trip to Marseilles.

In the two months since he'd wangled a job with Mr Obermeyer, Edmund thought he had schooled himself to be used to luxury. Since the day he'd clattered down the area steps to Mr Obermeyer's New York house and been swept up into the strangely classless yet hugely class-conscious world of financier and secretary, he'd taken to the differences between his old life and his new pretty well. If not exactly like a duck to water, he'd at least refrained from gawping every time Obermeyer flashed the cash or allowed Edmund to accompany him to some swanky restaurant or club.

But the Blue Train caught him out. What madman would build something like this, put it out in the open to be rained and snowed on, let people into its wood and enamelled beauty, knowing darn well that they'd only muss it up? This was its inaugural run, Edmund knew— Obermeyer had been first in line for tickets, despite his business not taking him to France at this time of the year. The train gleamed, and Edmund knew it would never be as beautiful as it was right now.

When he finished unpacking his employer's things and setting out clothes for dinner, he set off to find his own compartment, under no illusions that it would be a single, or in any way as salubrious. In that he wasn't disappointed. He was four carriages the other side of the luggage car, and even the corridor for the staff quarters was a damned sight more utilitarian than those in the first-class end.

He spotted the carriage's conductor at the far end of the corridor, making slow progress up towards him. Edmund watched as he stopped at a compartment, knocked, and inspected tickets. A swift inspection of the door closest to him revealed that this was his; only his own name was on the door, seemed he was going to be alone. Well, that was a relief at least.

He had a shock upon opening the door to find, in fact, he wasn't alone. Sitting on one of the seats was a young man of around three and twenty, his light brown hair in studied waves. Before he could say anything, the stranger jumped up, put his fingers to his lips in supplication of secrecy, then dropped down, sliding under the seat. It would have been a good ruse had he not been far too large to effect such subterfuge. His shoulders were clearly visible, being too wide to fit, and he was too tall for the space, causing him to bend his knees, which were also visible.

This happened in such a short time, Edmund—with his muzzy brain—hardly had time to process it, and the staccato rap on the door nearly made his heart leap into his throat. All he could do was to throw his coat down over the bench seat, obscuring what could be seen of the stranger before opening the door. He tried to look casual but it was hard, meeting the conductor's eyes, which held the same disdain now as the conductor of first class had in his, half an hour before.

"Billet, s'il vous plaît."

"I showed mine to the conductor in first class," Edmund said. It was a shame his stomach had recovered, for vomiting all over the pompous bastard would have made him feel a lot better. If people were hiding under every bench in every compartment, Edmund would be happy about it. There was a sound behind him which sounded suspiciously like someone trying not to laugh.

"Votre billet, monsieur. Maintenant."

The longer Edmund held out, the longer the man would be at the doorway, and he might step in at any moment. He had every right to do so, after all. With a sigh that was hardly fake, Edmund handed his ticket over and waited, glaring, as the conductor took an inordinately long time checking it against his list. *"Monsieur Dahsong?"* he said.

"Oui, Dawson," Edmund said. *"Secrétaire de Monsieur Obermeyer."* He glared at the man, as he knew he should have done before, but had felt too trampled by the rampant pink elephants of champagne so to do. Now he held himself tall, stuck out his chin, and used every ounce of his position with every bristling arrogant hair. He may have been a jumped-up Brooklyn luck-ridden flunky, but he was a jumped-up Brooklyn luck-ridden flunky to the richest man on this train, he was pretty damned sure. And a conductor—even one on the Blue Train—was only a man who punched tickets, same as any lowly ticket puncher on any tram, omnibus, or train in the world.

It didn't look like any suspicions had been raised regarding occupancy of the compartment, and the conductor eventually moved away with a reluctance that made Edmund wonder if he should have tipped him. Damn it, he would tip the man with Obermeyer's money for Obermeyer's service, and that was that. He closed the door and rested his back against it, breathing out with relief. "Bastard dictator," he said, with feeling.

"God, thank you," the stowaway said, collapsing back onto the seat. "You are a brick, truly you are."

The first thing Edmund noticed was his voice. Somehow he'd known the young man was English—perhaps it was his clothes, the restrained tweed rather than the rather more colourful lavender mix of his own apparel—but he wasn't expecting such a cut-glass accent from a stowaway. Cut glass had always been an odd term to use for speech, he'd thought—certainly weren't no cut glass in New York, that was for sure. But he'd learned to understand it after hearing the snobs in London. This man had it too, and Edmund's curiosity was pricked as to what the young man was running from, and why he'd chosen this train to do it on. Despite the relief and obvious friendliness, there were centuries of careful breeding behind those flattened vowels, and his voice could indeed have been etched in crystal.

"You're welcome," Edmund said, dropping onto the seat. "The French bug me already and I ain't—haven't—been in their country for more than a couple of hours. Any disservice to those snooty bastards out there, I'm happy to do."

The young man smiled and Edmund felt his stomach flip over at the sight of it. The guy was handsome too, not a chinless wonder like many of the snobs he'd seen around England, but with strong features. Crisp gold hair, fine white teeth, a little crooked, but Edmund's weren't perfect either. "I'm grateful. It's Jack," the newcomer said, sticking out a hand. "It's really nice to make your acquaintance."

"Likewise," Edmund said, taking the hand gladly. "Edmund." Jack's hand was as warm as his smile, and as soft as he'd expected it to be. *Nicely bred, and ain't never done a day's work and scared stiff of it too, I bet.*

❖

The afternoon and evening went quickly enough. Edmund shared his time between Obermeyer, dressing him for dinner and taking instructions as what to do when they got to Marseilles, and trotting along the rocking corridors back to his own compartment. He'd eaten in the less-than-first-class restaurant car set aside for staff and valets, but had put much of his food in a napkin, then shared it with Jack. They'd eaten the chicken straight from the linen, licking the grease from their fingers.

It was an odd feeling—eating in this way with his new acquaintance seemed natural, but watching Jack suck the meat from the chicken's bones was a little erotic. Edmund had pilfered two oranges, and Jack peeled them both while he listened to Edmund's story, offering Edmund the segments but none of his own tale. There were an awkward couple of minutes when the porter came to make Edmund's bed, but Jack slipped out and hid in the toilet until he'd gone.

In the dark, with Jack under a borrowed blanket on the other bench, they talked quietly into the night. Edmund found himself repeating the complaints he'd often made to Jimmy, about how he knew he should be grateful for such a plum position, but how it chafed him, being subject so much to Obermeyer's beck and call. Seeing men with less drive, but with sweeter tongues, rise up in Obermeyer's empire while, just because he was damned good at his job, Obermeyer kept him where he was.

It warmed Edmund to find that Jack was interested and sympathetic.

"So why don't you leave him?" Jack said. "Oh, I know that the money's good—"

"You'd be surprised." Edmund looked out of the window to cover his embarrassment.

"Well, then. You'd probably be better off doing something for yourself."

"Like what?"

"Oh, I don't know," Jack said. "Got to be plenty of opportunity in…New York you come from, is it?"

"Yeah," said Edmund, wishing the Brooklyn out of his voice for the hundredth time.

"Bars, or a shop, then."

"Have to say," Edmund admitted, "always fancied a little shop, hardware maybe, or groceries. Perhaps with a back room for friends."

"Sounds good," Jack said quietly. "What's stopping you?"

Edmund laughed at that question. "You sound like…" Edmund trailed off.

"Like who?"

"A…friend of mine. Jimmy."

"Is he an American too?"

"Nah. He's a limey. He was always saying that I could do better than Obermeyer. In some respects, he was right."

"But in terms of being the secretary to one of the richest men on Wall Street, you couldn't, right?"

"That's what I told him." Edmund felt a pang remembering Jimmy's face when he told him he was going on the Blue Train and didn't know when he'd be coming back. "I told him to come to the States, that's where we're heading from Marseilles. But he wouldn't."

"Wouldn't or couldn't?"

Edmund hesitated. Up to now he'd been angry, and he'd have said "wouldn't," but now, thinking back, he looked at everything Jimmy would have had to give up. Family, succession to title, no matter how slim a third son's chances were. Perhaps… "A bit of both, perhaps."

"And you couldn't, or wouldn't, stay."

"Yeah."

"You were good friends," Jack said.

"The best." Edmund was glad it was dark so no one could see how his eyes suddenly got moist. "Didn't know him that long, but it broke me up to leave him. He was a swell guy."

"Why didn't you stay in England with him?"

Edmund was quiet for a moment. It was a question Jimmy had asked him over and over. He was still struggling with an answer to that when Jack asked the question he'd been dreading—wondering how he'd answer it if ever he was asked outright.

"You queer, Edmund?"

The question ricocheted off the walls, and it seemed to Edmund that Jack had shouted instead of whispered it. By the time Edmund recovered enough to try to answer, he knew it was too late. He should have said "Heck, no!" instead of worrying about his reply.

"It's all right if you are. I won't say anything. I had you spotted straight away."

"The hell you did."

"Cross my heart. Don't know what it is. Oh, you don't swish or anything. You just have…something." There was a silence, then the secrecy of soft movement. The next time Jack spoke, his voice was close to Edmund's ear. "I meant it. It's all right. I'm as queer as they come. Wouldn't want you to be lonely. But if you think it's too soon."

Edmund could feel a hand sliding down the outside of the sheets, clasping around his own, fingers intertwining. It was too soon, really, but his voice said. "No, it ain't too soon."

Edmund sat up and the other man gave a short gasp, as if of intense disappointment, but all Edmund did was to pull up the blinds, letting the moonlight shine into the cabin. "I want to see you," he said. He reached out, pulling Jack towards him and putting his hands around his head. The curls felt crisp under his palms. Their noses bumped once as they sought each other's mouths. Edmund was the first to open his, teasing Jack's lips with his tongue, feeling the other man was playing with him, giving a show of reluctance to let him into his body. Once, twice, the lips opened a little, then closed. The third time was the charm as Jack's mouth opened, giving Edmund all the access he wanted. He was hard by now, feeling a little light-headed from the speed of it all. Jack slipped onto the bunk on top of him as they grappled with the sheets and each other.

Jack had less to remove and fewer buttons to deal with, his vest and briefs easy to put aside. Edmund's pyjamas proved a little more challenging in the dark. He sat up, pulled his top off, and shifted as Jack tugged the bottoms free of his legs. There was a delicious and decadent moment of freedom as his cock sprang free, seeking contact with another man. It didn't have to wait long. Jack slid back onto the bunk, took Edmund's cock in his hand, hard by the root, and slid it up then down again. Edmund pushed into Jack's hand, following the exciting pressure, the sweet rhythm. Jack's face was buried in Edmund's neck, and he could feel the gentlest of tongued kisses on his skin. With the heat rising in his groin, all Edmund could do was place absent-minded kisses on the side of the man's head.

Suddenly Jack rolled against the compartment wall, giving

Edmund a fraction more room. When Jack slid back into his arms, Edmund almost gasped with the shock of the Jack's body against his, warm, hard muscles over smooth skin with a dusting of hair here and there. His hands felt huge against Jack's flesh. Jack's naked body burned beneath his palms despite the cold of the night, warming his hands. Edmund wanted to touch him everywhere at once, learning the shapes, seeking the hidden places that the dark kept from him.

"Let's move to the floor," Jack said, his voice breathy and deep. "We don't want to be knocking against the compartment wall."

Edmund didn't answer, but they slid down, a blanket beneath them. Jack lay face-up on the floor while Edmund propped himself above. He used his lips and hands to move over and around Jack's face, working his way slowly down to his neck, down to his chest, licking and tasting and nipping. Jack's skin was a little salty, like he'd just swum the Channel. His nipples were firm little nubs, each surrounded by a ring of hair, and Edmund spent a long while on them while Jack groaned and pushed his groin up to meet Edmund's body, eager for any friction he could gain.

Down he went, his hands on either side of Jack as support against the rumble and sway of the train. He followed the sweet crease of Jack's belly, feeling the hair lessen under his mouth as he swirled his tongue around his navel, then picked up the trail of hair again, and as sure as a dog after prey, dropped down to the base of Jack's cock. Musky and sweaty, with high notes of pure need, a scent entirely Jack's own. With one hand gripping the base of Jack's cock, Edmund opened his mouth and swallowed as much of Jack as he could.

"Christ!" Jack thrust his hips again and Edmund moved with the motion, rocking his body to follow the line of Jack's. His mouth moved up Jack's shaft—hard, hot, bitter-sweet—and he let the suction of his mouth cling to the prominent crown, his tongue working around the sensitive underside. Jack was panting now, his fingers tangled in Edmund's hair, and he started to pump gently into Edmund's mouth. Edmund let him set the pace for a moment or two before taking control, moving his hand from the base of the shaft to the crown, tonguing and licking the top. Precum seeped from Jack's slit and Edmund lapped it away while keeping the relentless rhythm Jack so obviously wanted. When he heard Jack's breathing change to a shallow concentrated sound, he stopped as suddenly as he had begun.

Muffled curses sounded in the dark, and Jack's hands attempted to steer Edmund's mouth back to where it was needed. "Please," Jack said. "Don't stop."

"Only for a moment," Edmund said. He yanked a pillow from the bed, propped up Jack's hips, and with a spit-soaked knuckle investigated the delicious crease in Jack's arse. Finding his hole, he pushed his knuckle in and tested the welcome. It seemed Jack was more than ready, for he raised his long legs, draping them over Edmund's chest, and wriggled towards him.

Edmund need little more invitation than that. Waiting just long enough to dampen both his needy cock and Jack's entrance, he placed his cock against the hole and gripped Jack's hardness once more. Jack gave a sigh which sounded like surrender blended with bliss, opened his legs a little further, and with that, Edmund slid home.

The squeeze was delicious; Edmund loved this moment and would play a small game with himself when first starting to fuck. He tried to see how long he could wait with that arse clamped around the base of his cock before his body started to move, before his willpower not to move broke in search of further pleasure. He always wanted to draw it out, savour that feel of skin against skin, balls pushed up hard against a willing partner, but he always gave in. Like now. He pulled back with a contented sigh and pushed forward again. Slow at first, long, long and slow. Pulling out just enough to tease the head of his cock against the tight ring of muscle, then back in, back out. More and more. Faster and deeper. Jack put his hand against his mouth and each thrust drew a grunt of satisfaction from him, muffled under that gagging hand. Edmund tried to imagine how sweet it would be to hear him let loose, to really know how much pleasure he was giving.

Jack's cock was hot in his hand, and somehow he forced himself to pump Jack in time with his own strokes. For a blissful lacuna of time, there came an almost sacred moment when hand, cock, arse, heat, pressure, pace, need, want—all hung together in a perfect loop, one of those moments that should never end, when Edmund knew that nothing—nothing—would ever be as good. Then the magic broke and it was a rough, dirty, sweaty, but so very enjoyable race for the line as they fucked in earnest. His balls tightened, and his grip around Jack's cock echoed the motion. He lost his rhythm as he felt himself come, but he clung on, slapping himself against Jack's arse as each wave broke within him. He arched his back, trying to push more of himself inside, then fell forward, feeling warmth and wetness on his belly, smugly pleased he'd done as much for Jack as the man had done for him. He managed one wet kiss on Jack's mouth, but no more before he slid into a dream of rocking and fucking which went on all night.

❖

When he woke, Edmund found he was still on the floor, his arms and one leg wrapped around Jack. Sun slanted through the windows, setting Jack's hair ablaze with light. Edmund touched it gently, the curls as crisp as he remembered from their time in London. Funny how he'd had the courage to leave him behind then—he had the face of an angel when sleeping, and Edmund had left, like a coward, while Jack had been sleeping.

Blue skies were bright outside, a marked difference from the chill and cold of their embarkation. For a second, panic flooded through Edmund as he realised the blinds were still wide open from the night before. Luckily the train was still moving, slowly clattering over the rails, causing Jack's head to rock pleasantly from side to side on Edmund's chest. It felt heavy, and...right. He didn't have the strength to leave him again. He'd said good-bye to people too many times.

He heard shouting from outside. *"Messieurs and mesdames, Marseilles en trente minutes. Thirty minutes, s'il vous plaît."* And he shook Jack gently to wake him.

Jack sat up, looking delightfully mussed, as though he'd be quite amenable to a further ravaging should Edmund wish to do so. Oh, if only there were time! He gave Edmund a sheepish grin. "I suppose it's time to stop pretending now," he said.

"So...Jack?" Edmund asked. He reached forward and took Jimmy's hand. He'd been as surprised to see Jimmy as he would have been to see any stowaway—and the role-playing had both delighted and aroused him. Who knew Jimmy had such mischief in him? Seemed like he was a different man out of the feet of his family—and he'd played a different man so well.

"It's my second name. James John. Mother calls me Jack as father is Jimmy."

"Well, that makes sense." Edmund laughed. "I'll carry on calling you Jimmy, though, I think."

"After you left," Jimmy said, frowning, "the flat was so empty—and everything you said kept repeating and repeating. You were right, of course. My family don't need me. I wouldn't be leaving much behind. So I grabbed a bag. Left a note. All terribly romantic—and you played along so beautifully. Should I be worried about how quickly you tumbled into bed with a stranger?"

Edmund got up and started to rummage around for clothes. "If we are being strictly honest, the stranger tumbled into my bed. But all the same, a handsome stranger on a train? How could I resist? Not that I'm not pleased to see you, Jimmy, but are you really stowing away?"

"God, yes. There's no way I could afford the fares, and I'm going to need every penny. That is, unless you are going to support me. I'm already a reprobate, a law-breaker. The question is—do I stow away on the RMS *Scythia* and trail after you all the way back to New York, or are you going to leave that demanding bastard and we'll find what we can?"

Edmund stood up and pulled Jimmy to him, now uncaring they were both naked and probably causing consternation from the cows they were passing slowly in the fields outside the windows. "Oh, I'll leave that demanding bastard when we get to New York, I think. Meeting a handsome stowaway on board would be quite an adventure, don't you?"

THE TRAIN HOME
RICK R. REED

It was ironic, he supposed, that they were making this journey by train. After all, they had first met on a train, some ten years ago, when both of them were on vacation in England and taking the train from London to Brighton. There was a certain symmetry, a sort of coming-full-circle feeling to their current trip.

They were headed south and the train rolled along so smoothly that he almost didn't feel its motion. It was cruel, he thought, that they forced the two of them to sit in separate compartments, but that was just the way things were. They needed to get to where they were going, and since the arrangements were last minute, they were in no position to argue with the railway.

He sat back in his seat, grateful that he was spared having anyone else sit next to him, at least so far. Outside the window, autumn was in its full-blown glory and fiery reds, oranges, and yellows burst out of the hillsides, creating a northeast display worthy of a Charles Ives painting. The sky was that bright shade of blue, almost electric, that seemed to come only in the fall. It looked as though the birds, which he occasionally observed from his window, could be stained by the liquid color. Outside, and all about him, life bustled, hurtling forward in its restless ebb and flow, unaware.

He thought about Jim, in the other train car, wishing he could touch him, wondering if he was feeling as lonely, lost, and separated. He turned in his seat, pressing his head against the cool window glass, and shut his eyes. Whispering and promising himself he would stop should anyone occupy the seat next to him, he gave in to the urge to talk to Jim. He needed to talk to him, even if they were separated by several train car lengths, needed to make that connection.

He had to.

"Honey, I hope you're doing okay back there. Are you comfortable? The trip isn't long, so don't panic. We'll be together again soon. I'll make sure of that."

He glanced across the aisle. There was a woman in jeans and a sweater tending to a little boy, setting out a juice box and animal crackers on a tray before him. The boy bounced up and down in his seat, and his mother was busy trying to keep him quiet, occupied. He was sure she was too distracted to hear him.

"Remember that train trip we took when we first met?" He snickered, trying not to make any noise. "We both got on the train in London at St. Pancras station, and I saw you right away. That sunny summer morning, the station was filled with travelers like us, but somehow, you stood out to me, like there was a shimmer around you. I suppose there was." He closed his eyes, pressing his forehead harder into the cool glass. His whispering had a more furious intensity. "That shimmering was love, even though I didn't know it then." He laughed. "I would have just called it lust.

"But there you were in the busy station, with its airy domed glass ceiling. My God, it seemed like the summer light was shining down only on you. Who knows why? Back then you were just a boy, fresh out of McGill University, on a summer trip that was a graduation gift from your parents." He shook his head, but it was with pleasure at the images dancing across the insides of his eyelids.

St. Pancras Eurostar train station was gorgeous, a lovely melding of the old and the new, with an arching glass ceiling that at once mimicked and glorified the summer sky. Outside, its spires reached up toward that same sky, and the station's red brick Gothic architecture promised excitement, travel, and adventure. If he had only known how much adventure he would have when he walked into the station—life-changing adventure with love at first sight and naughty doings in the bathroom of a high-speed train. The smile spread across his face, and he warmed at the memory.

But the glory of St. Pancras station couldn't hold a candle to the real image of beauty: Jim. He had stood there in his simple white T-shirt and cargo shorts, his hairy, muscled calves drawing his eyes first. He drank in Jim's sculpted calves, defined by sinew and the down of pale brown hair. He remembered looking them up and down, watching as they disappeared into the loose khaki fabric on top and the hiking boots and slouching socks below. Jim had a worn backpack strapped to his broad back. Tan, defined biceps strained the simple white cotton of his shirt. "And when you turned my way, sweetheart, I was done, cooked, ruined for anyone else. That face, I suddenly felt, had been waiting for me all my life.

"You weren't doing anything special, just consulting a train schedule, but I swear my heart started beating harder when I saw you. Your curly blond hair, those blue eyes when you looked up, the broad, tan features that spoke of such youth and vitality. And yes, God help me, virility." He paused, shutting his eyes tight to better facilitate the memory of seeing Jim's face for the first time, and he recalled the pale blue of his eyes, the bushy golden eyebrows above them, the lashes too long for a man, but oh-so-seductive. Jim's full lips made him think immediately of kissing—for hours and hours. Even the imperfections, the slight crookedness of his nose and the gap in his front teeth, served to make him look more alluring, different from every other man on the planet—the one man who was meant for him. Of course, he didn't know that then, not quite. But he could think it now. He glanced over at the mother and child, who had gone quiet, the little boy's towhead nestled against his mother, his little mouth open in slumber. The mother, having a moment of peace at last, watched the landscape roll by, her gaze distant. He began to whisper to himself again.

"I had no way of knowing then that there was even a chance you could be mine, if only for a few minutes, let alone a lifetime. My gaydar did *not* go off, and I fully expected some gamine blonde, just as pretty as you, but more curvy in the bust, waist, and hips to come up by your side, wearing a sundress and offering you a sip from her can of Coke. You would press your heads close together, like conspirators, and laugh. You would steal a kiss and she would playfully slap you.

"But that wasn't what happened.

"You didn't see me then. Your world, if I can be so conceited and vain to say it, had yet to change. You were busy looking at the boards placed high above the travelers, the one which now informed us: *This train will be formed of 5 coaches instead of 10. This is due to a train fault.*

"I got pulled out of my reverie by the mechanical, Brit-accented voice announcing boarding for the train to Brighton.

"I took one last, longing look at you and thought if there was anything so beautiful that it could compare to the promise and glory of this summer day, that something was you.

"I hurried to board the train. A friend in Chicago who had moved to the States from Bath had told me that I'd love Brighton because it was sort of like the San Francisco of England. 'The place is crawling with gays,' Vincent had told me, so I was particularly looking forward to this part of my U.K. tour. Until that moment, I had imagined a smorgasbord of hook-ups with European men from across the continent. Vincent had told me how busy the bush-shrouded hills across from the nude beach could be of an early morning and how the bars there were crowded every night of the week.

"But suddenly the lure of promiscuity lost its charm. There was only one man I hoped to meet, hopeless as it was.

"Oh yes, my sweet, I was smitten. Even if, at that moment, I believed I had no chance of meeting you, let alone all that followed that afternoon and for the next ten years.

"Little did I know that once the train lurched into motion, and people began settling in for the hour-or-so ride, someone very special would occupy the seat across the aisle from me." He smiled at the memory and watched his younger self, a decade before, catch his breath as the young man from St. Pancras lumbered into his own train car, like a vision from a dream.

He could see Jim now in his mind's eye, struggling to get down the aisle of the train car with his backpack weighing him down. It was one of the large ones, and he would learn later that Jim had nearly everything he owned in it as he backpacked his way across the continent. The pack banged into seats and narrowly missed the heads of other passengers. He grew amused at Jim muttering apologies as he made his way down the aisle; there was something so boyish and genuinely kind about the man. "When you saw me, you smiled, and that set off an alarm within me, set the nerve synapses to firing, the heart to racing, the adrenaline to pumping, the pulse to jumping. And yes, I think that little shy smile of yours caused all of the blood from my brain to course southward. I shifted in my seat to relieve the pressure in my crotch.

"It wasn't just your smile that made my heart skip a beat or two, it was the way your eyes connected with mine, for just an instant.

"I hoped that you'd sit next to me, and already I was trying on lines that I would use to strike up a conversation with you. I searched for the perfect witty opening that would endear me to you, or just the right question that would reveal how much we had in common. In those fevered moments, I was already imagining how charmed you'd be by me, and we would both rearrange our schedules so we could spend the entire time in Brighton together, visiting the pier, the nude beach I had heard about, and of course, the glorious over-the-top majesty of the Royal Pavilion. I imagined surreptitiously holding your hand, stealing love-struck glances as we wandered the promenade along the beach. I would impress you with my geographic knowledge and tell you that if you looked hard enough, you could see all the way to France. We would shack up together in the gay bed-and-breakfast only steps from the beach I had booked. And thus, our life together would begin.

"I was, I admit it, a helpless romantic, even back then.

"As if to thwart me, you took the seat just across from me, placing your backpack in the aisle seat and settling yourself into the window seat. You got comfortable quickly, the seasoned traveler, and commenced to staring out the window at the pastoral British countryside flashing by. I was sad, thinking you'd promptly forgotten all about me. Still, no gaydar had gone off and I tried to be brave, thinking that in only about forty-five minutes, I would be in a beachside gay mecca and there, perhaps I would meet someone who was not only gorgeous, but gay as well.

"But no one, no imagined prince or stud, could make me reroute my hopes away from you.

"So I commenced staring at you, convinced there was nothing outside those windows more interesting to look at, and frustrated you wouldn't look my way, not for hours it seemed, until you did.

"My heart skipped a bit when those ice-blue eyes lit upon my mud-brown ones and our gazes locked, for a lot longer this time. A tiny smile played about your lips. There are all sorts of crude gestures and come-ons gay men can make to one another, but none can compare to the simple eloquence of the eyes. Strangers, whether they're male or female, may glance at one another, but propriety lets them look for only a measured number of seconds before it becomes rude staring. The language spoken by the eyes of two interested gay men becomes a ballet, often a mating dance, I suppose, with ideas and desires exchanged more freely and honestly than the spoken word could ever hope to achieve.

"We didn't have to say a word, you and I, to know there was mutual interest in one another. Our shy smiles only confirmed what our gazes had been bold enough to utter. The question then arose, wordlessly, between us: What were we going to do about it?

"It was at that moment I truly believed in the phenomenon known as telepathy. I think you were thinking the same thing I was.

"Confident that you had read my mind, I decided to put it to the test and stood up, a copy of *The Picture of Dorian Gray* discreetly sheathing the tent that had popped up in my shorts, a tent you and your cursed blue eyes had produced. I moved to the back of the car, sick with desire, anticipation, and hope—praying that you had caught the evil and naughty message I had broadcast your way. I didn't dare look over my shoulder until I reached the door at the back of the car leading into the next one. Fully anticipating that I would look back to see your head lolled to one side as you slept and knowing I had been wrong about *everything*, I leaned against the door for just a moment to see if you had received my message.

"And you *had* stood up. You grinned at me and your face was flushed. Again, language without words.

"I turned and continued back, hurrying and hungry with need, searching for a men's room. Tawdry, I know, but it was the only place I could imagine on this train where I could get you alone for even a few minutes. And I nearly trembled with need for that alone time. I prayed there would not be a line outside the men's room or a train employee lingering, leaning against the wall opposite the door.

"My prayers were answered. Hindsight reveals the universe conspiring to bring us together. No one stood near the men's room in the narrow hallway and I hurried inside, leaving the door open just a fraction of an inch. Enough, I hoped, that you would realize it was an invitation.

"After seconds that seemed like hours, you joined me in the cramped little washroom, locking the door and turning to smile at me. Up close, you seemed huge, almost unreal, a figure that I had only fantasized about come to life. In the close little toilet, I could feel the heat emanating from your body. I hadn't realized it until that very moment, but I was a starving man and I did not want to mar the intensity, this electric connection, with something as common and coarse as language.

"I spun you around so you faced the tiny sink and pressed myself against your broad back as I fumbled with the button and zipper of your cargo shorts. There was no script, no thought-out plan, just simple urgent need pushing us both forward. I still recall your sweet essence, your sweat, as I pressed my face close to your neck, struggling to push your shorts down as I drank in your scent. You whispered a snicker and paused to kick your shorts into a corner. You wore no underwear. I thought only briefly of how wild this was—and dangerous—and how time was of the essence if this encounter was to reach a satisfactory conclusion. But again, the blood that my brain might have used for rational thought was busy elsewhere.

"I sank to my knees. I wanted to send up a prayer of gratitude for the vision in front of my eyes. Two perfect, creamy white mounds of flesh rose up before me, their whiteness defined and highlighted by sharp tan lines, crisp along your lower back and across your thighs. I placed my hands on your perfect ass and, drawing in a breath, pulled the cheeks gently apart. Within nestled a perfect pink little pucker of muscle, framed in wisps of delicate wheat-colored hair.

"The picture was such a pretty one that I was powerless to do anything but stare at it, transfixed, for several long seconds, breath quickening. I was unsure if I should sully the image with my tongue, my face, but I couldn't help myself and I dove between your cheeks, tasting, teasing, pulling the flesh open with my tongue. I ground my lips and tongue into your hole and you pushed back against me, urging me deeper. Your hand fluttered about your cock, stroking it, then moving quickly away. My dick strained hard against the fabric of my shorts, and I looked down to see a dark stain marking exactly where the head of my dick was. I don't know if I ever produced as much precum as I did that one afternoon!

"You moaned softly and we both stopped—suddenly—as we heard a chorus of laughing male voices approaching the door. Footsteps and the bass of a group of young male voices grew louder as they drew closer, and we both froze at their approach.

"Someone rattled the doorknob and said loudly and a bit drunkenly, I thought, "*Occupato*. Onward, men!" Then the voices quieted as they headed away from the door. We both sighed out our relief and I knew, in that moment, if you were anything like me, you were trying desperately to hold in a yelp of joy at their retreat.

"I resumed my feast. You reached back to pull your cheeks further apart, granting me more access, access which I greedily took. You squirmed, bucking up against my face, and I reached between your down-covered thighs and up to feel the hardness my tongue had aroused. Your cock felt like a girder, so engorged it seemed in danger of bursting. The satin of your balls brushed against my wrist.

"I was in heaven. I continued to lick, probe, to grind my mouth against your open and delicious hole until you snatched me out of my reverie by whispering, frantically, 'Keep that up and I'm gonna come.' From your accent, I knew then that, like me, you were American. From your phrase, I conjured up an image of spinning you toward me, your cock slapping my face just before covering it in your seed. I was fully prepared and would have been grateful to take your onslaught. I think my mouth was already watering with anticipation of seeing your load arc out of your cock. Yes, I was a little delirious.

"But that was not to happen because you groaned softly another simple declarative. 'Please…more. I want you inside me.'

"Had you just said what I thought you did? Really? Here? Now?

"I closed my eyes and looked down at the tent of my shorts, wondering if we would have enough time. Was this safe? Would we be caught, as the saying went, with our pants down and be ejected from the train?

"It didn't matter. We were young, strangers in a strange land, unrestricted by whatever responsibilities awaited us at home, and filled with an almost blinding lust. From your frantic petition to me, I knew, with gratitude, that you were as perhaps as taken with me as I was with you. I closed my eyes, mentally whispering a quick prayer of gratitude to whatever God was listening but hopefully not watching, and stood.

"Quickly, with trembling hands, I undid the top button of my shorts, yanked down the zipper, and freed the cock that had been imprisoned and confined in too small of a space practically since the moment I laid eyes on you. There was no stopping me now. I don't even know if I could have stopped had a train conductor opened the door on our very public and very *verboten* encounter. You looked back at me once, over your shoulder, and the hunger I read in your eyes urged me on. I pressed my hard cock against the cheeks of your ass, smearing my precum across the creamy flesh. You reached back to take a fingerful of the stuff, bringing it to your mouth. I knew it would be futile to ask for something as simple as lube and was prepared to throw caution to the wind, to take you bareback with spit and worry about the consequences later.

"But you were not as heedless as I. You bent over further and for a moment, I thought you were doing so to grant me better access, but then I watched as you groped around in your pocket, pulling out a condom sheathed in foil. You brought the package to your mouth, tore it open with your teeth, and reached behind you to hand me the rubber.

"God bless you. At least one of us had the presence of mind to think of safety. My own mind was too fevered with lust to be in any way practical.

"I struggled to slide the condom over my engorged member, trying to unroll it the wrong way, and then finally rolling it down carefully and making sure it was secure at my pubes.

"And then I knocked at the door. You reached back with your hand, gripping me, and I suppose, checking to make sure I had sheathed myself in latex, and guided me to your portal. You positioned the head of my dick at that ring of taut pink muscle I could still taste, bent forward more, gripping the tiny sink, and sighed to signal me onward.

"I let a dollop of spit drop from my lips to my dick, moving it around with my fingertips. This, added to the lube already on the condom, would have to be enough.

"It was. Grasping my cock with one hand, I guided it to your hole, and pushed gently, harder, until I felt you open only slightly. I pulled back a fraction of an inch, letting you get used to my girth, letting your panting breath slow. I don't know if the care was necessary because there was only a token resistance and then you opened up to me. With a groan, I slid myself in, inch by inch, until I was buried in you, until my bush of wiry dark hair contrasted against the white of your ass cheeks. 'Oh God,' you whimpered, barely audible, wriggling and backing against me to ensure that every inch was buried inside you. There was a moment where neither of us moved, barely breathed. I could feel my cock pulsing and feared this would be over even quicker than I thought, but the pulsing slowed and I was able to move out, almost to the tip, then bury myself within you once again. You whispered 'Yes,' the word borne out on a mere puff of air, the 's' sibilant.

"And so it went. We both know the in and outs of the story, the thing that has been going on since the dawn of time, although I had to wonder how many times such activity had taken place in a crowded men's bathroom on a Brighton-bound train out of London. Once I was sure you wanted it, I pounded into you mercilessly, heedless of being heard. You bit your lips, reached back to pull me in deeper, and the two of us came together, our backs twins in sweat.

"The act itself probably took no more than ten minutes, maybe only five. I look back now and wonder how many people actually heard us. Our grunts, groans, and sighs that we were powerless to hold in, our shifting for better position, while our feet slid clumsily on the floor... wouldn't all of that had been audible, maybe even from as far away as the next car? I had been especially clumsy because my shorts were still around my ankles.

"But when we finished at the same time, again, we were unable to keep quiet, failing to keep our bliss a secret. We both trembled and bucked as we rode out the aftershocks of our orgasms, me with my arms wrapped tightly around your waist, you reaching back to clutch at my thighs to pull and hold me deep within you.

"When it was over, and my dick was softening enough that it was in danger of slipping out, I clutched the bottom of the condom, sealing it and ensuring it would not come off as I slid out, then I leaned even more into you and laid a kiss tenderly upon your neck.

"You turned, straining your neck, so that our lips could meet, our tongues could intertwine. In that moment, silly and romantic as it may sound, I knew this was not just some anonymous fuck born of passion, as passionate as it was, but that you were mine.

"Giggling softly, we both hurried to clean ourselves up, making use as best we could of the tiny sink and paper towels, and get dressed again. We smiled shyly at one another. I told you my name and you whispered, 'Jim' in my ear, and then licked the lobe to make sure I wouldn't forget.

"How could I?

"Sure that there would be a crowd outside the restroom, we opened the door cautiously, an inch or so at a time. At best, I expected a gathering with knowing grins on their faces, a round of applause, catcalls. At worst, I anticipated an outraged mother holding a babe in her arms, shielding its face with her hand, an angry conductor ready to eject us from the train, or a gaggle of eye-rolling teenage girls, tsking and red-faced.

"But there was no one.

"And it was then that I also knew that our coupling, crude as some might have labeled it, was meant to be. I believed—or maybe I decided—that fate had given us that small window of time alone to begin our life together. Those few minutes, in retrospect, had been a consummation, sealing not only our bodies together, but also our spirits. A seal that remained unbroken even today, as we travel along in another train and in another country. Our home.

"I didn't know it then, but I suspected it as you edged by me to hurry guiltily back to your seat, pointedly not looking back, that this was the beginning of something, the start of two lives merged that would only grow from this small, intense, and yes, silly, connection.

"And so it was. And now, here we are, on a train again, come full circle, ten years later…at the end."

The man opened his eyes as the train ground to a halt, feeling disoriented, as if thrust into a time and place he wasn't expecting. He felt as though he had been dreaming. But this was now. Autumn in New England. The day outside, with its bright leaves and blue sky, was ignorant of his journey and its significance.

Like that other day a decade ago, today was the start of a new life, a different one, changed. He smiled sadly at the optimism, joy, and hope he had felt at the birth of that other new beginning, on a crowded train in England, bound for the beachside charm of Brighton.

He let his thoughts drift to Jim in the car at the back and smiled wider, knowing it was only minutes until they would meet again on the platform. He imagined their reunion, how it would reverse how they started their journey. This time he would watch as Jim left the train instead of watching as he boarded it. There would be someone else there with him, he knew, someone who might lay a hand on his shoulder and squeeze as Jim came off the train, but that simple gesture would give him no comfort.

Wearily, he stood as the train completely stopped, the rocking motion and the clack of the wheels along the track now gone, making the silence rush up, almost louder than the half-noticed din of the train's motion. He stretched, grateful he had been alone for most of the ride. He looked around, reached for his hat, and put it on. The other passengers queued up, filtering out of the train.

A voice came over the intercom, tinny, squawking, announcing their station, and he sat back down on the edge of his seat, waiting, as he had been advised to do, until the train completely emptied of passengers. He folded his hands in front of him, gripping one to the other. He sighed deeply, at the end of which was a little falter of breath. He whispered once more to himself, "Save the tears for later."

At last he went into the cheery day, into sunshine and warmth with a chilly undercurrent, promising a crisp, cool night, the kind Jim adored. Outside, the air smelled fresh, cleaner than it had in the city, where he and Jim had left their home behind for this ride.

He turned and saw Jim's parents coming up the platform, the father gripping the mother's arm as if guiding her, helping her to walk. And perhaps he was; days like this one came rarely in a lifetime.

He continued back to the rear of the train and met with the man from the funeral home, barely shaking his hand, his gaze transfixed on the open door of the last train car, waiting for his Jim to emerge, even if he was in a box.

ROYAL SERVICE
DALE CHASE

He said he was a prince, which I didn't dispute because he had a good-sized dick. When I inquired as to lineage, he took me through a veritable maze of royals that ultimately led to the old girl herself, Queen Victoria.

"So you are…"

"Sixteenth in line," he replied, and I asked no more as he had entered me with such force that I fully expected the royal knob to emerge in my throat. He rode me from behind, which brought visions of him riding to hounds in jodhpurs and jacket, shiny black boots. He was certainly a horseman in bed, his formidable prick most often driving the cum out of me without so much as an encouraging hand.

Once he'd gained his satisfaction, he invited me to accompany him to Balmoral. "The royal train," he added as he lit a cigarette. He was terribly handsome and played on it to excess, which rendered me powerless. Commoner, I could but kneel before his royal personage most often to suck his cock.

Carlisle Edwin Joseph Saxe-Nevin was his full name, but Kit was how I knew him—Kit Nevin, college student reading law, as was I. He seemed in a single instant able to both embrace and denounce his royalty.

When he had me to his rooms, he thought nothing of calling in his manservant, Elston, while we lay naked in post-coital bliss. I saw he meant to impress me not only with his power over lesser men but his ease in self-display. On one occasion the servant took up clothes and drew a bath before retiring. As he went about his duties, Kit fondled me until I stood erect, at which the servant managed a glance, as I suppose his master expected.

"Do you fuck him?" I asked as we slid into the bath. "He's rather striking."

"Certainly not. I refuse to take a servant into the royal bed, however striking."

Kit and I had struck up an immediate friendship at college, punctuating it with sexual escapades as I'd never before known. Though Kit had a servant and private quarters, he nevertheless played at pranks and drank to excess no differently than we commoners. His sole entitlement was escaping punishment when caught. And he threw the best parties imaginable, encouraging them toward orgies where he used his endowment to excess.

Now school was ending and we were soon to assume our respective duties, his being swept into family estate matters, me, according to my lower status, starting work as law clerk in a solicitor's London office. But first we had a few weeks' breathing room, and the journey to Balmoral Castle was to launch us into our new lives. There would be formal affairs by night—parties, balls, and such—and manly pursuits by day—shooting, riding to hounds. I was also assured we'd have private time as well, though not able to share a room. "But on the train we shall share a private car," he said. "And the journey is one and one half days."

The London and North Western Railway, he told me, would, at Her Majesty's request, assemble her royal train to include her private car as well as those for her ladies in waiting, the prince, princess, guests, servants, and guards. "The old girl's car is twice the length of the others."

"Does the train have the corridors that are coming into vogue?" I asked.

"Good God, no. The Queen resists such progress. Until her two cars were joined into one, she would make the train stop before she moved from one car to the next even though the passageway was quite safe. She also refuses to eat aboard the train, so there will be a stop later for her to take supper at a station."

I had no experience with private cars, knowing only the common train, and while it brought one to his destination on time, the journey was accomplished in unheated cars with few amenities. Worst of all was the scramble for food, which was available only at ten-minute stops along the way. This resulted in mad dashes for questionable fare. "Must we also depart the train for meals?" I asked Kit.

"Not at all. My car will be fully stocked. There is a small compartment at one end, and Elston stays there so he can prepare my meals."

"What does he do the rest of the time?"

"Good grief, how should I know? Press pants, look out the window, play with his cock."

Kit's casualness toward the life of someone so close wore on me at times, but I allowed the attitude had been bred into him like some prized corgi. This failing served good purpose in that it kept me from falling for him entirely.

On the appointed day of travel, Kit called for me in his well-appointed carriage and was quite amused at my simple cloth valise. As always, I took his ribbing with a smile, noting his six leather cases would compensate for my inadequacy. We journeyed to Windsor and, as Kit had been late in calling for me, reached the royal siding at the castle's northern edge after others had boarded. I had scarcely a glance at the Queen's long twelve-wheeled red and black car before Kit pushed me up the steps into his own. Once there a signal was given and we were under way.

Inside the car I found steam heat, electric light, and sumptuous sitting room. A separate bedroom presented two ornate beds, and off this was a tiny toilet and w.c.

"We shall use both beds," Kit declared, "though not at the same time."

Elston saw to the luggage and I once again noted him an impressive older man, graying, reserved as his station dictated yet exuding a certain authority. His bearing seemed more regal than that of my friend and I couldn't help but feel an affinity toward him. When he carried baskets and hampers into his compartment, I tried to catch his eye to no avail. I admired this avoidance as he managed it with such ease that I felt no rebuff.

Rich cream tones were dominant in the car, both walls and ceiling done up in deep-buttoned quilted silk while the thick carpet was a fawn shade. Trim was a contrasting dark satinwood. Sitting room appointments included two luxurious armchairs, small tables, fringed footstools, a writing desk, and a sofa of such size that one could have made it a bed. A fully stocked bar stood at the ready, undoubtedly done up to meet Kit's specific demands.

As the train rumbled into the countryside, Kit undid his trousers and got out his cock. "Nearly noon and I haven't yet come," he declared, pulling himself. When I moved to lower the window shade, he stopped me. "Leave it. I prefer the light."

"But you'll be seen."

"By whom? And for how long? Why not give a jolt to the farmer in his field? Let him gain a glimpse of the royal prick."

Kit moved to the window and waved his member but found his audience none but grazing cows who, if their heads rose to the occasion, took no discernable notice.

"Undress," Kit said and I looked to the window. "Don't be such a prude," he chided. "If you're seen, it's for a moment in passing. When we reach a station, we'll lower the shade."

And so I reluctantly disrobed, as Kit did with far more enthusiasm. He then bade me bend over a chair so he might fuck in full display.

While I welcomed his cock, I suffered at the passing view and thus did not enjoy my usual arousal. Several times I glanced out to see men in carts or on horseback turned our way. "They see us!" I cried as Kit grew earnest in his thrusting.

"And it is likely the high point of their day," he declared. "Come on, Adrian, embrace the moment. Men live to fuck. Let them see the royal cock."

And with this he withdrew and pumped the thing until it spurted onto the window in great white gobs. As he emptied, I looked out to see a man who had stopped his wagon to observe the royal train shocked at the display. This caused me to drop into the chair in an attempt at concealment that led Kit to peals of laughter and more waving about of his prick. "Royal privilege," he declared.

"Would the Queen agree to such an attitude?"

"Ah, yes, the old girl. Well, my friend, she is two cars ahead and thus need not be troubled by youthful display, not to mention she is frightfully old and thus past concern about physical needs."

He flopped into the chair opposite me, swinging one leg over the arm to display his endowment. And I did enjoy seeing the rope of cock dangling over balls that seemed to perpetually ride high in the sac, as if always full and at the ready. I attempted to relax but was unable to escape the fact that we were sitting naked aboard the royal train.

"Hungry?" Kit suddenly asked. "Spending always brings appetite." He yanked the bell pull and I attempted calm as Elston entered. "Sir," he said.

"Tea and toast," Kit ordered.

"Very good, sir."

When Elston had departed, I made move to dress but Kit wouldn't allow it. "Why dress? I'm going to fuck you from Windsor to Ballater."

"I'm not comfortable in front of your servant."

"Silly boy. He sees only as I desire. You must discard your commonplace notions and live as a royal while in my company. We are above them. They do our bidding and expect nothing more."

I retreated then and, as the car was warm and accommodating, I attempted to embrace the situation. When Elston set the repast on the little table, I made no move to cover my privates. Kit sat forward in his chair, legs wide, to allow the royal cock a full dangle I was certain was intended to tease the servant.

I found myself quite hungry and ate the toast and drank the tea with hearty appetite. I then inquired of the rest of the train. "Are all the cars such as this?"

"Oh, no. The old girl's is beyond sumptuous, done up in royal blue and gold, everything either gilded or upholstered to the fullest with twice the room we have."

"How magnificent."

"There are several cars such as this one, and we have quite a good group on board. Lord Whitney is with Captain McClure and Major Bannock. Mrs. Halliday and Lady Forristal occupy another, and in still another are Sir Guy Mahew and Sir Thomas Wimble, who often travel together. Fucking is likely rampant throughout."

"You don't know that," I countered. "You play it up far too much."

He shrugged, then went on. "Other cars carry ladies' maids, dressers, servants, pages, and at each end of the train guards' cars. One can't help but envision the guards at one another or the servants imposing upon the pages. And who knows what Mrs. Halliday gets up to with Lady Forristal or what the maids and dressers do."

"Kit, you are incorrigible."

"And you love it."

"Do you ever think of anything but sex?"

"Not unless I must."

"I don't see how you managed to get through college."

Here he laughed and took hold of his prick. "Need I say more?"

"You didn't!"

"Pearson, Forestal, Draper, Goosling—"

"No!"

"Oh, yes, and Dean Burchard proved absolutely ravenous. Liked to take it on his desk."

How had I missed such carryings on? My mind hurried back, but all I saw were studies and lectures punctuated by assaults from Kit's formidable rod. "How could I not know?" I asked.

"Discretion," Kit replied. "Despite what you see here, I can manage to keep it under wraps until called for."

"Did you fuck them all?"

"Most. Surprising lot, the academics."

"Did you learn anything?"

"Intermittently, yes, but when one is destined for a life such as mine, one need not acquire a great store of knowledge. There are always lesser beings to handle the work."

We were quiet after this, looking upon the countryside as it trundled past, and I attempted to relax and enjoy this world Kit had welcomed me into. I also began to wonder how Kit would comport himself at Balmoral. If the privileged were indeed fucking one another on the train, would it continue at our destination?

It was scarcely noon when Kit poured himself a whiskey and chided me for not partaking. "A bit early for me," I told him, at which he downed his drink in one gulp, then poured another.

Kit always drank far more than I, and this I admired to the extent that all college boys see it as proof of manhood. But he ultimately lacked the capacity required of such indulgence and thus had more than once passed out in my company. I felt a thread of concern at his starting so early in the day.

"Come sit," he said and I followed him to settle onto the wide sofa that stretched along much of the wall opposite the two chairs. Kit lay back against the cushions.

"If you won't drink, then suck me," he said, grasping his cock.

The window blinds on this side were drawn, thus I leaned over and took the royal appendage into my mouth. Kit sipped his whiskey and watched as I licked and bobbed until he stood tall and wet. "Now sit on it," he commanded and I withdrew, face hot with a blush as he knew I loved to ride him.

"We'll be riding at Balmoral," he said as I stood to straddle him. "Practice," he added as I descended.

This position took his long cock into my passage much as it would a lance, spearing me with such pleasure that my prick sprang to attention. My breath caught as my innards attempted to straighten in accommodation of the formidable guest. Once I had the whole of him, I sat for a moment, breathing heavily. Kit, always impatient, thrust at me, which caused me to cry out, and I began to ride him, straining leg muscles to raise myself up and down until my thighs screamed for rest and I begged a moment's respite.

Kit bore a swoon from the whiskey and the sex, as if balanced somewhat precariously upon on the edge of an inebriated come. He began to squirm beneath me and I, in response, began to work my muscle, squeezing him again and again until he began to moan.

"Make me come!" he cried. "Ride me!" Thus I was forced to resume my squats, which led him in turn to spew filthy comments until he silenced into a strangled gasp as I received the royal spunk.

"I need a drink," he announced as soon as he'd stilled. I climbed off and started for the toilet, while his first priority was not washing up but more whiskey.

As we settled again into the chairs, Kit began to study me. He was such an unpredictable fellow that I knew not his intention. He could be planning a new sexual escapade or some prank upon his manservant.

"The atmosphere at Balmoral is most arousing," he began.

"Beyond what you bring to it?" I mused.

"Quite. Something about the old girl's territory draws guests to behave like rutting pigs. The place veritably reeks of cum, thus I am quite often erect." Here he became so animated that whiskey sloshed from his glass.

"What you are telling me is that I must be ready for you at all times."

"Most ready."

Kit rang for Elston and ordered a meal, which the servant seemed to have already prepared. Cold meats, crusty breads, and rich pies were laid before us and while I ate heartily, Kit nibbled. Wine was also served and I allowed myself a single glass while Kit kept to his whiskey.

"More!" he demanded of Elston, who refilled the decanter Kit had emptied. This prompted my friend to top his drink, which elicited a glance at me from the trusty servant.

As Kit went on about the Queen, I began to consider that his attitude toward her likely arose from the fact that she alone had sway over him. For one accustomed to ordering people about, he had no such power at Balmoral and thus fell to lewd attempts to degrade the old girl. As he ranted on, I thought instead of Elston, whose glance had set me wondering. Was the look one of concern at his master imbibing to such extent, or dared I think him stirred at pursuing his duties in the company of two naked young men? By the time Kit rang for him to clear the dishes, I was most aroused.

Elston was efficient with his silver tray but managed, as he leaned to take my plate, to gaze a long moment at my crotch. "Your napkin, sir?" he said, at which I grew hot with a blush but nevertheless removed the tented linen to reveal my erection. When the napkin went from my hand to his, Elston passed me a visual coupling that conveyed much promise. He then withdrew.

I turned in my chair to look out the window, hoping to relax my prick, which I managed by concentrating on a now more industrial landscape. A station then approached, which Kit announced as Leamington. As he made no move to lower the blinds, I leapt up and did so, which sent him into a fit of laughter. The train made no stop, however. It simply slowed as it ran through the station while officials stood gathered on the platform in honor of the royal passage.

"We shall fuck between Derry and Ambergate," Kit announced, "and we must do the deed at Sheffield, where the Queen will likely have her supper."

"Do others join her for the meal?"

"Yes, quite. The entire party will feast in her company while I devour your morsel of a prick."

Things came to pass just as he had announced. We fucked between Derry and Ambergate, him giving me a good one from behind as I bent over the little table. He continued to drink and I marveled at his capacity for staying alert with such excess while maintaining an ability to stiffen his rod. I was thus well used when the train stopped at Sheffield.

"Look out and see the progress," Kit said. We retrieved our dressing gowns so we might avoid shocking the party when we raised the shade. We then were treated to sight of a long red carpet at the ready for Her Majesty. Various uniformed station men stood to each side and soon came the guards. At last the Queen ventured forth. Though I had once seen her at some distance, I was treated to much closer view and saw how slowly she moved, how great her body. Clad in dark dress and cloak, she was indeed an old woman. Accompanying her were her ladies in waiting, the Prince, Princess, and other guests.

"There are Sir Guy and Sir Thomas!" Kit squealed. "Note Sir Guy's flush and the grin on Sir Thomas's face. Surely they've been fucking like rabbits and oh, here are Mrs. Halliday and Lady Forristal, and I say, does not Mrs. Halliday appear disheveled, perhaps with undergarments in disarray due to M'Lady's fingers of inquiry?"

"Oh, Kit, please. They all look quite normal and natural. Must you inflict your wickedness upon everyone? What I see are passengers showing nothing more than the rigors of train travel."

Kit shrugged. "If it pleases you to think so, then so be it, but it pleases me to think otherwise. Now lower the shade and throw off that dressing gown."

We shed our cover and Kit knelt to take my soft prick into his mouth. As he sucked, his hand found its way to my backside, where a finger soon found entrance to my passage. Prodding me such, he caused a welcome stir and I quickly forgot the royals outside, giving way to the royal inside my person. When Kit added a second finger, I spread my legs to assist, and soon I was quite stiff in his mouth.

As I had already come what seemed buckets, there was no immediate promise of climax but instead a languid sort of arousal that allowed Kit to minister to me at length. His own prick stood tall below, unattended for once, and I found myself in appreciation of his care.

"Let us retire to the sofa," he said, rising. He arranged me on my back, then climbed over me in reverse so his mouth might be upon my rod while offering his own to me. I began to lick his formidable instrument, then to suck the knob, and finally to admit as much of him as I could until he was well toward my throat.

His hands as we thus entwined moved about my body, caressing and squeezing, and we were in such position for some time until Kit issued an urgent moan and I received his issue, which I dutifully swallowed. When he had quieted, he stepped up his attentions toward me, removing his mouth in favor of his hand, which he wrapped around my swollen rod and pumped until I spurted for him. He then bent to lick what I had released.

We seemed at this point to share a wallow of sorts, merging into a fluid sort of coupling that existed beyond our respective cocks and bottoms. We continued on the sofa, my head upon his chest, and for a time enjoyed a welcome quiet. I nearly dozed and had no idea the passage of time until the train lurched, tooted, and began to move.

"She's had her fill," Kit declared. "I doubt she'll leave the train now until Balmoral. We'll arrive there tomorrow morning and she can breakfast at the castle."

"But there are more stops ahead."

"Oh, quite. Engines must be exchanged or some such and there are always stops to relieve the crew." He then rose and filled his glass. "Won't you join me?" he added.

I accepted a whiskey and we sat together on the sofa, me sipping the drink, Kit downing his quickly and taking another. When the hour was late and his words began to slur, I knew he was not to be long awake but I found I didn't mind because I'd grown tired of his rudeness about the Queen.

It was as I came to this conclusion that Kit rose and staggered about the compartment, now quite drunk. "Someone should fuck the old girl," he slurred. "Some poor bloke who can manage those skirts and find the royal cunt. Loosen her up a bit, don't you think?"

I agreed, as he was too far gone for reason, and he said, "Good man," before reeling, then falling to the floor. He lay giggling a moment before his eyes closed.

"Kit?" I said, nudging him even as I knew it futile. I rang for Elston. "I'm afraid he's done in," I told the servant. "Shall we get him to bed?"

"Very good, sir," Elston replied. When we had our drunken royal tucked in, I said, "A pity. He'll have a sore head tomorrow."

"Yes, sir."

We removed to the sitting room where Elston began to tidy things. "Have you been long with Kit?" I asked.

"Six years, sir. He was just a boy when I was taken on as his personal servant. I had previously served his uncle, who had died."

I could see he lingered in his duties and I likewise attempted conversation simply to keep him near. My cock was hard and I made no move for cover, thus when he turned to me he saw my intent.

"Were you subjected to such displays with your uncle as you are with Kit?" I asked.

He looked at my cock. "No, sir," he said to it.

"Rather an imposition," I observed.

"Of a sort, yes." He took a step toward me.

"Would it be such if I were to impose upon you?" I ventured.

"Not at all, sir," he replied. "Royals never display such consideration, thus your inquiry has great appeal." And with that he kneeled and took me into his mouth.

Kit had sucked my cock many a time but never like this. Elston's tongue was a voracious creature unto itself, ravenous upon my rod, licking and pulling and sending me to the heights of arousal until I erupted into his throat. That he kept to me and swallowed my issue was to his credit, and his ministrations as I softened were of such quiet intensity that I felt ascent even as I descended. I think he would have continued had I not gently pulled him off. "Will you bare yourself to me?" I asked and he nodded and stood.

I half lay in the chair as he slowly disrobed, folding his clothes neatly upon a table. When his under things were at last on the pile, I was presented with a broad and hairy chest above a thick plug of cock. He allowed me a long look, then brought a hand to it and began to stroke.

"Will you fuck me?" I asked.

"Gladly."

He motioned for me to move to the sofa, where he put me on my back and raised my legs. He then got into position and smeared his juices down his shaft before easing forward. As the fat rod penetrated, he spoke. "Does he tell you how beautiful you are?"

In throes of accommodating his girth, I was unable to speak and he saw this. "Because you are," he continued, now fully inside me. He began a slow thrust and said once more, "Beautiful."

He was unlike Kit or any of my other sexual companions—all boys, I now saw. I'd never had a man of such maturity. Bodies had invariably been sleek and smooth, and if any presented chest hair, it had been scant and fine. Elston, in contrast, bore the thickness of age, yet without a trace of fat. His pectorals were pronounced and his graying chest hair coarse. Beneath it hid nipples I longed to touch and possibly to lick and bite. That I received his cock while in such observation served to heighten his every attribute.

His expression while fucking remained constant. Pumping his cock in and out of me, he gave little clue toward arousal beyond the rod on which I lay speared. His eyes met mine, however, and I saw in them a measure of longing and an equal dose of care.

When I began to writhe and squirm, he increased his ardor and I saw his lips together, his jaw set. His thrusting became forceful jabs, and the harder he drove into me, the more I churned, until I let out a cry and a few drops of spunk. Seconds later he drove into me with such force the sofa complained while he grunted like a stevedore as he had his way.

When he'd finished, he collapsed upon me, breath labored at my ear until he managed a single word: "Magnificent."

I wrapped my arms around him and we lay some minutes before he raised up enough to speak. "May I kiss you?"

"You need not ask permission," I replied. "For anything."

His mouth upon mine was surprisingly gentle, almost hesitant, and I realized Kit had not kissed him. As Elston's tongue found mine, I responded fully and we lay for a while savoring this newfound communion.

The train halted, which bade me pull away from our kissing. "Oxenhome," Elston said, calling the stop. "We'll be on our way soon, but I should check on the master." And he rose and popped into the bedroom compartment, then came back.

"He is quite asleep," the servant announced. "I washed up and didn't attempt quiet but he never stirred. Knowing his usual habit, I'd venture he's gone until morning."

I couldn't help but smile and with this treated myself to an unembarrassed view of this man. He made an attempt at cover but stood with legs slightly apart as I took in the whole of him, noting the legs now, substantial and hairy thighs and the graying patch around his privates.

"Beautiful," I said and he smiled and came to me.

"The mistake boys make," he said, "is forgetting seduction. It is far better to cover oneself at times so there may then be the revelation."

He went to his compartment and returned wearing a navy dressing gown tied at the waist. Taking his cue, I sought my own somewhat worn plum garment. Once into it, I saw how enticing things became. The idea of him naked beneath made me want to get a hand inside.

"Tea," he announced and disappeared into his kitchen. I suddenly found myself famished and was grateful when he returned with a full tray. He seemed reluctant to take the chair opposite, never mind our intercourse, so I motioned him to do so. He sat with such care I saw he could not completely shed his lesser role.

He was not a talkative man, and I came to believe that normal discourse had been bred out of him much as Kit's flaws had been bred in. I did learn his family had been in service for three generations. "Mother is a lady's maid, father a butler. Only my brother resisted. He is a cobbler in Leeds."

"Do you ever regret following the family occupation?"

"Those in service learn to forgo retrospection."

I ate several sandwiches as well as three small cakes and two cups of tea. Elston likewise ate heartily and soon the plates were nearly empty. We sat back quite fulfilled.

"Forgive me, but I must again remark on your beauty," he said, "for it truly captures me. And while your fair skin and golden hair are most appealing, I must tell you that you also possess a passion I would explore further." And with this he took the tray and plates to the kitchen, then bade me stand.

When he reached for the ties to my dressing gown, I thought it to release them but he did the opposite, drawing them tightly. He then led me to sit upon the sofa where he joined me and ran a hand inside the gown, working along my thigh until he found my cock.

His fingers played about my hairy patch, everything slowly, gently. I soon understood what he'd meant about seduction. As he rubbed and fondled, I spread my legs to invite him further, and he strayed to my ballsac, where his touch was ardent yet light. "I wish to devour the whole of you," he said before kissing me. We were locked together thusly when the train lurched, wheels screeching as it abruptly slowed.

Elston paused. "Penrith," he said before drawing a finger back toward my bottom hole, where he prodded and played as the train resumed its speed.

At last he eased me onto my back and, while sitting at the sofa's edge, drew aside the top of the dressing gown to reveal my chest. Finding a tit, his tongue was but a whisper upon the nub until his lips descended and he began a gentle suck. That my prick stood but half-hard below seemed of little concern as he lingered up top, but at last a hand ventured into the folds to attend the rod. When he began to stroke, I told him Kit had taken too much. "I fear I am quite empty."

"That does not prevent me from enjoying you," Elston replied.

The train surprised us with a screech, as if to affirm my statement, but there came no stop. It continued its easy sway which I now saw lent itself to sexual play.

"Turn over," Elston then said. "Give me your bottom."

I did as asked but when I started to remove the dressing gown, he stopped me and I was thus positioned bottom high while still covered.

Elston got in behind and I felt him lift the gown to tease himself with slow revelation. The murmur this time bore a hint of the stevedore's grunt and then I felt his fingers on my buttocks, rubbing and caressing at length before pulling them open. "Ah, yes," he said. "The sweet pucker."

I felt him move closer and thus expected the fat prick but instead there came breath upon me and then his tongue. I gasped and he soothed. "Let me feed a bit, then you'll have the prick."

Though I knew this part of sex play, none of my men had so ventured. I also had no inclination toward the filthy hole, yet as Elston licked me I found myself in a veritable paroxysm of arousal. I grabbed my prick and began a frantic pull as the tongue played and prodded at my bottom hole. And then he did the unthinkable. He put his tongue where usually went his cock and proceeded to fuck me thusly.

Elston was not quiet in his tongue fucking, which I must admit enhanced the act. His snorfling sounded most porcine, and I felt overjoyed to join him in the wallow. Having come, I was now most pliable, and I venture Elston could have done most anything to me and I'd have offered welcome. But at last he put his cock in place of his tongue and began a thrust befitting the stevedore while still keeping the dressing gown intact.

As the train rumbled along, I likened Elston's thrusting to its rhythm, deciding train travel the ideal venue for sexual adventure. Elston didn't last long this time, no doubt due to his tongue play, and soon he issued his grunt and growl, dug his fingers into my hips as he reached his climax, which seemed, by virtue of his efforts, more powerful than before. Once quieted, he bade me turn over.

Onto my back I rolled to see his own dressing gown still tied, his cock having thrown open the lower portion, where it remained like some player refusing to leave the stage. I gazed upon the thing of my pleasure until it softened and allowed the gown to close.

"You are beautiful," Elston said to me before he withdrew to the bedroom where I assumed he would check on the master as well as visit the toilet to wash. When he returned he pulled me to my feet and kissed me at length.

"I am in your thrall," he said.

"Likewise," I managed, giddy at heart.

To say the night that followed was exquisite is to fail it entirely, for it proved a true awakening, my heart thrown open to welcome another most ardently. That sexual activity played a part must not obscure other rewards, and by the time the clock had moved past midnight, I knew myself in love.

"I'll wish us to continue at Balmoral," I told him as we lay together on the sofa.

Elston had no immediate reply. Rather, he considered my proposal at such length that it set my heart to rapid beating. "I cannot escape my station," he said at last. "I must serve the master."

"I would not ask such, but surely we can find means for a bit of private time. I shall have my own room. Can you not call upon me when Kit is asleep?"

Elston smiled at this. "I would venture you to be in his room most often."

I clung to him. "I cannot be without you. You have not only my body, you have my heart."

"And you have mine, but we must not discard practical matters," he replied, tightening his embrace. "The hour is quite late. You must sleep in the bed beside the master. He must find all as expected when he awakens."

This I resisted. "I cannot let you go."

"I shall not be far."

"You must promise we shall continue at Balmoral."

"If we are to have time together, you must manage to be in your room rather than the master's. Knowing you alone, I shall call late in the night."

"I fear we will get little sleep."

"All the better."

He, being the more disciplined, rose and pulled me to my feet. The kiss was most passionate, as it was to be our last for a while. "Go now," he said.

"I shall dream of you."

"And I of you."

We then parted.

The bedroom reeked of whiskey and while I settled into my bed, I found little sleep. Lying beneath rich linens, I allowed the train's rumble and sway to call up images of Elston's cock, which led me to think of him at the car's other end, likely feeling much as did I.

The new day found Kit retching in the w.c., which gave promise to lesser sexual demand. Our destination was mere hours hence, thus there would be time for breakfast and little more. Emerging at last, Kit looked awful, eyes red, face pale, hair a tangle. He fell back upon the bed and had me ring for Elston.

"Coffee," he rasped when the servant appeared. As I slipped on my dressing gown, Kit took note. "What's this?" he demanded. "You cover yourself?"

"The morning air chills me," I said which was partly true. Though the car was heated, it proved inadequate early on. "You would be best served to cover yourself as well," I added.

"Nonsense. We'll soon throw them off."

And so he was naked when Elston served coffee in the bedroom. When Kit tugged his cock in the servant's presence, Elston remained outwardly unmoved while I suffered newfound embarrassment on his behalf. "Breakfast," Kit then commanded, and Elston retreated to see to the meal.

At table I was near beside myself in Elston's proximity. The seduction of the previous night was magnified tenfold, and my prick was hard through most of the meal as Kit kept Elston in near-continued attendance, asking for this and that as if he were a puppeteer pulling strings. It became a true ordeal, yet I resolved to follow Elston's example and quietly endure.

Once Kit had his fill, he raised the shade and stood naked at the window. Fog lay across the landscape and for this I was grateful. "Where might we be?" I asked, hoping to stave off any sexual advance.

"Perth, Aberdeen, who knows?" Kit replied. "Elston, what's the next stop?" he asked as the servant cleared the meal.

"Carstairs Junction, sir."

"Ah yes, before Perth. Quite. That's all, Elston."

I stole a glance at my retreating lover and Kit caught my interest. "You mustn't be concerned about him," he chided. "He is the embodiment of discretion."

I thought back to the thick cock going at me and enjoyed a private satisfaction at having had the real man. "Of course," I replied to Kit. "Come, sit down."

My idea was to engage him in conversation to such extent that he might spare me sexual advances. Thus I asked how one such as me might manage riding to hounds, all the while hearing scarcely any of the reply, thinking only on Elston ensconced in his nearby compartment. Was he thinking of me as I was of him? Was he considering how our coupling might be accomplished at the castle? As Kit spoke of using one's knees and leg muscles to remain astride a horse, I couldn't help but consider Elston's hairy thighs as they drove his fat plug of cock into me. I called up the grunts that accompanied his climax and was glad I'd seen fit to don my dressing gown, as my prick was now quite stiff. That it was up for the man I loved gave me respite from worry at a royal imposition.

Fate was kind to me that morning as Kit became quite lethargic after the meal and his discourse on horsemanship. "My headache persists," he announced, "and my stomach grows queasy. I must rest." And with that, he retired to the bedroom.

Quiet descended upon the car. I watched the countryside amble by, the fog now risen to reveal green fields bordered by low rock walls. I welcomed the pastoral view and attempted to let it fill the morning, yet knowing Elston so close by undermined my efforts. I quietly looked in upon Kit, who lay in a heavy snore. I passed a few moments in his company before deciding his slumber was of such depth that I was free to do as I pleased.

Retreating to the sitting room, I could not bear to ring for Elston, whom I considered my equal. Instead I went to his compartment door, knocked lightly, and entered without waiting for a reply. "Sir," he said, quite surprised.

"Adrian, please. I am not your superior."

"The master?"

"Asleep. Deeply so, the night's indulgence still well upon him, which allows me to call upon you. I cannot bear to pass the remaining time apart. Allow me in, please."

I shut the door behind me and he took me into his arms, embracing me with much force before kissing me at length. Pressed against him, I felt him come up hard. "Fuck me, please," I begged and he released me, untied my dressing gown, and threw it open.

"I thought you preferred cover," I noted.

"At times, yes, but not now." And he began to quickly undress. Soon we were naked and in his narrow bed which, lacking the softness of those appointed for royals, allowed the train's vibration to come up through it.

"How you can feel the wheels below," I noted as he positioned me to receive him. "It gives one a pleasing sensation of being whisked away from life itself."

"That I may go with you," Elston said as he put his cock into me. His thrust soon rocked in time to the train's easy gait.

RESIST ME, PLEASE!
DANIEL M. JAFFE

I've got a problem. A sex problem. I always assumed it would ease with age, but I was wrong. Now that I'm in my seventies, the problem's as bad as ever. I've consulted doctor after doctor here in Philadelphia, but they can't help. My fault for choosing men doctors. Should have chosen a woman a long time ago. Obvious once I figured it out. That's why I'm taking this train trip across country. To meet with a woman specialist I found on the Internet. The only specialist I could find for CAAD, Compulsive Addictive Attraction Disorder. She's in San Francisco. (Where else?)

In case the name of the disorder hasn't clued you in, it's this: All men—gay, bi, straight, whatever—are compulsively, addictively, attracted to me. I've got to swat them away like flies. (If they're like flies, and I'm irresistible to them, that must make me a steaming pile of horse manure. Charming.)

The problem started on my bar mitzvah. I don't mean around puberty or sometime during my thirteenth year, I mean smack on my bar mitzvah as if some newbie angel was looking down and, in a bumbling attempt, fumbled his bottle of manhood cologne and doused me when he should have sprinkled.

My concentration was intense as I stood behind the lectern with Cantor Kahn beside me. Then, just as I finished reciting the blessing after my Torah reading and felt an incredible shiver of joy at officially becoming a man, Cantor Kahn copped a feel of my crotch. Right there while Mom and Dad looked on from the front row, oblivious and smiling. I jolted as if from electric shock and looked at Cantor Kahn, who brought hand to nose for a deep sniff. Admittedly, I must have looked dapper in my new navy blue suit and white prayer shawl that set off my thick black curls. But, still.

Then Rabbi Schmidt came over and shook my hand. Not only wouldn't he let go, but he yanked me close, hugged me tight. Embraced me like I was the Messiah or something. He nuzzled his nose in my black curls, sniffed deeply, fainted on the spot. I mean, he collapsed flat out. That diverted everyone's attention from me, thank goodness. "Is there a doctor in the house?" cried Cantor Kahn. Half the congregation ran up to the rabbi.

The women doctors attended to him while the men in the medical mob stuck their noses in the air like dogs in heat, and whiffed me. I had to flee the sanctuary like Moses chased by Pharaoh's horsemen.

That was the first time.

Then, of course, there were the male teachers in high school, who always insisted I sit front and center, and who were forever asking me to stay after class so they could lock the classroom door, drop to their knees in front of me, unzip me, and… And don't get me started on what happened in the locker room before gym class. (Nobody ever made it out to the ball field, but we always got our exercise.)

A month into college, the young women staged a mass protest and blockade of my dorm room because all their boyfriends were forever ditching them to spend the night with me in my official-issue single bed. Let me tell you, it got crowded in there. I did my best to satisfy everyone, and as a wiry young man, I stood a real chance at getting through the night with energy to spare. But I had my limits.

And you can imagine my work life. Male bosses and coworkers at the law firm lost lots of clients because they spent all their time trying to de-brief me. (The women partners in the firm actually adored me because their careers suddenly zoomed ahead.)

As I began to age, it became harder and harder to stay harder and harder, so the hordes of men took to beating each other up to see which ones could get my freshest and best energy. A real mess wherever I went.

Like I said, over the years I tried every (male) doctor I could think of, and all kinds of diet, exercise, hormone, gland, and skin treatments. *Nada.* I showered. I bathed. I scrubbed with Comet cleanser until I bled. I doused myself with ammonia, rubbing alcohol, cologne. To no avail. You see, I knew that it was my scent that did it. I learned that in the 1980s when I sent photos of myself in response to personal ads in the local gay paper. Not a single response. I'm not exactly a Samson look-alike, but I'm no troll, either, so *some*body should have responded based on my looks. In the Internet age, I tried camming on J-Gay-Date. com. Not even a nibble. Clearly it wasn't my looks. Skype proved it wasn't my voice, either.

It had to be my scent.

So, here I am on the Starlight Express chugging across country to meet Dr. Rosa Handelmeyer, the world's foremost (and only) expert in CAAD. I e-mailed her a detailed history of my troubles, and she replied that she has a surefire way to ease my discomfort, a patented medical approach so secret that she feared talking about it over the Internet. Fine. I'd take any risk. Castrate me if that'll help. (Well, maybe not.)

It would have been faster to fly cross-country than train it, to be sure. But I gave up flying long ago. There just isn't enough room in economy class for me to satisfy the hordes of men. Especially when the seat-belt sign is lit. I remember one flight to Fort Lauderdale when the stewardesses did their best at crowd control, but were thwarted by the stewards who kept pricking all the other men with their bronze wing stick-pins in order to get them out of the way. I nearly freaked when the pilot announced over the PA system, "Will the disruptive passenger in 24C please come to the captain's cabin immediately." Ever obedient to authority, I got up, shoved my way through the grasping masses, knocked on the cabin door, and went in.

They don't call it *"cockpit"* for nothing.

Sigh.

Driving cross-country would have exhausted me, what with fending off attacks at three thousand miles' worth of gas stations, motels, restaurants, etc., so the Starlight Express it is. Even if folks get out of hand, at least we're on the ground and I can barricade myself in my compartment.

I've taken some precautions: I chose a compartment at the very end of the caboose car, so there's no one behind me. I've brought three hundred energy bars with me, so I don't need to go to the dining car. I'm wearing five layers of thermal underwear in the hopes of stifling my scent.

Inside my train compartment, I even sealed the door tight with weather stripping. Trains are made of metal, so I've been figuring that I stand a chance at preventing my scent from drifting around the car.

But what I failed to take into account is the ventilation system that circulates air from one compartment to another and the corridors. And the fact that my five layers of thermal underwear have been making me sweat *a lot*, which only makes matters worse. And the energy bars have given me a permanent hard-on.

Since I'm not used to going more than fifteen minutes without an orgasm, I'm now feeling somewhat trapped and frustrated. At the first rap on my compartment door, I rip out the weather stripping and fling the door open. The official ticket taker, a young man in snappy blue uniform and cap, asks, "May I, um, see your ticket, please? And, if you wouldn't mind, your dick?"

He steps in and shuts the door behind him. Wrinkled and bald though I may be, I do my part in guiding America's wayward youth.

He punches a hole in my ticket, tips his hat, leaves with an "I'll be back."

Typical. Everyone wants repeats.

No sooner am I finished washing myself than I hear another knock on the door. It's starting. "Yes?" I ask.

"Sorry to disturb you," says a woman's voice. A woman's voice? Not a problem.

I open the door to see a really pretty middle-aged woman with long brown hair standing there. "May I come in?" she asks. "It's kind of private."

"You sure you have the right compartment?"

"According to my husband, yes."

Her husband? Instantly I know what's coming. I've traveled this road before. "Tell me," I say, trying to express a patience and understanding I don't really feel.

"Well, sir, you see…" And she gives the usual wifely spiel about how her husband is a wonderful lover and has never been interested in men before, but there's something about me that's driving him crazy and he can't get me out of his mind and can't I please please please come help them simply by being present while they make love so he can see me and smell me and imprint a fantasy he can then dredge up any time in the future while making love with his wife?

She looks so sad. The thought of condemning her to a sexless marriage breaks my heart. And—okay, I admit it—I get a pervy kind of kick from the idea of just being there watching. "Bring him here."

"Bless you, sir." She kisses my hand.

Her husband isn't a bad-looking sort, kind of dumpy with sparse frizzy hair and a body thick with pudge. They strip and I strip and the husband lies back on my bed while the wife mounts him and I stand off to the side playing with myself. The husband ogles me, sniffs the air of my compartment so hard you'd think I'm an uncapped poppers bottle.

They finish and dress. As he's about to leave, he turns to me and makes the sign of a cross over my forehead. "He used to be a priest," says his wife. "Bless you for saving our marriage."

Glad to oblige.

Just as I'm closing the door after them, a teenage boy with acne on his face and a hard-on in his pants comes to my door. "Mister?"

"How old are you?"

"Eighteen."

"Sorry, nobody under twenty-five. You young ones drain me completely."

"But I—"

"I know. I was your age once. Some shrinks call it Obsessive-Compulsive Disorder, but I call it Normal Teenage Nonstop Jerk-off Syndrome."

"There'll never be anyone like you." He looks up at me with such earnestness in his eyes, I want to cry.

Part of my problem has always been my deep empathy —how can I frustrate other men by turning them down? "Here," I say. "This is the best I can do." I stick my pinkie finger up his nose and tell him to sniff deep. He does, shudders, and covers his crotch.

"Remember that for next time," I say.

He takes my pinkie from his nose, gives it a quick suck, then leaves.

I lie down on my narrow bed and try to nap. Just as I'm picturing myself a modern Jacob wrestling with an angel—a muscular, bare-chested angel—another knock at my door.

"Who?" I ask.

"Me!" says a gruff voice. "No, me!" says another. "I was here first!" cries a third. And on and on and on.

"Go away."

The knocking turns into a pounding. Lots of pounding. Pounds and pounds of pounding on my door. (I'm tempted to say I feel like one of the three little pigs, except that simile wouldn't be kosher.)

"Go away!" I say, "This zipper is glued shut!"

We have our back and our forth, this mob and I, until I finally work out a compromise: "We're near Pittsburgh now. Give me till Chicago. Then I'll open the door and pull a choo-choo train, doing you one after another."

Fine. They leave.

Now what? I've got eight hours (this train's a local) to figure something out. I sit on my bed and pray, "Dear Lord, I'm so close to salvation. All I need is to make it to San Francisco in one piece and finally get healed by Dr. Rosa Handelmeyer. Please show me a way to arrive unscathed." And just like that, right smack on the luggage rack across from me, I see a vision of an angel beckoning Jacob up the ladder to heaven. Bingo.

I wait until dark, then quietly unlock my compartment door so the mob can just let themselves in without breaking anything. I write a note: "I can't take it anymore, so I'm joining my Maker. Poke around my used underwear to your heart's content." I chomp a hunk of energy bar and spit it out and use it to stick the suicide note to the wall.

I fill my backpack with essentials (i.e., energy bars, a blanket, and my cell phone in case of emergency), slide open my compartment's window, climb out, and make my way to the top of the train car where I sprawl like some contemporary aged Jesse James planning a heist.

Lying on my belly and wrapped in the blanket, I fall into a troubled sleep.

The stink of the Chicago stockyards wakes me at dawn. I'm glad for that stink, hope it will mask my scent while we stop in Chicago to discharge and pick up passengers. I keep my eyes open, peer down the tracks for trouble—none.

The train whistle blows, and we set off for the West, ever the White Man's land of fantasy and hope. Chug-chug-chug and chug-chug-chug and chug-chug-chug. The steady rolling of the train soothes me. I drift to sleep under the warming sunshine. After a while, I dream I'm hearing the trumpeting of *shofars*, then I see the walls of Jericho come tumbling down right on top of me, crashing onto me, weighing me down, nearly crushing the air out of me.

"Mmmmm," I hear, and I feel hot air in my ear.

What?

I awake and realize a group of men has piled on top. I crane my neck to see—yep, a bunch of ragtag hoboes. "Come on, guys, give me a break," I groan.

"Not until you give us your ass."

There's just no way around it. I'm too exhausted from my recent travails. So I say, "Fine." One after the other, they have their way with me. I'm not happy about it—bottoming has never been my thing—but this isn't the first time I've been imposed upon this way, so I survive. I just keep my mind on the prize, on San Francisco and Dr. Rosa Handelmeyer and release from this life of endless sex at everyone else's whim.

However, after all dozen hoboes finish and the first one says, "I'm ready for another round"—like I told you, everyone wants repeats—I get angry. Enough! As soon as he inserts himself into me up to the hilt, I clench tight, swivel my hips so he loses his balance, then release and fart him off the train. He tumbles with barely a scream.

"Who's next?" I ask, grimacing like a riled bear.

They all back away, jump to the next car, pull out cell phones, and start gabbing like a gaggle of junior high school girls.

My cell phone rings. "Hello?"

"This is Dr. Rosa Handelmeyer."

"Really? Dr. Handelmeyer?"

"I see that my hoboes arrived?"

"*Your* hoboes?"

"They're in my employ, yes."

"You sent them after me?"

"Yes, as part of your therapy treatment. I watched. You're really something."

"You watched them attack me?"

"Yes, via satellite feed spliced from Google Earth. You gave that one employee quite a wallop. He may have broken some bones in the fall off the train."

"There's a limit as to what I can endure."

"Really?"

"Yes, really. I just can't take it anymore. A lifetime of giving in to every Tom with a hairy dick just because I'm irresistible. I'm tired of the constant exhaustion, the glans chafing and occasional hemorrhoid. I didn't ask to be irresistible. It's not my fault. It's my body, and I've got a right to pull a Nancy Reagan and just say no anytime I want!"

"So you fought back."

"Yes."

"Violently."

"Sort of."

"For the first time."

"Yes."

"So now you know."

"What?"

"That you can. That you possess the ability to fight back and deny access. And that CAAD—Compulsive Addictive Attraction Disorder— is not *your* disorder. It's theirs. They should be exercising some restraint regardless of how irresistible you are. After all, if someone has an allergy, you don't say it's the flower's problem, do you?"

"Hmmm. Good point."

"We angels have rights, too."

"Angels? What do you mean, angels?"

"What do you mean, what do I mean? You mean you don't know?"

"Don't know what?"

"That you're a sex angel."

"A what?"

"A sex angel. No one told you? For God's sake, you should have been told. You were chosen at your bar mitzvah. Only the choicest cherubs are chosen to be sex angels, so you should feel proud."

A sex angel? Whoever heard of such a thing? "Dr. Handelmeyer, are you serious?"

"Totally. When you contacted me I thought it was because you knew I specialize in celestial treatments. Now that I know you weren't told about your gift, your problem makes sense. You've been feeling compelled to comply with every single sex request, haven't you?"

"Yes, ever since I was thirteen."

"It's true that our mission is to spread libidinal satisfaction throughout the land like an army of Johnny Appleseeds and Evelyn Eggplants. However, we have rights, too."

"So, it's okay if I just say no?"

"When you arrive at my office, we'll go through the handbook together."

"There's a sex angel handbook?"

"Now I'm really pissed. You should have been getting handbook updates for decades. I'm going to check our records and see which angel screwed up at your bar mitzvah."

"This is a lot to take in, Dr. Handelmeyer. All of a sudden, my life makes sense."

"Glad to hear it. Now, I want you to go back into your compartment and lock yourself in. Let the other passengers bang away at the door to their hearts' content. Between here and SF, you are not to satisfy any supplicant whatsoever. A good lesson for everyone concerned."

"Yes, Doctor."

She hangs up, I climb back to my compartment (my underwear had been shredded), and hunker down for the long haul to the coast.

Well, what do you know? I'm a sex angel.

A sex angel with rights. My mission is to spread happiness and fulfillment, yet I have the right to determine how and when and with whom.

I flex my shoulders in the hope I can sprout wings and zoom around my compartment in joy. No dice. But I'm happy, just the same. I'm so happy knowing there's nothing wrong with me at all. I'm my own normal, and there are a bunch of us. With our own handbook, no less.

I lie back on the bed, throw a boner, and offer happiness and fulfillment to myself.

Over and over and over.

Chug-chug-chug and tug-tug-tug and chug-chug-chug and...

ENGINE OF REPRESSION
GAVIN ATLAS

Christian fidgeted, avoiding the doctor's eyes by staring at the word "Misfit" on his own wrist. Black letters and all capitals. He winced at a memory of being tied up in a damp basement, needles stinging his skin. The tattoo had not been voluntary.

"I'm not ready to talk, Doc," he said. "I've only known you for a few weeks."

Dr. Hall nodded. "It's okay. Take your time."

The doctor's smile lit up his eyes, and Christian wondered if it were natural or if his expression was enhanced by so-called saint effects. It was legal for doctors to use them, right? *Now eighty percent more trustworthy*, a comedian had recently joked. Christian felt the air in the room change, a micro mist making it easier to breathe and relax. He inhaled.

"Jeremy told you correctly," Christian said. "The train dream is the worst part, or at least it's the worst of what he knows." Christian sighed, about to make the same complaint he'd made to every previous doctor. "If cancer is a thing of the past and every STI is now curable, why am I still fucked up?"

The doctor gave Christian an understanding nod. "So much of the mind remains a mystery. Each generation discovers more, but emotional trauma will always exist. Thus, so will neurosis. The fact you've identified the dream as a problem and are considering the correction process—"

"I don't think this will work, but I told Jeremy I'd do it if it meant that much to him."

"Good," said Dr. Hall with a sympathetic smile. "I imagine he's so glad you're willing to try."

Christian was silent, again wondering if Dr. Hall's charm was natural or enhanced. The room's systems continually monitored Christian's reactions and involuntary responses to subtle stimuli. A faint blinking light indicated the room had sensed his renewed reluctance and begun to recalibrate. The structured airflow and dim lighting of the office, the pleasant whirr of the placidity machine coming from behind him, and the engulfing comfort of the oversized chair adjusted to Christian's mood and subconscious preferences. The doctor smiled and waited for Christian to find his words.

"I can only have sex if I'm raped. If I'm not forced, it's…it's wrong. The train dream comes back."

Dr. Hall stroked his chin. "Again, I'm proud of you for the steps you've taken to stay away from men who rape you. I know treatments to counteract the pellet chemicals are painful, especially so long after the injection. I imagine Jeremy is proud of you, too. Have you thought about role playing where perhaps Jeremy is pretending to be forceful?"

Christian shook his head. "Not exactly. He doesn't want to risk that I'll associate him with rapists if he's rough. He did say if you thought it would help, he would try. He's so patient. We've dated for months now, and he's never gotten inside me. He says he wants me to jerk off when he's penetrating me. He says he won't enjoy it unless I come. I can't do that. It's not right. But he's very clear. He says he would love to top me every day all day, but the pleasure needs to be mutual. I wish I could give him what he wants."

"Okay, before we get to the dream, I'd like to hear about your rape situation." Dr. Hall folded his hands and frowned, pausing before speaking. "You should know I don't approve of the program, though I believe I am still able to discuss the aspects of the system without judgment."

Christian nodded.

"However, Jeremy is from a part of the country where they won't even discuss a rape program. How did you bring up the fact that you're a…participant?"

Christian took quick, shallow breaths. "I told him right away. I didn't want to keep something like that from him. He was perplexed, but he didn't seem to be too concerned. Now I guess he's wondering why it's not going away if I'm in love with him. And why would someone want that to begin with?"

"An excellent question, Christian. I know that circumstances for you were a bit unusual, but you still…allowed events to unfold. Why do you think that is?"

Christian blinked and steadied himself. He had to be honest. For Jeremy, he had to be. "Because I think, on some level, I must want sex." His throat nearly closed, but he'd gotten the words out. He took a deep breath. "I can't get over the feelings that it's wrong. That I'm disgusting. So if I'm raped, it's…it's not my fault. It's not my responsibility at all."

Dr. Hall stroked his chin and nodded.

"And it's more than that," continued Christian. This part was easier. "Studies show that cities with rape programs have many fewer incidents of true rape. So, I know this is screwed up," Christian said, his shame returning, "but it's like I've found a way to feel getting fucked makes me a good boy."

Christian could see Dr. Hall's face had reddened. "It makes me sad that you feel you have to be so self-destructive to be a good boy."

Christian looked away to give his parroted response. "The clinic's counselor says signing up for a tour of duty with the army is much more dangerous, and no one says they're being self-destructive."

Dr. Hall winced and shook his head. "I have it in my notes that your mother is a part of the train dream. I don't want to make an assumption, but nine times out of ten, when I have young gay male patients in your situation, their parents are members of the Revisionist Church. Are yours?"

"My father is a deacon actually, so, of course, they had to kick me out. My mother was devastated. When I told her, she…she was so upset I haven't heard from them. I'm worried that she's dead…that what I am killed her."

Dr. Hall cocked his head. "They threw you out. You don't seem angry. You seem worried about their welfare."

"They were both raised in the faith. It's not fair to blame them."

"Fair enough," said Dr. Hall. "Instead of blaming, we'll try to fix. Corrective Oneirology may be new, but it's successfully treated psychosexual dysfunction." The doctor folded his hands. "Are you comfortable enough to discuss the dream, Christian? Are you ready?"

Christian swallowed and took a series of deep breaths. "I'm on a train. Not a maglev or a hover train. One from the old movies that billows steam. It's hurtling along a track, much too fast to be safe. It's headed for a tunnel at the base of a volcano. It seems like we're out of control. And…and there are always some pirates."

Dr. Hall raised an eyebrow. "A train headed for a tunnel? Really? That's a rather obvious symbol."

"I know. But that's honestly my dream."

"Tell me about the pirates."

Christian shook his head. "Yeah, I don't get that. But there are pirates swarming the train. The seafaring kind complete with tri-corner hats and brandishing scabbards out the windows. And my mom is there. She's standing in an outfit that, I don't know, Queen Victoria might have worn when she was in mourning. You know, all black with a veil. And she's wailing and crying and wringing her hands."

"And what are you doing in the dream?"

"I think…I'm just sitting there, upset that my mom is so frantic. I'm helpless and can't speak. Or maybe, sometimes, I am the train, because somehow I know that train is nervous. It's unhappy that it can't stop."

"I see. You can't stop. You have no choice. Then what?"

"Then we enter the tunnel, and the train slowly disappears. The pirates and I are climbing rocks that glow a faint red. I rest my head on one and it's very warm. Then I wake up, and most times I start crying."

"Where is your mother when you're climbing the rocks?"

"I don't know. She's gone. I think she's dead." Christian began to cry. "I think the dream says I killed her. She was sobbing so hard and she was so upset that she couldn't breathe. So she choked and she died. Because I embarrassed her so much." Christian covered his face with both hands and rocked back and forth.

Dr. Hall spoke softly. "Christian, I'm so sorry you've been living with this for so long. But…I believe Jeremy said you had this dream even before they kicked you out. Since you were quite young."

"Yes. I've known for a long while that what I am is shameful. Abominable."

"Hmm, pirates. Are you familiar with the Peter Pan story?"

Christian stopped rocking and gave the doctor a surprised look. "Yes, it was one of my favorites. How did you know?"

"It creates a rather iconic image. Pirates capturing young men or, actually, boys. So a pirate might have a lot of power over someone innocent and boyish." Dr. Hall looked inquisitively at Christian.

The young man looked at his shoes. "I'm twenty-four now, Doc."

"Is it possible that a pirate, a dominant but friendly and trustworthy one, might be the right kind of a man for you?"

Christian laughed nervously. "Yeah, too bad they haven't been around for centuries."

Dr. Hall gave Christian a mischievous smirk. "Perhaps through the magic of dream induction and virtual reality therapy, we can find one for you. This particular dream sounds treatable. If you allow us to scan your dream while you have it, we should be able to recreate it quite accurately."

"You can?"

Dr. Hall nodded. "Absolutely." He picked up a digital pamphlet from his desk. He pressed a button, and with the flash of a red light, the contents were sent to the data pad in Christian's shirt pocket. "Transportation dreams, like trains or jets, usually represent movement toward the future. If the train is out of control, the dreamer might fear his life is out of control and perhaps headed for disaster. Since the dreamer is nearly never the conductor of the train, it means he thinks he's helpless to fix his situation. Such dreams are common, so we have a model train car at the center."

Christian took a deep breath, his hands gripping the arms of the chair. "But why would I want to live out the dream in an atmosphere that's even more realistic? It upsets me so much as it is."

Dr. Hall grinned and reached over to pat Christian on the shoulder. "I promise it will work out better when we guide it."

❖

It had confused Christian that Dr. Hall asked to meet with Jeremy alone at his next session. Afterward, Jeremy wouldn't discuss it. What did that mean? Now Christian was at the Dream Center for the first half of the procedure, the dream induction. He lay on a hospital bed with two IV units attached to his arm and sensors resembling electrode patches attached to his forehead. Worst of all, he'd had to put on special underwear that would measure and monitor his erectile responses while he was unconscious. The material was thin, scratchy, and constrictive. An assistant gave Christian an appraising look and then shook her head. He'd seen that before. Both the men he'd tried to date before Jeremy had asked him, "How could someone so handsome and muscular have so many problems?" The thought made him sad. What if this didn't work and Jeremy wanted to break up?

Dr. Hall entered the room, as always a friendly expression on his face. Christian fidgeted, uncomfortable to be only wearing the tight, almost sheer pair of briefs. He swallowed. "I didn't know you'd be here, Doc."

"This is still new technology," Dr. Hall said. "The center prefers to have their most experienced practitioners on hand."

Christian nodded as Dr. Hall patted his arm, reassuring him. "This is going to feel like you're having two different dreams, Christian. The chemical that will be introduced into your first IV causes you to experience hypnogogic arousal as you're falling asleep. You can help it along by thinking of sexual experiences that you've enjoyed or fantasies."

He'd read as much in the pamphlet, but now Christian's eyes widened in alarm. "Will everyone know what's in my head?"

Dr. Hall looked puzzled. "Well, of course not everyone. And we won't literally be seeing this particular dream like it's a video. But the brain has been so well mapped now that when a certain point is stimulated, we'll have a good idea what you're thinking. With the help of that pair of underwear, we'll know the intensity of your arousal at each thought."

Christian took a deep breath. This was going to be tough.

The doctor continued. "The second stage will be the induction of the train dream. Sometimes the sustained arousal will prompt the repressive response on its own, but if not, the chemical in the second IV should guarantee the train dream occurs. It will likely be more or less unchanged from its normal presentation. The analysis we do will take much longer and we'll scan much more deeply because this time we actually are going to try to reconstruct visual images from your dream.

We hope to recreate it as closely as possible when we do the oneiric correction next week during the virtual reality session."

Christian winced. "Are you sure this is safe?"

The doctor touched Christian's shoulder. "Absolutely. However, I'm afraid you might have a headache when you wake up, but we'll have an analgesic ready to go. It will only last a few moments."

The doctor waited for more questions, and when none came, he squeezed Christian's arm. "I'll start the first drug. Just relax."

Christian closed his eyes and thought of the night he'd finally tried to muster the courage to enter Depths of Darkness, a sex club reputed to be the wildest in the nation. He'd never even been in a bar before.

He'd lost his nerve three feet from the door, but he was close enough to attract attention. Blake was a giant of a man with a feral gleam in his eyes and a mean grin. Blake asked Christian his name and then put an arm around Christian's shoulder, ushering him, or actually, pushing him down the dark street to a darker alley. Guilty thoughts intruded. *I shouldn't have had so much alcohol. I shouldn't have even been in that neighborhood. This was my fault.*

The flow of the drug increased, and Christian slipped back into the memory of that night.

As Blake yanked down Christian's pants and bent him over against a graffiti-covered brick wall, Christian whimpered in protest. Christian had expected Blake to invade him with his dick with violent abandon, and that's what he got. Christian cried out with each massive thrust of Blake's dick. The burning of being stretched and the shock of each punch to his prostate was both frightening and exquisite.

What Christian hadn't expected was a rape pellet injection. With Blake's massive tool plowing his hole, Christian barely felt the sting in his thigh where Blake implanted the mechanism.

"You'll never be able to hide from me," Blake growled. "You've got a great ass meant to be fucked. My dick will be in it anytime I want, boy." This memory made Christian's dick stiffen.

Blake continued his assault on Christian's hole, bringing himself closer and closer to orgasm by telling Christian of dark deeds to come. "Anytime you leave your home, I'll get your ass. If you stay in and lock the door, I'll get your ass. Even if you try to move out of town, you're going to get fucked again and again and again." Christian moaned and swallowed as a hollow pang of lust in his gut made shame and guilt radiate through his entire body.

Christian was only barely aware that he was edging toward sleep. When his thoughts turned to his failure to have the rape pellet removed within the three-day limit, he wasn't sure if he'd conjured the image himself or if the drugs were causing the memories of both humiliation and incredible pleasure to flood through him uncontrolled.

He recalled calling a hotline. If he let three days pass, the pellet's chemicals would have saturated his body, making it even easier to track him. They also fomented production of a pheromone that made assailants perceive Christian as desirable and exciting to violate. He was told the pellet's agents sometimes enhanced the victim's pleasure as well.

Christian hadn't volunteered. He could have had the pellet removed and his system cleared free of charge. But Christian told no one, his silence allowing the reversal period to slip by. It was now legal for anyone and everyone to rape Christian. He slept at his apartment or in hotels, but an image passed through his mind of spending a few chilly nights on park benches to stave off possible assaults, as they were prohibited anywhere small children might be exposed to them. The defensive rationalization kicked in. *I'm stopping crime. I'm doing a good thing.*

The next image streaming into Christian's mind was that of several men breaking into his apartment, their pocket seeker-guides beeping that they'd found a rape addict. The first man had crazed eyes and, at least in Christian's memory, teeth sharpened to vicious points.

"This is the boy who didn't volunteer," the man said with a cruel grin. "Everyone is talking about it 'cause this is so much closer to true rape." The man panted and feverishly rubbed the bulge in his jeans. "That ass is gonna get multi, multi extra hits, boy. No point in ever puttin' on pants 'cause it's never gonna stop."

Christian wailed in fear as the man lifted his legs and spread them as wide as possible while his accomplices began to stroke themselves. Even with the regularity of furious penetration Christian had experienced since the pellet injection, this stranger's dick hurt. The look on the crazed man's face revealed he didn't care.

"Ooh," the man said, "I've never seen such a fine ass on an addict before. You have no idea what your hole is in for." The man's eyes bore into Christian's soul as deeply as his dick bore into Christian's ass.

A chugging noise began, drowning out Christian's cries for mercy. The memory of the strangers taking turns inside him as he futilely struggled ballooned into a three-dimensional reenactment. It seemed like Christian was no longer in the clinic bed, but back in his apartment, and the greedy, vicious grip on his aching thighs sent pulses of ecstasy through Christian as he writhed, breathless that he had no ability whatsoever to take his legs out of the air. His body was drenched in sweat and the euphoria of being entirely helpless to stop his ass from constantly getting fucked.

Then, the train dream. As always, Christian sat on a crushed velvet bench watching his mother scream in terror. She wouldn't look at him, and he couldn't move his arms to reach out for her.

The train hurtled through a barren landscape—a brutal, lifeless desert strewn with boulders, forever derelict on the barren ground. Each time the train rocked dangerously to one side, a sickening tension ran down his spine and into his gut. Through the forward window, he could see steam billowing. Moving shapes in the car in front of him resolved into pirates. His mother continued to scream, consumed in utter panic. Christian could do nothing to help her, and the guilt of his sins and the shame of his impotence consumed him with agony.

The pirates raced through the train, sticking their scabbards out windows and slashing at invisible enemies. He could hear them on the roof. Ahead, he could see the volcano looming, pouring smoke as fast the locomotive poured steam. A moment of confused panic seized Christian. Who was responsible for this train? And what the fucking hell did they think they were doing?

No, it was his doing. All his.

The train lurched. Christian's heart nearly stopped when he looked and saw they were now on a bridge. Rickety. Narrow. No guardrails. Each time the train tilted, he could see that the gorge was vast. He tried to tell his mother he was sorry. That it couldn't be his fault. He'd had no choice. He was a good boy. But no words came.

Then there was the beginning trickle of lucidity. Christian noticed he was in his underwear and out of breath. He was lying down on the couchette instead of sitting. The pirate captain entered the compartment and looked down at him. *That never happens*, Christian thought.

By the time the train entered the volcano and evaporated, he could hear whispered voices. "He's waking. Give him the painkiller now." Christian gasped at his roaring headache. "What the hell…"

"It's okay, sweetheart," a friendly voice said. His boyfriend, Jeremy, was rubbing his chest. "It's okay. You'll be fine."

❖

During his morning commute, Christian sat next to Jeremy on the monorail, Jeremy openly holding Christian's hand. The older woman across from them smiled sweetly. Why couldn't his family accept him if a total stranger could? Then Christian thought the woman probably wouldn't accept him either if she knew the perversion of his fantasies.

Christian whispered to Jeremy, "So now that you know that I kind of decided to keep the pellet, I'm surprised you're still with me."

Jeremy squeezed Christian's hand. "I told you I'd pay to have the chemicals flushed from your body. It's expensive, but you're worth it."

"But what about the way I think? I don't think I can change what I want."

"If you let the pellet wear off naturally, would you volunteer for another injection and get assaulted for another three years?"

"No. No, I wouldn't," Christian said, although a small part of him knew if some men injected another dose "against his will" he'd submit to another term.

Jeremy's face brightened. "Hey, maybe you are getting better."

Jeremy's happiness reached deep into Christian, and for a moment, he smiled. However, a trio of Revisionist nuns in billowing black robes boarded the monorail at the next stop, carrying an addict monitor in hopes of finding young women they could save from the program. The monitor went off, and the nuns actively searched about them, their hopes high. Then one of them noticed the light on the monitor was blue, not red, indicating the addict they'd found was male. The moment they realized it was Christian, they curled their lips in disgust. "Get help," the youngest one said with a sad frown.

"I'm trying," Christian whispered.

Jeremy was still smiling, unfazed, and he rubbed Christian's leg in encouragement. "You are trying, sweetheart. I know you are."

❖

Dr. Hall smiled as he ushered Christian into the Dream Center's train car. Christian was surprised to see the blond wood and red paint that usually appeared in his dream. The bench was red velvet.

The clothes Christian wore, a short-sleeve shirt and black pants, felt slightly sticky. They were made of something called "Dissolving Cloth," which made Christian feel both uncomfortable and excited. Dr. Hall swabbed Christian's shoulder with cotton. "This drug will put you in a semiconscious state to help simulate your dream." There was the tiny bite of the injection and Dr. Hall patted Christian on the back. "Like last time. Just relax and let things happen."

Dr. Hall slid the door to the compartment closed and Christian felt a rocking vibration accompanied by the huffing of a steam engine. He couldn't be moving forward, could he? No. He was in a stationary room in a stationary building. Outside the car's windows, a late-afternoon daylight appeared. No sun, but a dusty orange-white sky over a reddish brown landscape. Desert. Boulders. Christian was amazed they'd recreated such accurate detail.

The train pitched to the left and picked up speed. The scenery sped past faster and faster. Christian jounced left and right. His heart leapt as they reached the point where they were certainly careening out of control. The drug was making him woozy.

Then he heard an anguished cry. He blinked and there was his mother, dressed in funeral black and wringing her hands. Her mouth was contorted in fear and anguish.

"Mama, please don't cry." Christian could actually talk. "I'm so scared when you cry and I can't make it better. Please be okay."

For the first time ever in the dream, his mother turned to him. She blinked through tears. "Oh, honey. It's not you. My pain comes from far away. You've brought me nothing but joy."

Pirates began to run up and down the corridor, shouting, and Christian could see the volcano ahead. But his mother continued to smile. Christian's tension began to give way to confusion and then the beginnings of relief. The thought that the air mixture was probably enhancing the feeling of well-being only reached the fringes of Christian's perception. His brain began to accept the alteration. *Things are okay. My mother is okay.*

The unbelievable happened. The train came to a stop, and a door that had never existed before opened wide, allowing in streams of golden sunlight.

"Here's my stop, darling," his mother said, her mourning clothes had faded from black to gray to a pale rose. "There's a garden. And pretty birds. And, oh look, chocolate cake." As she stepped out of the car, she turned to Christian one last time. "I am happy. Won't you allow yourself to be happy, too?"

Christian sat there, stunned as the door slid closed. The train huffed to life, reaching unsafe speeds before Christian could even turn his head. The desert landscape returned although it seemed less harsh, suffused, now, with a pink-orange sunset.

There was a cloud of heavy mist, and when it dissipated, Christian's clothing had begun dissolving, in moments becoming as tattered as if he'd been shipwrecked for months. Soon his body was entirely exposed and available.

With the next giant jolt, the pirate captain appeared. The look in his eyes was hungry and appraising, but the smile that crept across his face appeared no less friendly than it did wicked.

"Offer yourself to me, Christian. Won't you?"

Christian swallowed and shook his head. "No. I can't."

"Why not, handsome?"

"It's…it's wrong."

The pirate blinked and smiled patiently. "Because your pleasure is wrong? Is mine right?"

Christian nodded, feeling a comfortable warmth that made him lie back on the couchette. His head spun. "Yes. If it's all for your pleasure, then I'm still a good boy. I don't…I don't want it, but if you take it, then I'm not bad. It's not my fault."

The train bucked, nearly throwing Christian from the couchette, but the pirate steadied him.

"Do you know what is more submissive than letting me fuck you against your will?" asked the pirate. "Giving me your pleasure. Let me see how much you love it."

"I can't."

"But you want to please me, yes?"

Christian nodded. "Yes, sir."

The pirate ran his hand down Christian's muscular bare flank. "Then it pleases me to see you enjoy this. Want this. Love this."

Christian shivered with heat and nerves. "But I'm a bad boy if I want it."

The pirate quieted Christian with a soft kiss on the lips. The train shook in response. "Handsome fellow, you know what this is. Uncontrollable lust. Uncontrollable train. Don't fight it."

"But—"

"What's the worst that can happen if you admit that you want sex? That you want to enjoy my body as much as I will enjoy yours?"

"I don't want to receive pleasure," Christian protested. "I'm not worthy."

The pirate gazed at Christian with a smile that was both friendly and feral. "Ah, but Christian, I am worthy, am I not? If I want you to be pleasured, to come for me, then you wouldn't be a good boy if you didn't give that to me, would you?"

Christian gasped and closed his eyes. The change in perspective was almost too much to comprehend. Enjoying sex would make him a good boy. Yes. And he wanted more than anything to be a good boy.

Christian lifted his legs and moaned. "Please," he begged.

The pirate unlaced and opened his pants. "You want me? You want me to take you?"

Christian whimpered. "Yes, please. I want to be good. Please."

The pirate rushed forward, attacking Christian with kisses to his face, lips, and neck. His hands reached down to grasp Christian's straining cock.

Christian jolted at the contact. No man had ever touched him sensually. No one cared about his pleasure. Why would they? The pirate's hand was warm, and the new sensation of someone feeling him was so good.

The pirate gently bit Christian's lip and then stared straight into Christian's eyes. Christian saw unadulterated lust, but somehow, there was also kindness. Patience.

"Do you like to be sucked?" the pirate asked.

For a moment Christian was sure the chugging roar of the speeding train had made him mishear. He couldn't believe this was possible, but it was. Christian's nerves returned and he shook his head. "No, no. I'm not worthy of that. Please let me pleasure you with my ass. That's what I'm good for. You know I want it so much, but it has to be something that will make you come. Not me."

The pirate arched an eyebrow. "If you want to be a good boy, you have to let me do what I want, even if it feels good to you." Christian's heart sped faster, but he said nothing.

As the train jostled beneath them, the pirate blinked slowly at Christian and caressed his face. "You say you want to please me with your ass? You want me to fuck you?"

Christian nodded, swallowing and panting with urgency. "Yes, please. Oh, please."

"Yes, sweetheart, I know you want it. But I'm going to drive you crazy with need."

The pirate slid his body down Christian's torso in one rapid motion. Before Christian could utter the word "no" his shaft was engulfed by the pirate's warm mouth.

Christian bucked like he'd been shocked with electricity, and the train responded by nearly rocking them off the bench. But the immediate panic, the sense that the entire world had made an unbearable shift, melted as soon as the signals from the nerve receptors in his penis reached his brain. Christian cried out in pure ecstasy. What was this man doing? This sensation was so incredible that Christian could barely breathe. The pirate continued to suck and lick while gently tickling, caressing, and lubricating Christian's hole. The pleasure was unendurable. Christian blinked away the beginnings of tears as he helplessly cried out again.

Christian thought it would never end, that he would die of pleasure before this man released his cock from his mouth. And the pirate was right. The longing to be fucked had risen to a raging need. He thrashed beneath the pirate's mouth. "Please. Oh, God! Please fuck me!"

The pirate sat up, a smirk of triumph and mirth on his face. "Now you're ready."

The pirate slid farther back, his hands sliding along Christian's thighs and calves, and then they captured his ankles, ferociously yanking them skyward. Christian sharply exhaled at the sight of the pirate's long, thick and curved erection.

Christian whimpered and panted in agonizing hunger until he felt the pirate's dick begin to push inside his ass. Bliss arced through him as he sighed in relief. His breathing relaxed and now he inhaled deeply; a delirious satisfaction like he'd never experienced shot through him to his chest and mouth. He moaned, feeling an unfamiliar ache in his toes. Somehow, his excitement had caused them to flex and curl, but he couldn't stop it.

The pirate's dick slid all the way inside Christian's hole, filling him completely. The stretching caused Christian's head to tilt back, and he let out a series of short grunts as his body adjusted to the penetration. The pirate remained still for a moment, kissing Christian's legs. Christian knew the pirate was trying to show patience and kindness, but he could feel the man's dick pulse with urgency. He pulled his thighs back, communicating to the pirate that he was welcome to ravish Christian's ass as hard and as fast as his heart desired. The train wobbled and rattled.

The thrusts began. They were gentle, but with his size, it was impossible for Christian not to feel the power of the pirate's lust and the sensation that he had surrendered his body to a man who would explore him more fervently than any other. Yes, as the strokes gradually quickened, it all became clear. Many men had shown Christian that his ass was worth fucking again and again, but this man's lust went far deeper. He loved Christian's ass. He'd capture and own his hole and his mind like no man ever had. But the pirate's gentle hands and the look of wonderment in his eyes told Christian the man wanted his heart as well. As the strokes became wild, fevered jabs, Christian felt a rise in his groin that had never occurred except when he was alone.

No, this can't be. I've never come with anyone else. I can't. The pleasure cannot be mine. Christian's muscular chest heaved with heat and confusion. What could he do to stop this?

The pirate must have been able to see the conflict in Christian's eyes. "Come for me, handsome. I want you, too. Come for me."

Christian moaned and whimpered. "I'm not...I'm not supposed to!"

The pirate thrust even harder. "Free yourself. Admit that you love having me in your ass. More than anything, it's what you want."

Christian bucked and his head thrashed from side to side.

"Christian, I want your ass more than life itself. I live to fuck you and love you and never let you go. I have to have you." The pirate stopped talking to catch his breath. He looked up and gasped. Then he increased his pace again. When he looked down again at Christian, his face had changed. It was Jeremy. It had been Jeremy the whole time. The light in the train car darkened as it sped into the tunnel.

"You can feel how much my dick needs to be in you, can't you? I must have your ass, Christian. You need a dick in you, I know. You need it so much." Jeremy growled and hissed as he drove in faster and faster. Christian had never had such an incredible fucking. So deep. So hard. Jeremy's dick seemed unstoppable.

"Oh, God," cried Christian. "Yes, yes! I do love this! I do! I love this! I love you!"

Christian gasped, his body convulsing as his orgasm began. At the same time, Jeremy moaned and growled, nearing his own peak. Christian's head snapped back as cum exploded out of him in waves, spraying his neck and chest. As Christian's insides tightened around Jeremy's dick, Jeremy roared and shot deep inside Christian's ass.

The train steadied. It glided now as it slowed, the din of the engine and the clacking wheels fading. Christian watched Jeremy as he panted, sweat dripping off his face. Then Jeremy looked him in the eyes and Christian saw the happiest smile he'd ever seen.

"Oh, baby, you did it," said Jeremy. "You let me love you."

"I want this every day forever," Christian said, his voice soft with contentment and exhaustion. Then he pulled Jeremy down to kiss him deeply as the train came to a halt amidst the steaming red rocks.

ONE NIGHT ON THE TWENTIETH CENTURY
JAY NEAL

Yes, sir, those were some times—good times, mostly, though it was a lot of hard work, but I've never been shy of hard work. It's tough to imagine now, but in those days trains had a sense of adventure about them, and the Twentieth Century Limited was the best of the best.

The Twentieth Century ran between Grand Central Station in New York City and LaSalle Street Station in Chicago. Train 25 left Central Station at 5 p.m. —train 26 left Chicago fifteen minutes before that— and they reached their destination sixteen hours later. The Twentieth Century was known as "the best train in the world"; it was so famous that people made movies about it. The Twentieth Century was the last word in luxury—it was travel perfected.

Every car on the Twentieth Century was a Pullman Sleeper. So you see, don't you, that being a Pullman Porter on the Twentieth Century was a special accomplishment. We were proud of the good work we did and most of the passengers showed us respect for it, although I have to say not everyone did. That was still a time of segregation and not just in the South. On every train there were wool blankets set aside for use by the porters; they were dyed blue so they wouldn't be confused with the passenger blankets, which were dyed a light salmon color—a not-so-subtle reminder that the two were not to be mixed. Most of the passengers called us "George"—in honor of George Pullman—but leastways they didn't call us "boy"!

Being a Pullman Porter was a respectable job. People like to talk today about how Mr. Pullman helped to create the black middle-class in this country. I suppose that may be so, but we didn't think that way back then, and I don't think that was his plan. He wanted to be famous for providing the best rail-travel service he could, and treating us a little better than in most jobs we could get at the time was just his way of doing it.

Expectations of porters were high. Using alcohol, or tobacco, or any kind of profane language while on duty meant getting fired. We were expected to present a neat appearance at all times and do whatever would make the passenger feel comfortable and welcome. I still remember the first words of our manual, the *Instructions to Porters, Attendants, and Bus Boys*: "Courtesy is an act of kindness, or a duty performed with politeness. One who is always courteous merely shows in a natural way his wish to be kind." Unfortunately there was no manual called *Instructions for Passengers*.

You know that we had our own union, the Brotherhood of Pullman Porters, formed in 1925 with Mr. A. Philip Randolph as our leader. The union became famous because it was the first union of black men to do collective bargaining with a company and win. In my time we just knew it as a way to keep standards high and keep us porters from working harder than we should.

We had two main jobs. The official one was making down beds for the passengers. Some porters made it a point of pride to do it the fastest they could; I heard about some that could do it in eleven minutes. I thought it was important not to waste time but to do a good job, so I generally took a little longer, but never more than twenty minutes. Finding just the right time when each passenger was away from his berth so his bed could be made down was the hard part. Everyone wanted his bed made when he was ready for it, but they didn't seem to realize that meant they couldn't be in their berth while it was being made down.

Once we got all the passengers into their beds, the unofficial job of keeping them in bed started. They needed the bathroom, or they needed a drink, or they needed a smoke, or they needed to walk out a cramp, or they needed to talk. Everyone had a different reason not to go to sleep. Maybe it was the excitement of being on the Twentieth Century that kept them awake.

Did things happen on that train? Let me tell you, everything happened one time or another on that train. We were like a hotel on wheels, and if there's one thing that seventeen years of working on that train taught me, it's that there is nothing you can imagine that people don't get up to in their bedrooms. We porters saw it all, too. Not because we were nosey parkers, but because we were servants who worked in people's bedrooms, and to most of the people on that train we were invisible.

Like I said before, we were the finest train on rails and every car was a Pullman car, so we had an elite class of passenger, richer and more powerful than most. That meant we frequently had big men from Washington D.C. on the train.

I remember one night in particular. I was working in the car named Hickory Creek, an Observation-Sleeper car—five doubles forward off an outside corridor that came out around the bar in the center of the car into the Observation Lounge. The lounge was furnished with the latest fashion in sofas and easy chairs and had modern indirect lighting and every appointment it took to be deluxe. You've seen this car; it has the rounded wall in the rear with lots of windows for looking out at where you'd been. That's why it was always the last car on the train.

I'd been promoted to working the Hickory Creek the same time as President Eisenhower's inauguration the previous winter, so this occasion I'm talking about would have been in January 1954. I don't think I'm ever going to forget what happened that night. I've never told this story to a soul before, but maybe the time has come.

All five rooms of the Hickory Creek had been rented that night to the staff of—well, let's just say a famous senator—make that an infamous senator—from one of the upper Midwestern states. He was at the height of his influence then, still worried about rooting commies and fairies out of the government. Leastways, that's what he claimed in public. He'd been on the train before, of course, although I'd never served him; he had a reputation as prickly and mean-spirited, and a poor tipper.

Too loud for my taste, too. When he and his group boarded the train, the senator made a big show of assigning his staff to their rooms. He was obviously used to directing people around and having them follow his orders. There were two women in his group; he put them together in the second room along. I imagine they were clerical assistants, or at least the younger one he called "Doris." The older one, "Mrs. Tallboy," was probably a valued personal secretary—clearly the most senior of the group.

That left five men to assign to rooms. The tall, rather gaunt man wearing the bow tie was to share the third room with the older, balding gentlemen. Political advisors? The fourth room was to be shared by two hulking men who looked like nothing so much as Chicago mob goons. I supposed they were along as hired heavies or bodyguards.

The fifth man was younger than the others by several years. I'd imagine that he was about twenty-five, not all that long out of college. I don't know why I thought he was a college boy. Maybe because he was dressed smarter than the others. He sure wasn't a laborer—his hands were too soft and his nails were kept too nice. To be honest he looked a little soft to me, but that wasn't unusual with the intellectual types.

"That leaves just the one room," the senator said, "so Edward and I will bunk in together."

Mrs. Tallboy pursed her lips. Perhaps she disapproved because she knew that they had rented all five rooms and that one was left empty with this arrangement. But perhaps she was the type who disapproved of everything. I didn't think much about it beyond the happy realization that the room left empty meant I'd have a quiet spot to catch a few winks of my own after everyone else was asleep.

"Okay, everyone, get your things put away and freshen up before dinner," the senator announced. "We'll reconvene at seven in the dining car. We have quite a bit to go over before we're back at home this weekend."

There followed the usual bustle of getting luggage wrestled into the right rooms and stowed out of the way. The effort did earn me thirty-five cents, the biggest fraction of which was not contributed by the senator, I might add.

I looked forward to a relatively quiet evening. They'd head to the dining car just before seven. I could make down their beds then and have a short nap before most of the evening crowd showed up in the Observation Lounge for after-dinner drinks and conversation. It was a good bet that Doris and Mrs. Tallboy would return soon after their dinner and retire early, but the men would stay behind for several hours talking and arguing and strategizing and drinking at their table the way political people do. Needless to say, the senator's bodyguards had no choice in the matter.

That was the way it happened. I made down the beds in their four rooms in less than an hour and withdrew to the empty room for my catnap. I was awake again by quarter to nine, in time to hear the door closing on Doris and Mrs. Tallboy for the night.

I got up and went out to the Observation Lounge to help out. The bar is staffed by its own porter to serve drinks and empty ashtrays, but people like to have more than one porter handy to wait on them if they happened to think of something that needed immediate attention—a shoe shine, a sandwich from the dining car, more cigarettes. The errands were petty, but the tips were a welcome addition to my very modest wages, and it was my prerogative as the Observation Car Porter to serve those guests and collect those tips.

As a rule we kept the lights in the lounge turned low so that guests could see the lights of towns and stations as we passed them. Low lights also kept the conversation muted so, although the mood in the lounge was usually festive, it rarely got very noisy. It makes for a peaceful way to pass the evening.

About one a.m. we turned up the lights some and got a little noisier cleaning up, emptying ashtrays and picking up empty glasses. It gave guests the idea that it was time to head to their berths for the night. They always get the idea quick enough but, still, it took some time to finish having fun and leave.

Everyone was gone by two, so I sent the bartender off to his bed while I took over doing the last tidying and stock-taking below the bar, where we kept the extra bottles. It was quiet except for the gentle click-clack, click-clack of the car wheels on the rails and I thought I was alone with the senator and his staff, content and asleep in their beds. I suppose I was until I heard the vestibule door open and somebody—or some bodies—stumbling in.

One of them tripped over something and didn't quite fall down. I recognized the voice of the senator, not trying terribly hard to be quiet. "Who keeps rocking the hallway around? Makes it damned hard to walk!"

I heard the door to the last room rattle, but they weren't ready to settle in yet. "Come on, Eddie, let's sit in the lounge for a minute. No one's there. We'll be more comfortable."

"It's late, Joe, and we've got a full day after the train gets in. Besides, everyone else has gone to bed and they've turned out the lights. Besides, you're drunk."

"Not too drunk and you know it, Eddie. Never too drunk for you. And don't forget who pays your salary."

"How could I forget that, Joe?"

I listened to them make their way around the bar into the lounge, then the sound of someone—the senator, I presumed—sitting down heavily in one of the easy chairs. I was still crouching below the bar and couldn't see them and, fortunately, they couldn't see me. That would have been the perfect time for me to make myself known and put a stop to things before they went too far, but I hesitated and missed my only chance.

It was so quiet I was afraid they'd hear me breathing, but they weren't hearing me or anyone else who might have been in that car, they were so intent on what they were doing. Had I been less naïve and maybe less scared I might have recognized the sound of a belt being unbuckled, a zipper being unzipped, the rustle of fabric from trousers yanked down. But that was all beyond me right then.

Oral sex was something I had not yet encountered at that time, either. I mean, I knew that whores and loose women sometime went down on men, but I'd never experienced that and I'd certainly never thought of one man going down on another man. I could understand how it might work but I'd never thought it might happen. I definitely never thought it might happen in my lounge car while I was crouched behind the bar listening.

"Eddie, you're a good cocksucker. You know exactly what makes me feel good. It's too bad women don't suck cock as good as you do. Too bad."

Curiosity may be dangerous for cats, but there was no way I was going to stay there a moment longer without doing something. Since there was no way for me to leave without being seen, looking was my only alternative. Slowly, ever so slowly, I raised my head to peek over the bar, holding my breath while I did so.

Picture this: They were on an easy chair across the lounge, half-turned toward me so I saw them in profile. Eddie was on his knees in front of the chair, his head hovering over the senator's crotch. The senator himself was sprawled back in the chair, head thrown back, eyes closed, mouth gaping open, one of his big hands weighing heavily on the back of Eddie's head as it bobbed up and down.

"You're such a temptress, Eddie, you always make me so horny."

Their activity went on for—I don't know how much longer. It was probably only a minute or two before the senator pressed his hand down on Eddie's head, stopping its motion.

"Eddie, I need to fuck you now in the worst way. Drop your pants and give me your ass."

Without complaint, Eddie stood and unfastened his trousers, which he then pushed to the floor and stepped out of. As the senator got up from the chair, his trousers fell around his ankles but he didn't bother to take them off. Eddie leaned over the seat of the chair, raising one leg onto it. He rested his arms on the back of the chair and laid his head on his arms.

The senator hobbled behind Eddie and slapped Eddie's butt once, hard. "Squat down so I can reach your asshole."

Eddie complied. I couldn't see exactly what happened next—I didn't want to see—but I could guess from watching the senator's face showing his strain and Eddie's face wincing at the same time. Soon enough the senator was holding Eddie's waist and thrusting his hips, and all became obvious even to me.

The senator's lust seemed to me urgent, almost animal-like. It also seemed furtive, or guilty, but maybe that's only because I knew who the senator was, knew the opinions that he expressed publicly. In those days this was something that would have ruined his career in an instant if it became known. It wouldn't have gone too well for me either if he'd seen me, seeing what I was seeing.

Eddie, on the other hand, seemed almost to have no interest in what was happening. Maybe he was simply resigned to this fate. I wondered what strange force had brought these two together in this way.

The senator moved his hands up to hold on to Eddie's shoulders. "What we've had has been great, Eddie, but I can't let you spoil everything."

His thrusting grew still more urgent, his breathing more like panting. "I can't let you do that, Eddie. I saw you talking to that reporter. I can't let you tell, Eddie. I can't let you tell anyone, ever."

The senator slid his hands from Eddie's shoulders until both of his hands were wrapped around Eddie's neck. He squeezed. My God, I could see the muscles in his hands tense as he squeezed and began choking the life out of Eddie while I watched. I watched and did nothing.

The senator groaned, evidently finishing taking his pleasure from Eddie at the same time that he took Eddie's life away. I was shocked beyond breathing as I watched the senator bend over Eddie's still, lifeless body. My eyes were too blurry, too filled with tears to tell whether he whispered something in Eddie's ear or kissed him good-bye. But why? Eddie was already gone by that time, gone beyond hearing, gone beyond feeling.

I felt weak and sank to the floor behind the bar. Through the haze of my exhaustion—or was it terror?—I heard the senator make his way noisily and unsteadily to his room. The sound of his door latching shut was the last thing I heard before falling soundly asleep.

When I woke, I felt heavy and my bones ached from the awkward position of my sleeping. The sounds I heard were the sounds of people getting ready to leave the train. I had slept through breakfast and my morning duties.

I looked out into the lounge with trepidation, but Eddie's body was not there. Had the train's staff removed him? No, everyone I saw was behaving normally; I heard no outcry, I saw no shock, no investigation.

Perhaps, I thought, I had imagined the whole thing, but even as I grasped at the idea I knew that it was not possible. It was too real, too terrifying for my limited imagination—how could I have imagined those things?

As we reached LaSalle Street Station, I had my confirmation. The passengers in my charge gathered their things and prepared to leave the train. When they had gotten on in New York, it was the senator and his staff of seven who came on board, but now there was only the senator and six others who were leaving.

There was no Eddie leaving the train with them, but it was no triumph to have my confirmation. Where was Eddie's body now? Who knew? Mrs. Tallboy's lips were firmly pursed; she had to know. She was the type who knew everything and arranged the senator's life. My bet would be that the senator's goons threw Eddie's body off the train in the middle of the night and the middle of nowhere. I never heard another thing about a body being found, so I'll never know.

To my dying day, I will regret that I never did a thing to stop it. I worked out the rest of my time as a Pullman Porter without another incident at all like that, without any fuss. All I wanted was a quiet retirement and that's what I got, that and the nightmares.

I haven't told a soul since then—I didn't see what good it would do anyone except maybe get me killed. But they're all dead now, dead and buried—or not buried, in Eddie's case. I'm telling you now, so maybe Eddie and I can both get some peace at last.

SHADOW MAPPING
J.D. BARTON

Elias Coustineau walked the length of the track as far as he could see and felt his erection rise whenever he placed a foot on the rail, which shook from the vibration of an approaching train. The mountain air had shivered down from certain frost to only mildly chilly, so he was dressed casually in his uniform of blue jeans, work shirt, and sweater. He didn't think about it much anymore, but the imminent arrival of the train always made him hard.

The reason why always eluded him. Maybe it was the mythology of trains or maybe it was the cute guy he once saw sitting by a window, staring at him as if he was just another touch of local color. He honestly didn't know. He just knew that he was always aroused by the smell, the power, and the speed of the train as it zipped past him.

So he continued to walk the tracks for as many reasons as there were railroad ties curving up the mountain on which he had been born and raised. Boredom. Curiosity. Ghosts. Horniness. Whatever.

Usually, after he had walked through the cool night air and watched the locomotive rush past him, Elias would run into the woods, lean against a straggly pine tree, and jerk off until his whole body shook. He knew it wasn't much, but for a nineteen-year-old mill worker stuck on the side of a mountain, it was enough to get him through the week. The tedium of his life begged for any sort of release, so slipping away after Saturday dinner with his folks had become a sort of art form for him. His window screen was now permanently attached with chewing gum, and he was always sure to return home before the first streaks of sunlight.

But tonight, he saw the ramshackle train station as he looked around and realized for the first time that it was barely holding up against the elements. Its cement platform was decorated by white splashes of bird shit, and its remaining lightbulb hung like a barely gleaming noose in the middle of the ceiling. Elias inhaled the sap from the pines and told himself that he was standing right in the middle of nowhere, which was how he felt about his life—it was nowhere. So he waited for the train.

Sooner than he expected, he saw a pinpoint glimmer of light coming up the track. He ran toward it and felt his whole body tense up at the imminent arrival of the train. His hand swiped the denim of his zipper and felt his cock stretching its limits. Then he backed up against another tree and closed his eyes as his hands crunched into the rough bark and his shoes dug into the clay soil beneath him. He didn't have to wait too long before his nose picked up the scent of the heavy white smoke unfurling from the train, filling him with expectation and excitement.

Within seconds, the locomotive was right in front of him, and he stood as still as he could against the tree. The ground and his whole body spasmed from the arrival of the gargantuan machine with its yellow squares of light blazing from the side. And although Elias was several yards away, the sensation of the train made him feel as if he was only a few feet from its dark presence.

His hand brushed his crotch and stroked it gently as he looked at the long, dark vehicle and felt its power go through him. There was nothing else to compare it to in his small, contracted life. No man he had ever seen was half as strong as this machine. No force, whether it be church or school or family, transported him so thoroughly. When Elias saw the train pull up, its strength infused every cell of his body. And even though it was his cock that was obviously responding, his heart began to race to its spinning wheels and his eyes watered from the heated wind that accompanied the locomotive. He knew there was nothing else that brought him so completely to life.

Yet this night his rising passion was abruptly cut short when he realized that the train wasn't just rushing past him as usual. Tonight it was unmistakably coming to a stop right in front of him. The squeal and clatter of its clashing metal announced its abrupt intention, and it slowed down, then crept up to the skeletal station, as if it was suddenly exhausted and needed to rest. When it stopped, it sighed as if satisfied with itself.

With his heart roaring in his ears, Elias quickly ducked behind the pine tree and felt the blood drain from his cock. He held his breath as he peered around the tree to see what was happening. No one had arrived or departed from the dilapidated station since his childhood, and in the entire time he had been train watching, it had never stopped. Not once.

For years, the boys in his class at school had spoken of the headless ghost that supposedly haunted these tracks. He knew the story by heart—how the ghost was a conductor who was decapitated in an accident and held up a lantern, walking up and down the tracks, looking for his head. But in all the time he spent in this spot waiting for the train, Elias had only seen that one cute guy by the window and a few errant fireflies. He held no fear of the area until tonight.

Fear froze him to his spot behind the tree as his blood hummed loudly in his ears. There was something else to the story that he struggled to remember, something about the consequences of actually meeting the ghost. Death. Pain. He couldn't recall. His thoughts crowded together until all he could do was stare at the motionless train and wait to see what would happen next.

The shadow of a form glided across the yellow windows, moving quickly, then slowly, then loping from coach to coach. It was a single form, with no other obvious passengers on the train. Then it was gone. Elias blinked his eyes several times until he told himself, that no, he had not imagined it. There was definitely someone or something on that train. Gingerly, he let go of the tree and started walking toward the station, determined to decipher what he had just seen or run as quickly as he could back down the mountain.

His breathing increased with every step, and he made mental notes of what he would do if he actually met someone or *something* in the station. But nothing could have prepared him for what he did see.

He approached the vast, empty space of the station, its one bulb now swinging wildly, and he stopped in his tracks, his breath catching when he actually saw the man. He was almost as tall as the station. His arms were casually crossed in front of him, and his face was pocked with small craters indenting the tanned skin. He was dressed in dark pants and a flannel jacket with a railroad cap pushed back a few inches on his slick, balding head. His body was rangy and stocky all at once, with mounds of muscles pushing against his clothes, and Elias noticed that the man's thighs and arms were as thick as tree trunks. He couldn't help it as his eyes grazed down to the man's crotch and saw a nice smooth bulge. The man's fingers stroked his zipper and Elias saw that they were long and tapered but strong-looking. Still shaking with fear, he couldn't help getting a hard-on at what he saw.

He walked over to Elias, and with every step. the aroma of oil and smoke and hickory increased, burning his eyes and making his mouth water. Then, just as the man came face-to-face with him, he spat a toothpick onto the floor, clamped his massive hand onto Elias's shoulder, and began pushing him out into the night.

They walked past the train, so close that Elias could almost touch it, but the man was guiding him somewhere in the woods. His fascination with the man evaporated and the fear returned when he thought of all the things that could happen. His body began to tremble, and he tried to slip loose from the man's grip, but it just grew stronger. When they reached the tree that Elias had hidden behind, the man shoved him against it, then put his mouth beside Elias's ear and said in a sandpaper voice, "I saw you waiting."

"Who are you?" Elias managed to squeak out. But the man didn't answer. Instead, Elias felt the warm sensation of the man's rough hand sliding down his belly and into his jeans, the calluses nicking his skin.

"I'm the Conductor," the man growled into his ear. Then he lightly gripped Elias's cock, which was now as hard as a piece of coal, and he maneuvered a finger under his balls and started stroking the tender skin he found there. Elias felt as if he would break into a million pieces from fear and lust, but he didn't care. He stood against the tree and inhaled the musk of the man and willed him to continue.

The Conductor removed Elias's pants and threw them into the woods. Next, he slipped off the sweater and work shirt and slid his hands up and down the slender torso. Elias could hear the Conductor's breathing turn shallow, and suddenly the man was naked as well. Elias almost went crazy when he saw his body, with its dark mat of hair covering his chest and his cock long and thick and hard traveling up and down on Elias's tender belly. Without any provocation, Elias dropped to his knees, unaware of the cold night spangling around him, and took the Conductor's cock into his mouth. At first he was afraid he would choke on its size, but the Conductor made it easy for him, slipping it in and out of his mouth like a piston starting up—slowly at first, then with a measured intensity.

Elias took to sucking cock with a natural ability that surprised even him. His tongue licked down the thick shaft, then he grasped the mushroom head and flicked the slit until a slick film appeared. He painted his lips with it, then grabbed the surprisingly smooth balls and stroked them with his middle finger until he found his own rhythm and guided the Conductor's cock down into his throat. Then he began sucking the Conductor's cock with an assurance he had never possessed before.

As it slipped in and out of his throat, Elias allowed himself the pleasure of absorbing all the sensations he had only imagined in his fantasies. He let the saltiness and sweat of the skin leach into his mouth, allowed the hardness of the shaft to open his throat, and tickled the spongy head with his playful tongue. Just then he noticed the long blue vein striping the underside of the man's cock and traced its course with the tip of his tongue. He could feel it pulse in his mouth and that thrilled him even more, increasing his need for the Conductor's cock. He sucked him for what seemed like hours, content to let time and the evening pass him by. But the Conductor had other ideas.

Elias felt the man's balls turn rock hard, and his cock swelled in his mouth. He knew what was going to happen next, but nothing had prepared him for the coming explosion, for the Conductor came with a force that almost lifted Elias off the ground. Suddenly streams of sweet and sour cum erupted into Elias's mouth and filled it until he almost gagged. Then the man rocked his cock into his mouth like a runaway train until every drop of cum was spent and Elias swallowed it all, licking the shaft of the cock out of his mouth and sucking the last drop off the tip, eliciting a startled gasp from the Conductor that made him smile. And for a moment he felt his own head fill up with a white light, making it seem like a cloud that could just float away into the night.

He kept his eyes closed as the Conductor, with a surprising gentleness, raised him up, placed him against the tree, and dressed him. The cold air became a reality to Elias once more, and as he shrugged his coat on he said quietly, "Who are you?"

But when he opened his eyes, disappointment settled on him like the morning dew dotting his face, and he sat up slowly and looked around. The sun poured down through the latticework of tree limbs above him, and he told himself that it must have been a dream. Yet he could still smell the oil and smoke on his clothes.

The next Saturday night, he ran to the station and saw that it hadn't been a dream. The Conductor was waiting for him in the woods, smiling and already removing his clothes. All trepidation was gone as Elias allowed the Conductor's slender fingers to remove his sweaty, smoky garments. And before he knew it, he was covered by the Conductor's strong body, his tongue going into and out of his mouth and the wide cock pressing into his own, almost making him come from its pressure. But then the Conductor did something he had not done before—he grabbed Elias under the arms, picked him up, then turned him over and threw him on the floor of the forest. The force of the action made Elias lose his breath, but before he could regain it, he heard the Conductor spit and then suddenly his naked body was on fire.

He started to scream, but the Conductor had wrapped his ample hand around his mouth and then, as the Conductor's cock slid deeper into Elias's ass, he started to fall away somewhere dark and soundless. But after a few minutes or maybe hours, he couldn't tell which, Elias felt his whole body relax. It was as if the Conductor was becoming a part of his skin, melting away the bones, making every other feeling disappear except for the rhythmic thrust of his cock.

Then Elias felt that deep part of him that he'd only found with his fingers come alive as the Conductor's cock massaged it, turning the fire into a warmth that coated his entire body. He heard no other sounds except the Conductor's breath beating against his back, reminding him of the smoke from the train. The pine needles cracked under his hands as he pushed his ass up to the Conductor, unquestionably asking for him to fuck him harder. And he did.

As relaxed as he became, Elias was aware of what was happening to him. The Conductor heaved his cock in and not-quite-out of him with an amazing rhythm. First it was slow, then he would speed up as if he was afraid he was coming, then he would burrow deep into Elias's ass and hold it there until Elias almost came from the hot cock melting into him. Once more, time disappeared and Elias was gone, only existing inside the well-timed rhythm of the Conductor fucking him. He became vaguely aware that he had been lifted up and was now being fucked against a tree, the bark rough against his skin. But he didn't care. All he knew was that the Conductor, with his beautiful hard body, was so deep inside him that when he did begin to come, he almost didn't notice it.

Yet when he came, Elias felt a new round of fire and warmth rocket throughout his body. He opened his mouth to yell, but the sensation of being fucked by this man in this manner took his words away and they both rocked against the tree as the Conductor emptied into him, releasing a river of cum so far inside him that Elias could have sworn he was now one being with the man who was slamming into him. His body turned liquid and suddenly he fell slowly to the ground, aware only of a breathing sound above him.

Now that Elias knew that the Conductor wasn't a dream, he rushed through his week and ran to the station every Saturday night. There was nowhere he else he wanted to go. And every Saturday night, the Conductor taught him a new lesson. He learned how to finesse sucking cock and balls and how to fuck the Conductor as well as he had been fucked. And the smell of oil and smoke and hickory seemed permanently imprinted on his skin, a thought that made him smile to himself. He forgot about the boredom of his life and felt a constant, soothing buzz at the pit of his stomach. He would lie in bed at night and wonder what new trick the Conductor would teach him that week and then try to imagine how it would feel.

One week, he arrived early at the station and waited for the Conductor to appear. And when he finally did, the train depositing him like a dark dream, he walked up to Elias and simply stood and looked into Elias's eyes as if he wanted to ask him something, standing so still and quiet that Elias almost started to ask him what was wrong. But just as he opened his mouth to speak, the Conductor took his hand and began walking them into the woods behind the station. Elias noticed that they walked much further than they normally did, since the Conductor usually couldn't wait to rip their clothes off. But he figured they must be going to some secret place that only the Conductor knew, and the thought made him proud, thinking he was the only one who would know about it.

Just then, they stopped at a dark, nondescript opening in the woods. It seemed no different to Elias than the other places they fucked, and he almost said as much until he saw the patch of red mud on the ground. The next thing he knew, the Conductor was undressing both of them and laying them down in the mud.

Even with the difference in their heights, their bodies seemed to align automatically, and Elias always enjoyed the heft of the man's body on top of him. But this night, he didn't stay on top of him for very long. The Conductor took fistfuls of mud in his huge hands and coated his body with it. He painted every inch of Elias's body, including his face. Then he did the same with his own.

He lay down in the mud and pushed his ass up in the air, and Elias knew what he was waiting for. So he fucked him, amazed at the sensation and extra friction the mud gave, and continued to fuck him until flecks of mud broke away, as if the Conductor was shedding an old skin. The Conductor writhed around in the mud as if he'd never seen it before, rubbing his face in it and bunching it between his fingers, but Elias ignored the strange reaction and continued to fuck his ass.

When he finally came, Elias buried his cock deeper into the man as they both fell into the mud and lay there. For a few minutes, Elias thought the Conductor had gone to sleep, but then suddenly, the Conductor stood up and stretched his arms wide. He resembled a statue to Elias, a particularly beautiful one made of clay. He began to smile at the sight. But then the Conductor dissolved into a shower of metal and sparks of light. The red clay fell away from his body and a yellow light appeared in his eyes. The aroma of oil and smoke overpowered Elias as he scooted away and felt for the tree behind him. Just as he opened his mouth to cry out at the sight, he became blinded by the yellow light. And before he knew it, he was waking in the woods with the Conductor nowhere in sight.

That was the last time he saw the Conductor. And although he still went to the station every Saturday night, he never appeared again. As the warm weather arrived and the mountain flourished with wildflowers and the mist of spring, Elias resigned himself to going to the station more out of habit than desire. Then he remembered the first impression he had of the Conductor as a shadow walking through the train.

So he began walking up and down the railroad track, mapping every step the Conductor might have taken through the train. He felt the roar of the engine shake through him and smelled the aroma of oil and smoke and hickory when he closed his eyes.

One Saturday night he mapped the shadow of the Conductor until he could swear he could feel and smell him. So he kneeled down on the track and unzipped the Conductor's pants and took him in his mouth. At that moment he was more than just a lonely mountain boy—he *was* the mountain and the train and the rail and the hungry need of the Conductor.

Lost as he was in his fantasy, he didn't see the ball of light racing up behind him. Nor did he feel the heat of the train as it pounded down the track. All Elias knew was that he was ready to explode into light and so was the Conductor, who was still in his mouth, smiling down at him in the dark.

The mountain boys only go up there on a dare or a drunken spree now. But when they do, they are always struck dumb or scared stiff because whenever they look down the track, they can see two lights. And as they get closer, these two lights merge in and out of each other like miniature suns. Then the train roars up the mountain. And if the boys stay long enough, they can see two shadows floating through the coaches.

The ones who stay after that never talk about what happens next. But the man and the boy who approach them in the dark make sure that they stay awhile and make sure they remember the shadows on the train and the lights in their eyes.

GERONIMO'S LAUGHTER
JOSEPH BANETH ALLEN

W ith his mouth opened wide in anticipation, Ed Christensen was doing his extreme best to be a patient man.

"Just need a few moments more," Mark Wilson reassured him before inserting a periodontal probe and mirror into Ed's open mouth. "I need to make sure the crown covering the nano-transponder has set securely. Then it's a green light and you're out of here."

Ed let the corners of his mouth twitch upward to show silent appreciation. Mark quickly made a few exploratory taps and wiggles with the probe tip against Ed's lower left mandibular premolar. Satisfied the crown securely covered the nano-transponder he had implanted in the tooth about two weeks ago, Mark withdrew the dental instruments.

"You're good to go," Mark cheerfully told him. "Good luck on your time hop."

"Thanks," Ed replied as he got out of the dentist chair. "So far Professor Manibusan hasn't texted me yet about finding my bones on the old Atchison, Topeka and Santa Fe Railway rail line strutting alongside the Kaw River. So I'm assuming I'll survive this trip into Past Time."

Ed brought his hands together in playful appeal to the almighty. Despite being a veteran time hopper, he was a bit unnerved that Henry Manibusan, his former professor and one-time lover, was still traipsing up and down the banks of the Kaw River in search of the signal from the nano-transponder that would lead searchers to his mortal remains—if they existed in the present.

Mark chuckled. "Sometimes I think the only reason why Dean Rosado insists on outfitting every temporal historian with a nano-transponder is so that she has an excuse to send good old Henry far out into the field."

"Can you blame her?" Ed laughed. "His 'authentic' Roman gladiator orgy still remains one of the most popular YouTube videos seventeen years after it debuted online."

Mark's almost casual use of Professor Manibusan's first name hadn't escaped Ed's notice. As a rule, the Emeritus Historian of MIT's Department of Historical Temporal Investigations only allowed his past bedroom conquests to be so informal with him.

Ed was more than a bit intrigued by the unexpected revelation. "I didn't know you knew Professor Manibusan."

"Oh, not really," Mark quickly said. He nervously twirled the traditional Neo-Christian gold wedding band on his left index finger. Neo-Christians had assimilated the ancient, but quaint Hebraic belief that the index finger was the most prominent of fingers to display a church-approved sacrament on. "I took one of his Introductory to Temporal Field Archeology classes as an elective. Just was investigating a possible field of interest back in my undergraduate days when I had no clue as to what I wanted have a degree in. Nothing more to it than that."

Mark turned away, but not before Ed had caught notice of a deepening crimson blush now spreading across the dentist's face. It wasn't too hard to see why good old Henry had taken a shine to Mark and marked him for seduction once he had set foot in the professor's undergraduate class. Curly blond hair framed a square-jawed face with ocean blue eyes. His middle-aged body had not sagged a bit, still exhibiting the muscular firmness from his youth.

"Just let me update your medical records real quick, and you can be on your way. So which train are you catching?"

"The California Limited," Ed replied. "I'm hoping to get some leads on the disappearance of two Pinkerton agents who were traveling along the route on November 7, 1895. They were investigating sabotage attempts on the rail line by the Molly Maguires—a rather secretive union of coal miners who disrupted rail service whenever they could. I'm including a chapter about it in a book I'm writing on the great unsolved railroad mysteries of the nineteenth century."

Mark turned back to face him after signing off electronically on Ed's travel papers. The embarrassed heat of his blush had now been cooled a bit by a tentative smile. "As it happens, I've pulled the biweekly shift in the quarantine quarters. Perhaps I could swing by your quarters one evening after your return and get a firsthand account of how your trip went? Temporal Field Archeology is still sort of a backdoor hobby of mine."

"Look forward to giving you all the details," Ed said. He smiled as he shook hands with Mark and departed the examination room.

Ed found himself humming slightly. Being cooped up in quarantine for two weeks prior to departing and after returning to Current Time definitely wasn't going to be so mind-numbingly dull this time around now that he had a bi-closeted married stud to pass the time when he was writing.

He swung his left arm to ease a bit of stiffness that still lingered in it from all the booster vaccinations he had received prior to entering quarantine the week before for yellow fever, malaria, typhus, and other diseases common in the late nineteenth century.

Upon arriving at the airlock leading into the Temporal Causeway Chamber buried deep under MIT's Exotic Matter Research Facility, Ed paused to give himself and his attire a final critical appraisal by studying his reflection in the full-length mirror near the final check-in station. Dressed in black slacks, black tailored traveling coat and a freshly starched white shirt trimmed with a black bow-tie and topped off with an equally black bowler hat, Ed thought he looked the exact part of a nineteenth-century university professor on travel. The gold chain that linked a pocket watch with a small penknife in his vest pockets was a smart touch.

He had even grown a mustache while he waited in quarantine to give his boyishly round face a bit of the adult gravitas the era expected and demanded from all of its scholarly gentlemen.

"Great timing for insertion, Ed," said Ann Walker. The pert, auburn-haired departure technician's green eyes twinkled mischievously from behind her monitoring console. She always made bad puns to all departing and arriving time hoppers. Ed suspected it was due in part to a faulty humor gene adversely affecting her neurological chemistry or a bad source code. He still wasn't sure whether or not she was one of those still-rare female über computer geeks or a humanistic android. Nobody in the department, not even Henry, really knew for sure.

"Your final clearances, along with your Saratoga steamer trunk, arrived just a moment ago." Ann gestured to the well-traveled trunk waiting for him just inside the Temporal Causeway Chamber's outer airlock door. "Now, if you'll step into my parlor, Mister Fly, I'll send you on your way."

Ed playfully rolled his eyes and went in. By the time he laid a hand on the trunk, the airlock door had closed behind him. He felt the air temperature drop to near freezing.

It was the warning cue that he about to transition in the time stream from inside the Temporal Causeway in Current Time down to the train station in Chicago for the California Limited on the morning of November 7, 1895.

His ears popped as the atmospheric pressure in the airlock decreased. He steadied himself against the trunk, thankful he'd remembered not to eat anything twelve hours in advance of this time hop. Transitioning to another time on a full stomach always caused him to have dry-heaving fits upon arrival.

Like most time hoppers, he had only the rudimentary grasp of how saturation of the molecules in his body by the Higgs Singlets Field provided the unique ability to jump out of the normal three dimensions of space and one dimension of time. By traveling through the hidden dimension in M-Brane space, a Higgs Singlets Field allowed for the reentry into space and time dimensions at a point forward or backward from the time of entry.

He swallowed hard and blinked. People now milled around him on the station platform.

Ed had safely arrived at the train station for the Atchison, Topeka and Santa Fe Railway rail line. He could discreetly check a newspaper for sure, but it was a foregone conclusion that he had arrived on the right day and the exact predetermined time.

His sudden appearance on the station platform had not attracted any attention, unwanted or otherwise. One of the nice built-in rules about hopping back and forth through time was that the universe always cloaked the sudden arrivals and departures of hoppers like him from those people and other observers who resided in Past Time. As the bronze memorial plaque just outside the Department of Historical Temporal Investigations main entrance attested, causality usually protected herself quite well from any and all temporal paradoxes.

Ed quickly took stock of his surroundings. Porters were busily assisting passengers and carrying luggage aboard the Limited. Engineers went over final checks of Number Three—the powerful coal burning engine that would carry the train on its two-and-a-half-day journey to Los Angeles.

He spotted the ticket counter about halfway between his location on the platform and the Limited. Ed waved an available middle-aged black porter over to watch the hefty Saratoga flat top steamer trunk while he went to purchase to a ticket for his berth aboard the train.

Only a quiet, nondescript married couple was ahead of him at the iron-barred ticket window. Once Ed's turn came, a balding middle-aged ticket clerk sporting an ample black-and-gray-speckled walrus mustache acknowledged his presence with tired brown eyes.

"Good morning, sir. Destination and fare class?" the clerk asked. "Will that also be a one-way or round-trip ticket?"

"Los Angeles, first class, one-way," Ed replied. He always found it a bit disarming to purchase one-way fares in Past Time. A similar last-minute purchase in Current Time would raise more than a dozen red flags across the cyber networks of the numerous scattered Homeland Security Agencies still tasked with preventing terrorist attacks.

"That'll be twenty-five dollars, sir," the clerk replied. Ed got out his money belt and counted out three crisp ten-dollar bills. He resisted the urge to quip that money was newly printed as he slid bills into the smooth hollow recess under the bars of the teller window. In less than two minutes, the clerk proceeded to pound the keys of an Underwood typewriter until the train ticket had been filled out with all the pertinent information.

"Your ticket and change, sir," the clerk said. He slid the completed ticket and five Morgan dollars out to Ed. "You're in sleeping compartment 16-A in Section Three. Show your ticket to a porter to get your luggage loaded aboard. The Limited is scheduled to depart within forty-five minutes."

"Thanks," replied Ed. "Seems like I've got plenty of time to catch a bite at the Harvey House."

As Ed made his way back to the porter, he automatically adjusted the time on his pocket watch to read 9:15 a.m. against the clock tower in the station. It was more out of habit to have the exact Past Local Time easily accessible if he needed it. He showed his ticket to the patient porter and tipped him with two of the silver dollars.

Ed didn't bother to keep a pair of laser-focused eyes on the porter as he easily hefted the steamer trunk on his shoulder before striding off to the passenger section of the Limited. Customer no-service was an invention of the late twentieth century, not the nineteenth. Ed briskly walked over to the Harvey House, enticing aromas emanating from their open doors. He had to sate the growing hunger pangs his stomach was now sending him in more frequent intervals.

Ed spied an available seat at the U-shaped counter as soon as he walked inside the restaurant. A waitress wearing a long starched black dress with an equally stiff white apron immediately walked up to him and presented him with a menu once he had eased himself on the stool.

A white ribbon held her dark blond hair securely back behind her neck. All the waitresses, known as Harvey Girls, were clad in similar attire as his waitress. Although the height of the counter prevented him from actually spying a glimpse of their shoes and stockings, Ed knew from historical documents that those undergarments and shoes were also black.

He ordered a roast beef sandwich and a cup of coffee black with cream. Coffee was the only way he was going to get the caffeine his body craved during this Past Time jaunt. The waitress who took his order placed a coffee cup in front of him with the handle facing eastward. It was a signal for the waitress who followed behind her to fill the cup with strong black coffee followed by a good dollop of fresh cream.

Harvey Girls didn't engage their customers in idle small talk. Even if they wanted to, the stern drill sergeant of a matron who watched over their every interaction with customers would have immediately nixed it. In less than three minutes of passing silence, the waitress who had taken his original order had returned with a hefty roast beef sandwich on a blue-patterned china plate.

Ed had devoured the sandwich and drained his coffee in less time than it took for his order to be filled. He placed one of his remaining three silver dollars next to his empty plate on the counter before heading out to catch his train.

On the outside, the Limited certainly lived up to its billing as "the Finest Train West of Chicago." Even though the train had been in service for about three years, it seemed to Ed that the exuberance of a brand-new vehicle about to be driven off the lot emanated from Number Three.

He quickly counted the number of cars attached to the train engine bellowing out tufts of steam. There were only nine sections attached to Number Three, and two of those were observation cars fitted with illuminated "drumheads," which bore the train's name juxtaposed over the company's logo. If he had arrived during a peak travel period, his task of trying to learn the identities of the Pinkerton agents who had gone missing would have been harder. He would have had twenty-three sections of train to explore. Ed allowed himself a slight smile.

Upon arriving at the entryway to Section Three, Ed showed his ticket to one of the two porters waiting to assist passengers. Both wore name tags that identified them as "Don." All porters on nineteenth-century trains were known by a single name to make it easier on passengers. How "Don" ended up being the name porters were identified by was still a mystery that eluded Ed. The older of the two men looked at the ticket, smiled, and asked him to accompany him aboard the train.

Don pointed out the location of the various amenities available to first-class passengers aboard the Limited as they made their way across the sections to compartment 16-A in Section Three. Section Four housed an onboard barbershop, a beautician, and a steam-operated clothing press. Each passenger section was lined with mahogany paneling and had its own shower-bath. His room was just four doors down from it. A sturdy red carpet designed for constant foot traffic and ease of cleaning covered the floor.

"We've also got electrical lights in the rooms, just like the Royal Blue Line," Don proudly confided to him as they approached his cabin. Ed smiled his appreciation for being able to indulge in at least one of the newest in modern amenities. He was going to have to rely on an open window to cool his cabin down. Air-conditioning was still a few decades away from being invented, let alone being incorporated into train interiors.

Don handed him the cabin key after opening the door for him. Ed thanked him and gave him a silver dollar as a tip.

"Thank you, sir. Switch for the lights is right by the door frame.

Just ring the buzzer if you need anything," Don said. He pointed to both before closing the door behind him and leaving Ed alone with his steamer trunk.

The first-class cabin was equivalent in size to a modern walk-in closet. Adjacent to Ed's right side was a couch lined with plush red velvet cushions. Depending upon his mood, he could sleep on the couch or pull down the overnight bed. Mahogany paneling also lined the walls and floor. A narrow closet concealed the standard water closet.

Ed sat down and opened the trunk. He was anxious to begin the legwork in flushing out the identities of the Pinkerton agents who had disappeared aboard this train about two centuries from Current Time. He ignored the clothes and scientific books he had packed and went immediately for his sketch pads, pencils, and pastels.

His plan to identify the lost Pinkerton agents was a relatively simple one. Complete physical descriptions, along with photographs of operatives, were kept at the Pinkerton Agency's main corporate offices in Chicago in case identification needed to be made on a deceased agent. The case files on the agents investigating anti-railroad activities by the Molly Maguires agents probably on board the Limited right now in Past Time had gone missing at the Pinkerton field office.

All Ed had to do when he returned to Current Time was scan his various drawings of all the male train passengers into his computer. Female and minority agents weren't a staple among Pinkerton staff in the nineteenth century. A facial recognition software program he had commissioned from one of the Computer Science Department's graduate students would take care of the rest of the work, comparing his drawings to photos of Pinkerton agents he'd already uploaded weeks before onto his computer.

A loud blast of the train whistle broke through his thoughts. Ed checked his pocket watch. It was ten o'clock. The Limited's departure was heralded by a sudden forward motion that jerked him against the couch back before it smoothed out.

Ed watched from his cabin window as the train pulled away from the station. He waited until the station had completely disappeared from view before gathering up his drawing materials and finding his way out of the cabin and to an available seat on the nearest of the observation cars.

Seven hours later, a full spectrum rainbow of pastel and charcoal dust stained the tips of Ed's fingers as he added the final touches on the last drawing for his portfolio. For good measure, and as a precaution against snoops with prying eyes, he had also included drawings of the female passengers, the porters, a few interior sketches of the observation cars and dining car, and some hurried drawings of the landscape the Limited had effortlessly passed by. He had even managed to get a drawing of the quiet, nondescript married couple who had been ahead of him at the ticket window back in Chicago.

A digital camera camouflaged as a fountain pen or a book might have made his task of recording faces easier. Yet the task of contriving two hundred or more ways to get up close and personal with strangers while being able to discreetly point and click would have made the job nearly impossible. True, a few people had casually passed by and looked at the various sketches he piled up on the portfolio while he sat drawing away, but nobody had bothered him.

"If it's no trouble, sir, I'm curious as to see how you drew me," a young man's voice inquired.

Somewhat startled by the unexpected intrusion, Ed looked up to the man who stood in the aisle across from his seat in the observation car. Ed definitely liked what he saw.

The stranger carried himself with a confidence few men in Past Time, let alone Current Time, had by their mid-twenties. Wavy black hair neatly offset a pair of storm-gray eyes and a firm square jaw. Uneven scruffs of new black beard growth gave sharp definition to his cheeks, chin, and neck. Spry muscles nicely accented his lithe frame, which just reached about five foot six. The brown suit pants and white shirt he wore, with matching tie, had been expertly tailored to highlight as well as fit his body. Ed had already captured all of that on paper. Now the real thing set his heart and cock racing.

"Sorry 'bout spooking ya. Just curious, that's all. Name's Nathaniel Royce. Friends call me Nate." He gave Ed a smile that must have set many young women's hearts aflutter.

"Pleased to meet you, Nate," Ed said. He gestured for Nate to take the vacant seat in front of him. "Edward Christensen is my given name, but I prefer my friends to call me Ed."

He offered his hand, and Nate took it in a firm grip that lingered a second or two longer than normal societal protocol of either Past or Current Time usually permitted.

"So what made you draw just about everyone onboard?" Nate asked once he was seated. "Are you an artist of some kind?"

"No, not really." Ed laughed. He began going through the portfolio for the sketch he had drawn of Nate. "Drawing is just a hobby of mine. It helps to make the time pass quicker when I'm traveling alone. I'm a botanist. I usually study plants at my lab back in Cambridge."

Nate's casual ease dissipated a bit. He looked a bit worried, as if he suddenly realized he was out of his depth. "Oh, you're a learned man. No doubt you're a professor from that newfangled college they just started up there. Maybe one day I'll get to visit out there. Know I'd like to."

Ed immediately picked up on the reason for Nate's distress. Striking up a conversation with a stranger with seduction as the intent was always, at least for Ed, a daunting task at best. Barriers of wealth and education still strongly segregated the social classes in the nineteenth century. The fact that Nate was traveling on a first-class fare and dressed accordingly indicated some level of personal wealth, but was not indicative of his educational background. Ed suspected the young man was largely self-educated. No doubt Nate was probably mentally kicking himself for committing the social blunder of striking up a conversation with a so-called "social better."

"Some of my colleagues back at the newly minted Massachusetts Institute of Technology might debate you about the level of my intelligence." Ed laughed, ceasing his hunt for the sketch of Nate. He had made a snap decision based on his reading of the situation and decided to act on it. He'd already completed his main objective for this Time Hop. Hell, good old grandfatherly Henry got away with introducing Alexander and Hephaestion to the notion of a three-way romp during a previous Time Hop. Surely he could partake in a little harmless, mutual one-on-one fun with a hot young stud who had already indicated by touch what he wanted.

"Looks like I left that drawing in my cabin," Ed said. The little white lie had rolled smoothly out of his mouth. His tongue discreetly played across his upper lip—the suggestion visible only to Nate. "I'll take you there if you still want to see it."

"Sure, I'd like to see how you drew me," Nate replied. He smiled again. "Lead the way. I'll follow from behind, my good sir."

A vibrant reddish orange sunset peeked through the half-drawn window shade of the cabin by the time both had stepped inside. Sometime during the late afternoon, a porter had come in and prepped the cabin for Ed's nightly repast—which included lowering the concealed bed and making it fresh for sleeping in. Even the window had been cracked open to let fresh air in.

Ed went to close it. There was no doubt that any noise he and Nate created over the next hour or two would be more than thoroughly muffled by the sounds of the Limited steadily going over the tracks, yet he didn't want to add more risk to the one he was already taking in this Past Time era. Sodomy was still a capital offense in 1895, and he had no desire to have his or Nate's neck stretched out on a rope.

He heard the door click locked as he turned back to face Nate. The young man's fingers were fumbling a bit as they worked to free the buttons on his fly.

"Here, let me help," Ed said. Kneeling down, he caressed the outline of Nate's cock against the fabric of his pants—eliciting a soft moan from the young man.

With the last button freed, Ed eased Nate's pants and underwear past his hips and let them fall down to his boots. Nate may have been small in stature, but his uncut cock rivaled many men of average height Ed had hooked up with back in Current Time—even good old Henry's. It was surrounded by black ringlets of pubic hair.

"Nice," Ed murmured as he began massaging Nate's scrotum. The young man gasped as Ed's tongue teased and probed upward from the base of his cock. Ed knew that Nate had been expecting a simple blow and go, but he was going to get and give up so much more.

Ed stole a glance upward as his tongue slipped under the cock's foreskin as precum began dribbling out of the piss slit. Nate was quivering in orgasmic anticipation. He paused only for a moment to moisten the fingers that had been massaging Nate's scrotum, then he resumed sucking the quivering cock. An unexpected jolt rumbled throughout the car, allowing Ed to position Nate against the bed.

"Ohhhhhhh, unnnghhhh," Nate moaned. His half-closed eyes flew open in wide surprise as one of Ed's wet fingers penetrated the outer walls of his quim. His legs and buttocks momentarily tightened up instinctively against the unexpected intrusion before intense waves of orgasmic pleasure sent him collapsing against the bed—right where Ed wanted him.

Ed discovered that his initial suspicions about Nate were correct. The young man was a complete virgin when it came to anal sex. Ed slipped a second finger in. Nate's back arched upward. He moaned, trying to at least say no, only he couldn't. He was enjoying being finger-fucked too much. A hand slid under his shirt and began tweaking his nipples.

"Ahhhh...yes, fuck me, Professor, please now, sir, yes," Nate rasped just as a third finger slid inside his quivering, now cock-hungry ass.

Ed paused only long enough to strip off his clothes. He grinned when Nate stared wide-eyed at his thick, nine-inch cut cock.

"Not yet boy," he told Nate. "Class has only just begun."

Quickly unbuttoning Nate's shirt, Ed pulled it off the young man and ordered him onto the bed—whose height and breadth in the cabin just barely had enough room to accommodate them both. Nate meekly complied. Ed straddled Nate's smooth chest and pinned his arms to the side.

"Professor's cock needs to get all wet before it fucks your virgin hole, boy," Ed said. He bounced his cock head against Nate's lips. "Now open those lips."

Nate only hesitated a second before taking his first lesson in sucking cock. He knew learning how to ride the professor's cock would be his second lesson.

❖

Pale orange sunlight leaked through the closed window blind by the time Ed had woken up from the nap he had taken. He was not surprised and a bit relieved to find Nate had departed while he slept away in the early morning hours after a few sessions of robust fucking.

Nate had proven himself an eager student. They had talked a bit after their first sexual bout, and Ed genuinely liked the young man. A pretty good mind ticked behind that hot young body. Yet it was better that Nate had left of his own volition. Sure, Ed would have enjoyed working out the stiffness of his morning wood with Nate, who had all the makings of becoming a great power bottom, but parting after sex in Past Time was always more awkward than in Current Time.

Ed stretched before getting out of bed. The sheets were a bit stained with blood from Nate's cracked cherry, but he wasn't worried about that. Like all pre-teenagers in Current Time, he had received his TIPS—therapeutic interfering particles—vaccine and the annual adult booster shots. TIPS prevented the transmission of all sexually transmitted diseases and even eliminated those already in a person's bloodstream.

Ed rummaged through his discarded pants pockets for his pocket watch. A quick glance told him he had about forty-two minutes before the Higgs Singlets Field sent him shivering back into Current Time. There was more than enough time to make use of the shower-bath and get cleaned up. No sense in giving Ann something to gossip about when he and his luggage and drawings arrived back in the Temporal Causeway Chamber.

He pulled out a robe and a fresh pair of clothes. After donning the robe, he left the cabin and made his way to the shower-bath. Thankfully, it was unoccupied. Once inside, he disrobed and turned the shower spigot on before setting aside his change of clothes.

The Limited was giving her passengers a relatively smooth ride on this stretch of the rail. Ed smiled as he recalled taking advantage of a few jolts on the rail last night, using the added momentum to plow his cock deeper into Nate's hungry hole. He had gotten a few bruises himself when he bumped his head and shoulders against the confines of the nook the bed resided in. He welcomed the warm water coursing down his body as it worked out the stiffness and kinks.

Ed checked the time again after he had dressed and left the shower-bath. About fifteen minutes remained before he would be snatched out of Past Time. He had nothing further to do to prep. All his gear would be snatched up along with him.

Grabbing a light breakfast in the dining car was out of the question, though. Being tossed around in M-Brane space always caused him to hurl once he was back within the safe confines of the Temporal Causeway Chamber. Ann would provide a mop and bucket but absolutely no sympathy.

"Just keep walking, Pinkerton scumbag," a voice ordered from behind him. Ed turned sideways and caught a glance of the man holding a gun against the small of his back. It was the porter who had shown him aboard the Limited.

"Beg your pardon, I'm not—" Ed started to protest. The gun barrel now poked hard against the back of his head. He got the hint Don was giving.

"Shut your hole and keep walking straight ahead all the way to the last luggage car," Don curtly told Ed. "Otherwise I'll plug you before we get to where we're keeping your partner."

Despite feeling his heart literally leap into his dry throat, Ed did his best to remain calm as he walked through each section of the Limited at a leisurely pace. Don didn't seem to be in a hurry to reach their destination, and if Ed could manage to stall for enough time, not only would he safely be hauled back into Current Time, but he would also learn the identity of the lost Pinkerton agent.

Nobody impeded their progress to the luggage car. Don called out once they reached the closed door. It opened and Ed was roughly pushed inside. His mouth gaped at the scene now playing out before his eyes.

Nate was on the floor of the luggage car, roughly bound and gagged with rope. His right eye was badly bruised and swollen shut. Blood trickled out of his nose and the corner of his mouth. Standing over him, armed with service revolvers, was the married couple Ed had encountered at the ticket window yesterday.

Ed couldn't believe it. Not only had he discovered the identity of one of the Pinkerton agents who had been presumed killed aboard the Limited on November 8, 1895 by Molly Maguires saboteurs, but he had fucked him.

And Ed was royally screwed as well.

He had been pegged by Causality as the second murdered Pinkerton agent—lost, it would seem, to the memory of time.

"Help me get the door open," Don told the husband. "We'll shoot them and dump their bodies out. Nobody will find them alongside this stretch of the rail."

Ed and Nick watched helplessly as the husband handed over his gun to his wife.

Nate shivered a bit as Don and the husband unlatched the side door to the luggage compartment. The wife smirked over what she saw as cowardice. Ed thought at first the young man was being overcome by fear of his own impending mortality when he realized he was cold and shivering too.

Ed let out a sudden gasp as he realized that he had saturated the

Pinkerton agent with a minute smattering of particles from the Higgs Singlet Field last night. It was not enough to pull Nate fully into the M-Brane dimension, unless Ed got close enough to literally drag him there, and maybe, just maybe, into Current Time.

Henry hadn't found his remains along the old Atchison, Topeka and Santa Fe Railway rail line strutting alongside the Kaw River prior to his departure to Past Time, so there was an outside chance his crazy scheme would save both of them.

With the door now open wide enough to let two men through, Ed dropped to the floor and began rolling. His actions caught Don and his fellow Molly Maguires saboteurs by complete surprise.

"Hang on, Nate!" Ed screamed as he grabbed hold of the ropes restraining Nate. They kept rolling toward the open door and certain death from the fall.

Ed felt the air temperature drop to near freezing. He could tell Nate felt it too.

It was the warning cue that they about to transition in the time stream from Past to the airlock of the Temporal Causeway Chamber in Current Time. His ears popped. Nate grimaced as his ears popped from the pressure change. They came to a halt against the solid metal wall of the chamber. Ed's desperate gamble had worked—Causality had been satisfied by their rather abrupt departure from the Limited.

"Ann, in case you haven't noticed, I need a medical team here, pronto!" Ed called out.

He gave Nate a tired, reassuring smile as he steadied his breathing.

Ed's career as a Time Hopper was undoubtedly over. Yet he had managed to save Nate. He hoped he could make it up to the young man for taking him out of his time. He knew that he'd spend the rest of his life in Current Time trying.

Ed removed the rope gag from Nate's mouth. Nate's good eye hinted at many unspoken questions and fears.

"You told me when we first met that you wanted to travel out to Massachusetts," Ed told him with a lopsided smile. "Well, Nate, welcome to Cambridge."

THE ROUNDHOUSE MEN
DUSTY TAYLOR

The Mojave Desert, California, spring 1925

I knew from the get-go that I would be looked upon as an outsider by the president's entourage, so I did not trouble myself on that account. Rather, I determined to hold my own as the only slide-rule engineer, indeed as the only actual trainman in the delegation, and spend as much time as possible with my engine. Still, heading forward from the president's private railcar, I had to pass through the saloon where his personal retinue waited. And since it would have been discourteous to simply bustle through, I accepted their offer of a glass of Madeira.

The five were both older and younger, though all carried the pallor of marble staircases and wood paneling and each displayed some quantity of gray in his hair. Their suits fairly gleamed in comparison to my shopworn coat and hat. As we clacked along the Santa Fe main line, I could but smile at the little capsule of Pennsylvania luxury that seemed to bolster their confidence as much as it guarded their comfort.

"To William Wallace Atterbury," said the youngest, and we all raised our glasses.

"The most influential man in the world," added another.

"And to the great Pennsylvania Railroad," said one of the elders, "agent of all our futures and fortunes."

"To Little Jenny," I said. "May she be ever victorious."

"Hear, hear!" we all agreed. We drank in unison, whereupon silence commenced. As the outsider, I felt it was not my place to initiate conversation, and so I sipped my Madeira and appreciated the soft cushions and supple springs of the saloon car.

"I understand," said one of them, "that since you have no assistant motorman, the General has ordered you to sleep in the engine to ensure her security."

"He has," I replied, "though I see little likelihood of anyone attempting to make off with her in the night." The joke fell flat, and the faces of the men darkened.

"I believe the intent is to guard her secrets; to keep the prying eyes of our competitors from peeking under the hood, as it were," said an elder.

"Gentlemen, the L5 design holds no great secrets. And any engineer worth his slide rule can read her from a distance. Besides, the point of the Panamint races is to bring together trainmen from around the world so that we can learn from one another."

This time it was the youngest who spoke. "The General's chief concern lies in stripping the New York Central Railroad of its seven-year championship. As you must know, they are our primary competitor on the roads, just as that wretched little engine of theirs is our primary competitor on the racecourse."

My patience was strained, and I sensed a chasm opening between our points of view. The man closest to my age smiled and tried to lighten the conversation.

"By chance, did the General happen to offer you a cigar?"

"He did," I replied, and took the big presidente out of my vest pocket. "A Havana, I would say, though I am no expert."

"He must hold great confidence in you, to be so friendly," said the younger.

I was done with civility. "Gentlemen, Atterbury has ordered me to win both the unlimited electric pennant and the grand champion trophy, and I have given him every assurance that I shall. There is no question in the matter. It is what Little Jenny was designed to do, and barring disaster or high water, she will succeed."

A collective cringe followed my bald reference to their beloved president, and I determined to take my frayed cuffs and sweat-stained derby back to my engine. I rose and downed the last of my wine.

"I am curious," said the middle man, "to know your opinion of Mr. Atterbury, or 'the General,' as we so affectionately refer to him."

"He has an amazing vocabulary," I said in mock admiration. "For an executive, that is." The five remained silent until I left the saloon.

❖

I felt an acute need to be among men of my own kind, and so headed forward through the Pennsy cars and past my engine, safely cocooned in its heavyweight carrier, to the Santa Fe locomotive that pulled our little delegation. It was a big Pacific type, and I had admired her lines when she picked us up in Topeka. My hands took on a coal soot patina from climbing over the tender, and the fact of it pleased me. The big engine had a healthy smoke plume, blown high and away.

"Good day, gentlemen," I called out as I dropped down into the cab, where I was met with a smile and a scowl. The smiling man gripped my hand and shook vigorously.

"Good day to you, sir. I take it you're a Pennsy man?"

I returned the smile and the handshake. "I am indeed. Seth Davidson of the Juniata shops, Altoona, Pennsylvania."

"I'm Voss Carter, fireman of the Atchison, Topeka and Santa Fe. Pleased to make your acquaintance. This is Jefferson Levitt, engineer of thirteen seventy-three."

"A beautiful engine, sir. I always did admire the big Baldwins. Eighty-inch drivers?"

The man nodded but kept his right hand fast on the throttle and ignored mine. We were traveling along at a good clip, upward of ninety miles to the hour, so I took no offense.

"Yes sir, she's a beauty!" Voss chipped in. "Why, she's a shoo-in to win the Pacific class, and a good bet for the unlimited steam pennant." He fairly bounced from foot to foot with excitement. "Though I sure would love to see what you've got inside that heavyweight carrier."

I guessed from Voss's garrulous enthusiasm, as much as his partner's silence, that he was starved for conversation. "If you could be away from your firebox for a spell, I would be pleased to show you my engine." Voss looked to Levitt, who dismissed him with a wave, seemingly eager for a few minutes of solitude.

"Hot damn!" Voss cried. "I've been itching for a peek into that heavyweight ever since we picked you up!" And with that, he bounded up the monkey-ladder and over the tender.

Voss trotted the catwalks ahead of me, hopping from car to car with the sureness of a seasoned trainman. All around, the wide desert broiled under a merciless sun and wildflowers tainted the sage-spiced air with occasional drifts of sweetness. Down the line, Voss waited for me atop the heavyweight car.

"I'll leave it to you to do the honors, as it were," he said.

"Come ahead," I replied and began to throw open the vent caps that ran the length of the car. At the far end, I dropped down to the platform and opened the door.

"I knew it, I just knew it!" he cried. "She's an electric. You're going after Old Maude's trophy." I smiled in response. "Double-ender too. And just look at them drive-wheels! Great God almighty, you just might be able to do it. Side-rodder, so I'm guessing they're jackshaft coupled, am I right?"

"You are right, sir."

"So then it's just a question of horsepower, and there's enough room under those hoods for a couple of big Westinghouse motors, so I'd say it's a done deal. Yes sir, Old Maude will finally meet her match!"

"You really know your engines," I said, genuinely surprised.

Voss put his left hand on my shoulder and stuck out his right. "Seth, my friend, engines are my life's blood. And I must say it is a genuine pleasure to meet a Juniata man. Why, those shops are the envy of the entire railroad industry."

I accepted his firm handshake with gratitude. And as I began to suspect that he might be a man's man, or at least open to the idea, I decided to try a gesture that was well known back in Juniata. I took the cigar from my vest pocket, broke it in half, and offered him the good end. "Share a smoke with me, Voss?"

He took the half cigar and returned a surprised smile. "Why, I'd be honored, Seth. I surely do thank you."

"Unless you have a match, we'll have to go back up to the engine," I admitted. "Not only is fraternization frowned upon by my associates, I simply do not care for their company."

"Not to worry," he said, stepping back out on to the platform. Voss climbed out over the safety chain and clutched the grab iron on the side of the car. "I can't quite reach from here, so you'll have to take my hand." I did so, and he stretched himself down until he was almost under the wheels. "Don't let go now, or Santa Fe will be short one fireman for the race." We both laughed at the joke, but I felt a genuine affection for this man so confident as to trust his life to the hand of a stranger.

"That'll do the trick!" he called out over the clack of wheels on the rail joints. He held the broken end of the cigar to the bearing box on the nearest wheel. In seconds a thin wisp of smoke trailed from the spot and Voss set to puffing on the stub until it was fully ablaze. "Haul me up!" he called, and landed on the platform with the cigar clenched in his teeth. He spread his arms in triumph.

"I never would have believed it," I said.

"Do you get out on the main line much back home?"

"Not near as often as I would prefer," I admitted. "I spend my days between the drawing board, the machine shop, and the dynamometer shed."

Voss shrugged. "I reckon that's as good a life as any for a trainman. Me, I need the wide open and fresh air."

"I'm rather enjoying them myself. Say Voss, could you lean in and give me a light?"

"Hellfire, Seth, I plumb forgot!" He stepped close and puffed at the cigar until its cherry glowed bright. The wavering platform made it hard to bring the ends together, so we held each other by the shoulders. The tips met, and we both puffed mightily until mine was lit as well. We stood there in silence for a moment, wry smiles passing between us until we both began to laugh like schoolboys. Presently, we found ourselves leaning back against the safety rail, side to side, arms thrown intimately around each other's shoulders.

"You're going to like Panamint, Seth."

"You've been before?"

"This'll be my fourth year. You'll see engines from all around the world and meet some mighty fine trainmen too. Yes sir, we surely do have us one hell of a time."

We passed a friendly silence until Voss decided he was due back at the engine. He seemed reluctant to break our half embrace. I know I was.

"I thank you for the smoke, Seth. This surely is a fine see-gar. I've got to be back to my firebox, though, or I'll never hear the end of it."

We shook hands again, a long, friendly grip. "I'll see you in the roundhouse, Voss."

He threw me a wink. "In the roundhouse, then," and he climbed up and was gone. I passed the remainder of the journey on the platform, enjoying a content that stayed with me all the way in to Panamint.

❖

We arrived before noon, though the qualifications had already begun, and the yards and sidings were all abuzz with activity. I supervised the unloading of Little Jenny while Atterbury supervised me. He thereupon retreated to the cool of his private car and was not seen for the remainder of the day.

"I do declare, he's a regular shrinking violet," commented Voss, who had installed himself at my right elbow. "Who would credit it? The chief of the greatest railroad in the nation, here among the finest trainmen in the world, not to mention the fastest engines ever built, and he won't come out of his caboose. Who would credit it?" There was good-natured laughter all around and great interest in my engine. Since Little Jenny was an electric, she would not be berthed in the big forty-stall roundhouse. Rather, she sat between a tiny Pacific Electric steeple-cab named Electra and a massive bipolar from Milwaukee. The champion Old Maude sat on the other side of the bipolar. The four were the only electrics in the entire competition.

Voss introduced me to some of the men he knew from previous competitions, and we bragged up our engines and expectations with good-natured rivalry. A quantity of Egyptian cigars had arrived with the crew of the Algerian Garratt, and there was much discussion as to whether the apparent admixture of camel dung with the tobacco was of positive or negative effect. Word came around that Union Pacific had broke out a mess of frankfurters and sauerkraut, so Voss and I, accompanied by a distinguished man with graying hair, decided to stroll over and try our luck.

"Say, Lee," said Voss to the man, "have you met Seth Davidson here? He built that Pennsy side-rodder they just set on the tracks. Seth, this is Leland McGowan, of the Southern Pacific. He's one of the Panamint champions."

"Pleased to know you," I said, shaking his hand.

"Good to know you, Seth. Call me Lee."

"You wouldn't by chance belong to that sleek little Alco Atlantic

I saw back yonder, would you? She looks like a champ if ever I saw one."

Lee grinned. "Southern Pacific, thirty twenty-five, at your service. Three-time grand champion, ought-five, six, and nine. Not much in the running these days, I'm afraid. Looks like it's going to be up to you to unseat Old Maude."

Word was out that a real contender had rolled in and everyone was excited at the prospect of seeing the end of New York Central's winning streak. I found myself somewhat of a celebrity among the trainmen and received a good many handshakes and pats on the back. After our lunch of hot dogs, Voss set to whispering with Lee, who nodded and smiled as the two conferred. Their manner made my ears fairly burn, for I got the distinct impression they were discussing me. At length, Voss clued me in.

"Say, Seth, what would you say to taking a nice cool swim with a few good friends?"

I was caught off guard. "Where, out in the sand dunes?"

Voss kept his tone low. "There's a spring about three miles north of here, and a service rail that takes us right to it. Now, if we was to take out in the heat of the day like this, wouldn't nobody be the wiser and we'd have the place to ourselves. What do you say to that?"

The thought of it might have made me blush. Voss had more than won me over with his easygoing manner, and Lee was as handsome a man as I ever had the pleasure to meet. "That sounds like a grand time to me. I'm in."

Lee leaned in close. "We'll need one more to make good time with the Kalamazoo. Shall we try to find Coop?"

"Hell, he's always game for a getaway," said Voss.

❖

Jeremiah Cooper was an easy man to find, or more accurately he would be a hard man to hide. We heard his thick Louisiana accent booming around by the switchman's tower, swearing a blue streak between his boisterous guffaws. "That's Coop," said Voss. "He was a navy boiler tender back in the war with Spain."

"He's a permanent resident at the Panamint shops," explained Lee. "This is the high point of his year."

We found him regaling a handful of railroad executives. He had them trapped on the steps of the switchman's tower, which they probably had climbed for the view. Now they were seated on the steps, reluctantly enduring a sermon of debauchery and violence as found in the Philippine Islands. As we approached, I was amused to recognize Atterbury's retinue, looking slightly wilted and eager for escape to their saloon car.

"Coop!" shouted Voss. "Let them fellers alone! Holloway needs you over to the powerhouse right away."

Coop took his foot from the bottom step and turned to face us. He was a bull of a man, massively muscled and over six feet tall. He sized up our little company and a knowing grin spread under his handlebar mustache.

"Oh, yeah! The powerhouse! Hey, we better get right over there before Holloway get mad and come after us." He winked at Voss, who had trouble holding his laughter. Atterbury's men fled as soon as the bottom step was cleared and were walking back to the Pennsy train as fast as dignity would permit.

"There they go again, them shrinking violets!" cried Voss.

"Hey, where you go?" Coop called after them. "I ain't tell you what her daddy done yet!" We all shared a laugh and Voss introduced me. The others were all old friends.

"Pennsy man, you say? We ain't never get a Pennsy train out here before."

"Just wait till you see it, Coop," said Voss. "He's brought a right beautiful electric to take Old Maude's trophy. But for right now, we was wondering if you could help us man the Kalamazoo."

Coop smiled and threw me a wink. "You guys feel like a dip? Sure, I go for that!"

We ambled over to the maintenance of way sheds and found the handcar around back. We set it on a track that stretched away toward the dunes in the north.

"All right, gents," said Lee. "We've got three miles of hard labor in the heat of the day, with a cool plunge at the finish. It'll be upward of one hundred and ten under that sun, so hats on and coats off. If we make speed, we'll be there in ten minutes. Everyone up for the challenge?"

We were. Coop and Lee took one side of the handle, Voss and I the other. In seconds, we had the car rolling away at a respectable speed.

There seemed a general competition between the two opposing sides of the car, each pair of us trying to take the lion's share of the work yet show no fatigue. I was pouring sweat, but in the dry heat it evaporated instantly. Voss and I rode backward, and the breeze on my back and shirtsleeves made the heat endurable.

It seemed as though ten minutes had passed ten minutes since, and we weren't there yet. "Anyone need a rest?" called Coop, "just let go and set a spell. We can take turns if we need to." Nobody was about to admit being tired. My arms were getting weak, but the pace was beginning to slow. Apparently I wasn't the only one flagging. Still, the four of us kept hauling, all presenting a stiff upper lip.

"Is that water I smell?" I asked across the pump handle.

"Sure smells like it to me," said Voss, "and not a minute too soon, by my reckoning."

"Aw hell, you guys tired already?" chided Coop, but even he showed fatigue.

"We're there," puffed Lee. "About thirty yards to go. God Almighty, this heat is a killer."

We coasted the last few yards and left the handcar on the track. I dropped to the ground and my knees almost gave out. But upon looking around, I saw no water hole, only a series of low, black iron tanks. Pipes and check valves pointed around to the other side of the row, and it was there the boys were heading.

"Hot damn, that's what I came for!" said Voss as he stripped off his shirt. We came upon a smaller tank, about waist high, that the larger tanks drained into. It was open to the sky, and the sweet smell of clear water hit me like a wave. I began to peel down. Lee was already naked and plunged in head-first. Coop crooned a French melody as he slowly stripped off his clothes, smiling all the while at Lee, who floated face-up in the pool. "Last one in is a gandy-dancer!" called Voss as he vaulted the tank wall and splashed in. I slipped over the side and was instantly refreshed. The water was warm but still much cooler than the blistering heat of the day. Voss sidled up to me in the tank, and we all laughed at Coop, who was undressing with exaggerated slowness and grinning at Lee.

"You know, Seth, we're all good friends here. Coop and Lee been particular friends for years, and every year is like a reunion. I was telling Lee about how you seemed like a right friendly fellow, and that

I thought it might be nice for us all to have a getaway and get better acquainted."

"I appreciate it, Voss, but you don't need to sell me. I've been around enough to recognize men of my own stripe."

Coop was now naked and flexing his muscles for us all. He was truly a sight to behold with his sailor tattoos and dark furred chest. Not only built like a bull, he was hung like one too. We all cheered and whistled. Suddenly, he grabbed his nose and leapt into the tank with a huge splash. Some fifty gallons of water cascaded over the rim and hissed on the hot baked earth. He came up in front of Lee, who placed his hands on his shoulders and drew him into a bear hug. The two of them laughed and rocked together, then kissed and began to talk in lowered voices.

Voss extended his right hand to me over the water. "To old friends, and to new."

"Friends old and new," I replied as we shook.

"I surely am pleased you came up to the engine to say hello or we might never have met."

"If it weren't for my need to escape the shrinking violets, I might never have sought you out," I said, our hands still clasped.

"Ha ha! I do declare! Well, to shrinking violets then!"

"Shrinking violets," I replied, and kissed him hard and long.

The ice being well broken and the situation made clear, we enjoyed ourselves freely in the desert isolation. Voss was a strong and sturdy chap, not shy about his needs and desires. His cock poked me while we kissed and I took the hint, taking him in my hand. He was hard, and in seconds I was too. Voss's hand found me and we stroked each other under the water. He stopped kissing and whispered in my ear.

"You know, Seth, what I would most like right now is to swallow you right down to the root."

I stood up in the tank and found the water level came up to my scrotum. Voss fixed his lips around me and went to work. His mouth felt cool and contrasted wonderfully with the dry heat.

"Oh, so that's how a Pennsy man like it, eh?" Coop said with a smile. "You see that, Lee?"

"I sure do, and I like what I see. He's going to fit in just fine with the roundhouse boys."

Voss sucked me like a man who hadn't had it in a long time. He took me in deep and his stubble chafed at my thighs. It had been a while for me too, since I had spent over a month of evenings balancing Jenny's rods and drivers. Was that why Atterbury chose me over the others on the design team? For my obsessive dedication? I wondered, but not for long. Voss sucked me back into the present and for a time I forgot all about the engine, the race, and my prospects for the future. Suddenly I was getting close to the edge, so I pulled away.

"Slow down there, pardner. You're like to finish this race before it even starts."

Voss smiled. "I hope you'll forgive my enthusiasm."

I pulled him to his feet and went down before him. Not a cock in the pond hung soft, and Voss was no exception. His shaft fairly throbbed with excitement. I threw my lips around it and started puffing. Voss let out a loud moan, which caught the attention of Lee, who was giving his every inch to Coop from behind. Lee gave me a nod and a conspiratorial smile that told me we would take our turn later. Voss grabbed my hair and rammed himself deep, unable or unwilling to hold back. He howled and slammed himself against my tonsils. Water splashed around the pool and wavelets tickled my ears. I felt his hips buck, and he blasted my throat with a salty load. I sucked him right to the end, until he pulled out and sat back against the rim of the tank.

"I do declare, Seth," he panted, "I surely did need that. Yes sir, skinning one off by my lonesome just don't compare."

I smiled, and Coop laughed out loud. Lee was too far gone to pay any attention.

"What's so funny? Why, I know every man in this tub has done it time and again, especially on them long cross-country hauls."

"It's just that I had barely got started, Voss. I figure I still owe you some."

"Aw hell, you can pay me back later," he said. "Besides, I don't go in for that fancy stuff. Get in and get it done, that's what I say."

"You talk too damn much, Voss. I don't know how you manage to get nothin' done!" Coop hollered, then whooped out a laugh.

Suddenly Lee tensed and pushed himself hard against Coop's tight butt. He sort of growled through clenched teeth as he came, and Coop crooned at him. "Oh yeah, just like that," he said. "Just like that there, Lee, just like that."

For a minute we all leaned back and caught our breath. Lee caught my eye and threw me a nod. "Now, as far as I can tell, Seth still hasn't been properly initiated yet. And it would be impolite for us to let him to go back to the roundhouse with a loaded pistol in his britches."

"That's my Lee," said Coop. "Always put the needs of others before himself." He bellowed again and poked Lee in the ribs.

"If I could have the honor," Lee said. "I've never sucked off a Pennsy man before."

I laughed with him and the others, then he got down in front of me and picked up where Voss had left off. Lee was slow and thorough, exploring my every wrinkle and ridge with his tongue. He wrapped his arm around my waist and held me tight. His other hand held me by the balls and gave well-timed tugs that seemed to wind me up tighter and tighter in anticipation of a big let-go. It was clear that Lee had experience in the finer points of cocksucking. I found myself rapidly approaching the point of no return, but this time I didn't fight it. I let him work me right up to the edge, at which point he pulled hard on my ballsac and sent me the rest of the way home. I came hard and from deep down, hitting him with several long spurts. Lee took it all in, then slowly backed off and took to floating on his back with a happy smile on his face.

Coop and Voss had been watching quietly. "You one of the boys now, eh, Seth?" Coop said with a wink.

❖

We soaked our clothes in the tank for the trip back to the shops. That, along with the general good feeling we all shared, was enough to make up for the lost urgency that had got us there so quickly. Still, we were all fagged by the time we got back. And since Lee had a race that afternoon and Coop was busy in the shop, Voss and I stretched out on my cot in Little Jenny's cab and took a nap.

We were awakened by commotion in the shed. The doors were thrown wide and the big bipolar was nudged in by the Panamint switcher. In minutes, it pushed Old Maude back into her stall as well. Voss and I went among the crowd for the latest news.

The Milwaukee bipolar had beaten Electra the day before, and Old Maude had just now dispatched the bipolar with equal ease. As my engine was the only AC electric, she was in a class by herself and needed no qualifying runs. It was now a done deal. Pennsy 3930 and Central 6000 would face each other in the morning, and the unlimited electric pennant would go to the winner. A substantial purse of bets had been placed, and while the odds favored Old Maude, the majority of bets were for Jenny.

I walked over and found the Central engineer tending to his engine. He was a little man, about my age, slim and dark haired. Old Maude was a beautiful machine, a double-ender like mine, but much shorter and with smaller drive wheels. She gleamed bright black, with "N.Y.C. & H.R. 6000" sparkling white on her side. Oddly enough, the crowd was gathered around the bipolar's just-defeated engineer, and Old Maude's man was all but ignored.

"A beautiful engine you have here," I said. The man looked up and smiled.

"Pennsylvania Road, I presume?" he said, extending his hand.

I nodded and shook. "Seth Davidson, out of Altoona."

"Dudley Hayes, of Troy, New York. Thank you. I must say, you have an astounding engine there yourself. I was looking her over earlier. Hard to believe she's brand-new, what with side-rod drivers and all. Would you believe this engine of mine is twenty years old?"

"Hard to believe indeed, innovative as she is. Just like that bipolar, real innovation in practical design. I admire that above all else."

"Innovation isn't going to beat your engine, though, is it?" he said with an ironic smile. I simply shrugged, as it would have been immodest to agree. "Not with those big drive wheels," he went on. "I don't mind. I've had my run, and folks here would just as soon see the back of me, figuratively speaking, of course."

He was right. No degree of innovative design could overcome four Westinghouse motors and eighty-four-inch drivers. Like a high stakes gambler who could raise his opponents until they all simply folded, Little Jenny had already won the grand championship, though she had yet to even leave the engine shed.

❖

I paid a visit to the shrinking violets in their saloon, with Voss still faithfully on my elbow. Whether it was the heat or the general excitement that had thawed their icy manner, a change had taken place.

They were almost friendly toward me, and downright diplomatic in shaking Voss's hand.

"The General has been closely following the preliminary races and is quite confident of our position. In the interest of good sportsmanship, he has contributed a case of champagne to the evening's festivities."

"Well, ain't that generous." Voss beamed.

I lowered my voice. "Gentlemen, I had come to impose upon you for a case of rye, which might also be a fitting contribution, if the saloon is well enough stocked." They assured me it was, and that both cases would be delivered in time. Voss was overflowing with friendly enthusiasm.

"Gentlemen, I surely do hope you all can come to the dance tonight. Smack Henderson's band came in with the New York Central. You know, with Louis Armstrong and Coleman Hawkins? Yes sir, the roundhouse is going to be jumping!"

The youngest violet puzzled. "But it was my understanding that due to limited facilities, women would only be present on the final day of the races."

"Oh that is true, sir, there are no women in Panamint this evening. But no roundhouse man worth his steam would ever let a lack of womenfolk stop him from going to a dance."

"You mean it is to be a stag dance?"

Voss winked. "Yes sir, but you can still come in your Sunday suits. And as an added bonus, you can spit on the floor with absolute impunity!"

❖

Henderson's band was not the only one in attendance, and the roundhouse roof seemed at times in danger of being carried away on a flood of celebration. Mariachis had come in on the Rio Grande, Appalachian banjos on the Wabash, and Cajun fiddlers on the Susquehanna. The shorter tank engines and Atlantics left room in front for music and dancing, while card games, hard drinking, and braggadocio favored the relative quiet between the longer Pacifics and Mallets.

All forty doors stood wide open to the cool evening air, and the sounds of the big blues band filled the open circle. A wrestling match was under way down in the turntable pit while wagers changed hands above. In all corners, trainmen from around the world kicked up their heels in their finest suits, shirtsleeves and suspenders, or striped overalls. Men from the south and west could be spotted by their Stetsons, while those of the north and east favored the derby. An assortment of boaters, flat-caps, and a fez or two were sprinkled throughout, and at least one man sported a turban. The excitement was infectious, and Voss and I took a few turns around just taking it all in.

"Levitt will be playing cards tonight," Voss was telling me, "so we prob'ly won't see him around. He's a mean one at poker, let me tell you."

I thought about the serious, silent engineer I had met earlier in the day. Undoubtedly he was a fine poker player and a fine engineer too. There was a chance I would race him in the morning.

"Hey, ain't them your fellas?" said Voss, pointing. It was, though this time the shrinking violets stood tall and proud. Atterbury was with them. He caught my eye and smiled, adding a slight nod and a wave. Apparently his attitude had loosened, and I was pardoned for leaving my engine unattended.

"What do you say, Voss, shall we dance?"

"I thought you'd never ask."

We started off by the banjos where a free-for-all stomp was well under way. Several jugs of corn were circulating, and we took our swigs. When the banjos took a break we headed for the fiddles, where Coop had appointed himself guest conductor. Bourbon was being passed around, and those dancing as ladies tied bandanas on their arms. I led Voss for a few dances, but it became clear that the liquor was gaining on us. If we didn't slow down, it would be a short night.

"What do you say we head back to my engine," I asked.

"That sounds just fine to me, Seth. We've got a big day tomorrow."

We found Dudley Hayes tinkering around his engine. "Say, Dud," Voss called over, "why don't you join us for a drink."

He looked up and smiled. "Don't mind if I do."

Voss had squirreled away a bottle of Atterbury's champagne, so we popped the cork and passed it around. Dudley examined Jenny's control panel and regarded the huge step-down transformer that dominated the cab. "A clean design, that's for sure." He noticed the cot where Voss sat. "You sleep in here too?"

I smiled. "No worse than a Pullman berth."

Voss shook his finger. "Now don't go gettin' no ideas, Dud, I've already called shotgun and this here cot ain't big enough for three. If you want to stay over, fetch your own bedroll."

Dudley blushed and smiled, but said nothing. There was room enough for us all to sit down and tell railroad stories while we passed the bottle. Dud was a friendly chap, and we enjoyed a pleasant hour or so until a bellowing voice split the night.

"Voss, you in there?" Coop hollered up from the shop floor. "Levitt is looking all over for you. He want you back at the engine, say you gotta run drills tonight."

"Well, gentlemen," said Voss, struggling to his feet, "that's my date and I've got to go. I'll try to get back when we're done, but I can't make no guarantees."

"If not, then I guess I'll see you on the course."

"On the course," Voss agreed, and hurried off.

"Looks like I'm sleeping alone again," I said, stretching out on the cot.

"Well...I mean...you know, uh..."

"Dud," I interrupted, "If you'd like to stay, I'd appreciate your company. If not, then that's all right too."

"No, no," he assured me, "I understand how it is. It's just that, well I never, uh..."

"But you're interested, I take it."

He hemmed and hawed a bit. "I guess I'm interested, all right."

"How about you hand me that bottle and stretch out a bit."

That was all it took. Dudley laid into me with all he had. His lips were all over my face, he bit at my neck and his fists tugged at my hair. It was like a joyful discovery for him, and I was quite flattered. He kissed me with an adolescent passion that must have been pent up for some time. I gave back in kind, but let him call all the shots. It was well worth the buttons I lost when he tore my shirt open. He was strong for his size, with powerful hands and hard forearms. Out of his shirt, his dark chest hair swirled in a symmetrical pattern, thickening as it disappeared in his waistband. He eased me out of my trousers, then shucked off his own.

If I had held doubt of his attraction, it disappeared when I saw him naked. Dudley's bone stood erect before me, witness to its owner's desire and intention. I rolled onto my belly. He took the suggestion and lay down atop me, his member parting the crease of my buttocks. Though the day's heat had lessened, we were still sweating. Our skin slipped easily, and with a pleasant friction. He slid himself slowly up and down my crack, letting the head of his cock poke at my asshole. He was working himself up, and judging by his grip on my shoulders, he was about ready. I raised up a little when he poked at me, and caught his prick with my pucker. Unless he backed off, his next thrust would put him inside me.

He didn't back off, but drove his cock firmly into my ass. I accommodated easily and savored the rare sensation of a long, slim cock inside me. If Dudley was indeed new to ass-fucking, then he was a born natural. He kept up a perfect rhythm, like a steam piston on a side-rodder, gradually picking up speed. I clenched up on him, and he let out a moan. His right hand reached under my belly and gave me a similar squeeze. My balls swelled in anticipation as his rhythm began to falter. Soon he was bucking erratically, ramming himself to the hilt as he blasted me with loads of hot jism. He fell forward, but gripped me again, this time stroking me furiously. In seconds I was there, spurting long ropes onto my cot.

"My God," he panted. "I never would have guessed it could be like that. That just doesn't compare."

I was dizzy with ecstasy. Whether it was the heat, the sex, the hootch, the excitement of the day, or all of them together, we both collapsed in a sweaty pile on the cot and were quickly lost in sleep.

❖

"Hey, sleeping beauty!" a strange voice called. I awoke to find Jefferson Levitt standing over me, and Voss pulling up his trousers. "Get yourself buttoned up. We've got a race to run. And as for you," he sneered, turning to me, "I'll see you on the racecourse."

"Sorry, Seth, I've got to get going. I'll catch up with you later."

I was confused. "What happened to Dudley?"

Voss smiled. "Such a gentleman! He gave up his bunk when I got back. You were already asleep."

❖

Jenny beat Old Maude quite handily. Had we not done it, any of the newer Atlantics would have. Maude's time was simply over.

Tragedy struck when a Cotton Belt Atlantic destroyed itself on the course, taking with it Santa Fe 1468. A drive wheel had come apart at speed, which sent the coupling rod free to vault the engine into the adjacent track before piercing the boiler and causing a general explosion. As the speeds were in excess of one hundred miles per hour, 1468 was unable to escape destruction, though her engineer and fireman were able to throw themselves clear and escape with their lives. As a result, Levitt's 1373 claimed the unlimited steam pennant and was set to race Little Jenny for the championship.

Since the steam tracks were still fouled with wreckage, 1373 ran on the DC track next to mine. Levitt chuffed his blowdown valves, sending up great clouds of steam. Black smoke blasted from the stack. I had seen it all before. With my hand on the selector lever, I waited patiently for the flagman to signal.

The flag dropped, and I engaged the first transformer tap. The wheels slipped only a little, then bit the rail and rolled. In seconds, I moved to the second tap and speed increased. I was already ahead, as 1373 was experiencing considerable slippage. Still, I knew that once her wheels caught, she would pass me, though probably not for long.

She steamed by me in mere seconds, sending dust-choked steam everywhere. In a minute or so, she would be all out, probably over a hundred miles per hour, and hold steady for the rest of the race. I was up to the fourth tap and still had a lot of voltage left to burn.

I caught her just before we entered the timed course. Jenny pounded the track viciously. Half a ton of side rods, no matter how well balanced, produced thundering vibrations at high speed. I passed her on my ninth tap, three notches left to go. At most I would need one more, and only if she rallied and pulled ahead. But it seemed as though it wouldn't be necessary, as she simply dropped farther and farther behind. The grandstand approached on the left, the finish line dead ahead. I passed it some four or five lengths ahead of Levitt and Voss, smiling to know that my future with Pennsy was now well secured.

I determined to look up Dudley when I got back home. After all, we were practically neighbors. Altoona to Troy was just a day trip by train.

THE LAST TRAIN
WILLIAM HOLDEN

The last train of the night is approaching. It rumbles through the tunnels of Boston. I stand and wait for it with my legs spread straddling the third rail—the electric rail. I feel the pulse of the electricity vibrating around me, entering me, seducing me. My body or what I call my body blends in with the dark, damp caverns that are the bowels of this city. I am Nate, the Midnight Barker. I own the night, and for now Boston is my home. Every night when the clock strikes twelve, I take over the subway looking for the one young man who will make the one-way trip to my Netherworld—the most pleasurable hell he'll ever know.

I've been here for months waiting, wandering the passages beneath the city looking for the one to come along to give me what I need to survive. I'm not complaining, you understand. It's not as if the dank, stale air below the city isn't a welcoming environment. On the contrary, I'm finding myself quite at home here. There's a quaint coziness about the burnt electrics, rotting soil, and seeping sewage that I just can't find anywhere else. My complaint comes from a different place, a place of hunger—desire.

I'm not alone on this quest. The human world is too vast a place for just little ole me. I couldn't keep up with the demands. Well, I could, but that would take all the fun out of it. So I have my boys, the ones I've already taken, out scouring the world for other lost young souls that can fill the void. The problem is it takes them so much longer. They're new at the arts of seduction and selection. They don't have the hundreds of years of experience that I do, nor the charm, for that matter. So I am out once again looking for young men whose desires are deep enough to let us feed.

The vibrations of the oncoming train echo around me. Its thunderous roar consumes the air in the tunnel. The train makes the curve. The lights are upon me, yet the conductor is blind to my presence. The force of the wind billows through my hair, my cape, my being. I flicker to allow the train to pass through me. The impact is forceful. It takes my breath away. I ejaculate as the subway car swallows me. The train's wheels thump against the rails. I feel the pulse within me as if it were my own heart pumping blood through my veins to keep me alive. The electricity that races through my body heightens my senses.

There are few people on the train this time of night, which makes my job easier. I begin my search, one person at a time as they sit in the car unaware of my presence. I pass through them, the men anyway, tasting them, caressing them; searching for the right one. Night after night I have foraged the subway, and every night since arriving I have come away empty-handed. Or should I say with an empty stomach.

Tonight, I feel, will be different. There is something in the air that hasn't been there before. I can sense it, almost smell it. It's getting closer to me as the train continues to invade my body car by car. I take a deep breath. The desire of a young man fills my nose. The deep, heavy scent of the male body in heat ravishes my groin. My stomach grumbles. My cock aches. I'm almost upon him. He's in the last car. It enters me. I see him sitting alone in the back. He looks up in my direction as if he can see me. His pale green eyes smolder with a sexual energy that ignites the air. His scent intoxicates me. I taste him as I pass through him. He's just had sex. I can taste the spilt cum as it lies drying against his skin. His body spasms as I exit it. I turn facing the back of the train as the last car leaves my body. His desire and sweat cling to my tongue. He looks out the back window. He knows someone is out there watching him. He felt me inside him where I still linger. He's had a taste of what awaits him. He'll soon need it, crave it, and before long he'll be begging me to take him. I watch him shrink into a tiny speck as the train disappears down the long, dark corridors under the city. The vibrations have stopped. The tracks are quiet. I saunter down the damp, musty tunnel with his scent clinging to my body. He won't get far now that I've tasted him. I have established the connection. Our journeys are one. I shall pay him another visit tonight, this time on his turf—his bed.

I take myself above ground. The late-night August air is warm and humid as I make my way across town. I squat down next to his triplex, peering through the small ground-level window into his one-room apartment. I see him sleeping in the dim light of the moon's rays. I shimmer and slip inside the building. The house is still. The thick, heavy air of his room hits me as I slip through the door. His scent drifts around me, through me. He never showered. His body still reeks of cum and sweat. Our brief connection in the subway this evening wasn't long enough for me to know much about him.

I stare at his beautiful sleeping form. His left foot sticks out from the covers. I kneel down at the foot of his bed. The warm leathery smell of his foot makes my mouth water. My tongue expands. It slithers and weaves itself between each of his toes. I savor his salty skin. He pulls his foot away in his dreams. It slips underneath the covers. I need to know more. I walk to the side of his bed. I place my fingers against his temple. I flicker. My fingers sink into his skull as they make their way into his brain.

His name is Rafael Sanchez, born twenty-six years ago tomorrow. I'll have to remember to wish him a happy birthday. He becomes restless from my invasion. I slip further into his brain to quicken my invasion and to get a better look around. He goes by the name of Rafe. His memories flash in and out of my mind. It is then that I realize why he tasted so good earlier tonight. Sex is his life. It's his business, and by the visions his mind is invoking, he has an insatiable appetite. This new information has many possibilities for me. I may need to alter my plans for him. Do I know how to pick them or what?

As I remove my fingers, he rolls over onto his back. A scattering of dark hair crosses his upper chest. I want to peek below the sheet. I resist the temptation. I stand in quiet contemplation against the shadows of his room. I watch the rise and fall of the thin sheet that covers his body. I notice a sudden movement between his legs. His dreams are becoming erotic. His cock lengthens beneath the covers of the night. It bobs up and down, brushing against the bedding. A small wet spot spreads through the cotton fibers. A half smile grows across his face. I lick my lips, wanting to enter him, to experience his dreams or become a part of them. I refrain. There will be plenty of time to enjoy him later.

I look away from the seduction of his body. His clothes lay on the floor next to the nightstand. The scent of his body hovers over them.

I squat down next to them. I inhale his body's perfume. His musk is a mix of stale sex, sweat, and ass. It blends to make a perfect pre-dinner cocktail. I take his white ribbed briefs in my hand. I inhale the odors of his crotch. I take another long, deep sniff before slipping them into my topcoat—a keepsake, if you will, of my night out on the town. Rafe mutters in his sleep. He's becoming restless. His eyes flutter open as he sits up in his bed. I blend into the shadows and leave his room before he has time to register my presence. I return to the quiet tunnels of the subway where I wander alone waiting for our next encounter.

Rafe boards the train at Brookline Village heading inbound. It's the last Green Line train of the night. I sit at the other end of the car watching him. His dark brown hair is tossed and tangled. It falls around his face, obscuring my view. His black T-shirt is tight across his body. It hugs his toned chest and the six-pack that he carries. His nipples press against the thin fabric of his shirt. My mouth waters at the thought of slipping them between my lips. His faded blue jeans are torn and ratted in all the appropriate places. He wears ankle-high black boots on his large feet. I remember the taste of his feet from last night. My groin aches with the anticipation of what's to come—or who. Tonight, I will take Rafe to my world, a mirror image of his own, but beyond anything he will ever experience. I can feel his beating heart. I can taste his desire. It's time to take him on a little ride.

He looks over at me. He can feel my eyes caressing him. He likes the attention. His mind tries to decipher why I look or feel so familiar. He remembers the intense pleasure from last night as I passed through him, though he doesn't know where the moment came from. The train is speeding along the tracks below the surface of the city. It rocks and sways with the twisting turns of the tunnels. I stand on solid footing. The motion of the train goes through my shadow. I walk toward him. The lights of the subway car blink on and off as I approach. Our eyes remain fixed on one another. I stand in front of him. I feel the rush of nerves pulsing through his body. His rugged, musky scent engulfs me. He's eye level with my crotch. He looks up my shadow body. He stares at the face I spent hours painting on with meticulous detail, a face I must wear whenever I travel in the outside world.

"Who are you?"

His rich, smooth voice resonates through me. The deep, velvet tones caress my ears. "I'm Nathaniel, but please, call me Nate. All my boys do."

"Do I know you?"

"We met for a very brief moment last night, too brief to truly get to know each other the way it was meant to be." I can see his mind trying to make the connection with what he felt last night. "Yes, that was me who gave you that moment of extreme pleasure."

"I don't understand."

"Of course you don't, but you will." I run my fingers down his cheek. A heavy coating of morning whiskers covers his skin. I lean down and kiss him. His stale breath sweeps over my made-up face. His mouth opens to mine. I slide my tongue through his mouth and taste the remains of another man's cum

"We can't do this." He gasps as he pulls back, separating our lips. He looks around at the scattering of people in the car with us. "Not here."

"Yes, here." I follow his eyes around the near-empty car. "I can get rid them. It will be just the two of us. Let me take you on a ride you will never forget. A birthday gift, if you will." His facial features strain with curiosity at my mention of his special day. "I suppose I know more about you than I've let on. Come with me. Let me show you the true meaning of pleasure."

I don't give him time to respond. It wouldn't matter anyway. He's coming with me whether he wants to or not. I straddle him. The heat of his body surrounds me. It pulls me into him. My tongue slips back into his mouth. Rafe moans. His voice vibrates against my tongue. He gags as it stretches and slides down his throat, the muscles tightening around it. I attach myself to him and flicker, bringing him with me to my Netherworld.

I lean back and look at Rafe. The passage between our two realities has disoriented him. His eyes are full of fear and confusion as he looks past me at our new surroundings. I love these moments with a newbie—they're priceless.

"What is this place?" Rafe's voice drifts through the thick, damp air. He squints, trying to focus on what lies behind my veil of deception.

"It's my home, Rafe. Do you like it? You see, our worlds are not so different," I lie. "Our worlds are mirror images of each other—parallel universes, if you will." I clutch his chin, bringing his attention back to me. I must shield his eyes from our true surroundings. He cannot know the horrors or pleasures that await him in my world, at least not yet. "I know you want me, Rafe. I can feel the desire seeping from the pores in your skin." I watch his lips tremble as they try to form words. I grip the edge of his shirt and pull it up over his head. I become intoxicated with the scent of his body. His armpits, stale with deodorant and sweat, wrap their heavy fragrance around me. I run my tongue through the thick mat of damp hair. His body shivers against me—through me. I savor the oils of his armpit as my hand runs down the blanket of soft hair that covers his chest and stomach. I feel his cock pulse with life as my fingers run along the waistband of his jeans. He shivers with nonstop ripples of desire no human has ever experienced. Sweat beads at his hairline before running down the sides of his face. I lick it up, tasting the fear and pleasure that his body is trying to flush out of its system.

I raise myself off his lap and sink down between his legs. I release the one button on his jeans. His body flinches. I tug the zipper down. The sound of its metal teeth vibrates around us. The bulge of his crotch is large and continues to swell from my touch. It stretches the thin material of his black boxer briefs. I feel the heat leaking out of the cotton fabric, ripe with his musk. He licks his lips, throwing his head back against the window of the train as I pull his pants and underwear down to his ankles.

His cock is thick and meaty. It slaps his stomach with a wet smack. I grasp the base of it and pull it toward me. Its large piss-slit spreads open. His precum escapes to the tip, pooling between his cock's lips before sliding down his shaft. I run my tongue up the length of his cock, gathering his precum on my tongue. Its potent flavors awaken my hunger—it's time to awaken his.

I pump his swelling cock, greasing it with his own lube. The veins in his shaft are a dark purplish red. They pulse with need. I stand up and straddle his body. I solidify my shadow even more so I won't pass through him during our ride. I raise his arms above his head and bury my face once again in his sweaty armpit. I suck the moisture from his skin. I lower myself onto his lap, feeling the thickness of him pressing against my ass. I rock up and down with the rhythm of the train and I open my ass, allowing his cock to slip inside me.

Rafe's eyes are closed. His moans rise above the other sounds in the car. Sounds I have yet to let him hear. His body shines with sweat as the electric rails spark, sending a bluish glow through the tunnels. I run my tongue down his neck, tasting his salty skin. I lick the soft, silky hair that lies across his chest. I roll his left nipple between my lips. I bite it and he arches. I let his body slip into my shadow but only for a moment, feeling the pulse of his blood rushing through the veins of his body.

His heart beats faster as the pleasure mounts to heights he's never known. His groans of agonizing pleasure escape through parted lips. Sweat drips down his chest in long, thick, salty rivers. His cock is swelling inside me. It's expanding and throbbing. His pulse becomes mine. His mind is a blur of images and emotions. He throws his head from side to side as his groans turn into painful screams of release.

He awakens in the subway car beneath the streets of Boston with the screams caught in his throat. I stand in the shadows and watch him. He sits up. Sweat has saturated his clothing. Beads of perspiration hang from the curly strands of his hair. The other passengers stare at him as he releases a deep, guttural moan. He shivers as he begins to ejaculate in his pants. His body shakes uncontrollably as the orgasm races through his body. As the final spasm dies, he looks around the train, realizing he is back in his own world. It was his usual twenty-two-minute commute, but in my world his ride lasted much longer. I stand in the tunnel watching the last train as it fades into the darkness. I can feel the pangs of hunger rippling through Rafe's body. His appetite for me has begun.

❖

The last train of the night isn't due for another few hours. I stroll through the damp, unused tunnels beneath the city as a way to pass the time. These areas of the subway system are barren lands, forgotten portions of subway lines never realized. The air is still. The only movement here comes from the rats that scurry from place to place in search of food or water. It's been two days since Rafe tasted my world.

His hunger for me continues to gnaw at him, growing with intensity and fervor. He's scared at what he feels but knows he cannot escape it. He has avoided the subway hoping that the hunger will subside—knowing that it won't.

I make my way back to the buzzing sounds of the electric rails. The dark tunnels sporadically illuminate from the electric flares caused by the dripping water and ancient exposed wires coiled around the ground like thousands of angry snakes. The snapping and cracking echo in the silence. The air shifts. Someone has violated my space and entered the tunnels. I inhale the new scent. I recognize the redolence; Rafe wanders somewhere in the distance. He has come for me. I can feel his hunger— his desire. I change my direction and go to him.

Rafe is coming toward me. I stop and blend into the shadows, listening to him approach. His footsteps crunch under the stones that cover the ground. His silhouette rounds the corner of the tunnel. He pauses. I hear his breath in the silence, hear his heart beat through the still air. I step out of the shadows. I feel him shiver from my sudden presence. The air circulates with his energy. I wait, for he must come to me. He takes a step forward. His footing is unsure, hesitant. He cannot fight what must be. He gives in to his desires and comes to me. We stand face-to-face.

"I had to find you." His voice quivers with a nervous excitement.

"Of course you did. I've been expecting you."

"Why am I here?"

"You tell me."

"I don't know. I can't get you out of me. When I'm asleep, I dream of you. When I'm awake, I think of you. When I fuck one of my clients, I'm fucking you."

"Your desire for me has consumed you. That's good." I stroke his cheek with my finger. "What is it you want from me, Rafe?"

"The other night…wherever that was…your train…your reality… it was like nothing I had ever experienced. I want to go back. Take me there again, please. Nothing else will ever be able to satisfy me like that night."

"There's no turning back this time."

"From what?" Rafe's eyes flinch with my words. Fear causes his hesitation.

I decide to ignore his last question. The answer could give him a way out, and then I would have to take him by force. That is such an unpleasant thing to do—not that I wouldn't, but I prefer if they come willingly. I pick him up and push him against the cold, damp wall. His eyes smolder with sexual energy. He wants this. He wants me. His heart pounds in his chest. His blood rushes through his veins. I feel the heat of his body filling the air of the tunnel. His scent is intoxicating. The wind increases through the tunnel. My cape billows in the breeze. The last train is making its final run of the night. Rafe must be prepared to board.

I slip my hand down his pants. My fingers sink through the thick tangles of his pubic hair. I reach the base of his cock, hard and pulsing with desire. I flicker, slipping my finger down his piss-slit. I stroke him from the inside out. His legs buckle. I hold him up as I continue to prime his cock. I pull my hand away. The wind swirls around us as the train approaches.

Rafe pulls his T-shirt off. His body is warm and damp against the chill of the air. I run my tongue down his chest, following the thin line of hair that runs down his stomach, stopping just above his navel. I feel his fingers grab hold of my solidified body as I remove his shoes; the heavy scent of his feet drifts up around us. I unbutton his jeans and tug the zipper down. He's not wearing any underwear tonight. His thick cock bobs in the air as I tug his pants down to his ankles. The familiar sent of his crotch engulfs me. I bury my face below his low-hanging balls. I inhale the deep, musky fumes of his ass.

The walls begin to vibrate. The electrical rails sizzle and snap as the last train continues its nightly run. Rafe groans as I stretch my tongue and run it over his tight, hairy ass. I taste his ass sweat. I slip my finger up his ass. I fuck him with my finger extending further into him. Crystal-clear drops of precum form on the tip of his cock, and then dribble down the shaft. I run my tongue along the pulsing veins. His precum flows into my mouth. I lick the tip of his cock before bringing the head into my mouth.

Rafe tightens the grip on my head as I let the entire length of his cock slide into my mouth. I start off with long, slow glides up and down his shaft, pulling more of his warm precum into my mouth. I swallow every drop. I soon learn that he is the aggressive one in the party. He takes over fucking my mouth, pounding my face with his damp, sweaty crotch. I flicker again, expanding my finger in his ass. It swells and grows inside him, pulsing and pushing his orgasm closer to the surface. His moans of pleasure increase as I feel his orgasm rise to the surface. He begins to ejaculate as the train rounds the corner. Wave after wave of his hot, white cum splashes into my mouth and falls down my throat. He thinks he's finished—he's wrong. He tries to pull out, but I refuse to let up on his cock. His moans turn to screams as he experiences pleasures that his mind cannot process. His voice echoes over the noise of the train as he begins to come again, filling my mouth and stomach with his seed—his soul.

Rafe continues to ejaculate as the subway cars rush by us, throwing up dirt and debris. His body quivers as he begins to come again. I must be careful not to take it all. My plan for him does not include taking his life. As hungry as I am, I must keep him alive. I pull him into me and flicker as his orgasm—his life—nears the end. I attach his essence to me and pull it away from his body, creating a mirror image or semi-body of his human form. We enter the last car of the train.

I stand behind Rafe, or what has become of him, and look out the window of the last train. His near-lifeless semi-body is lying near the rails where we left it, shimmering with the sweat of our activity. I lean into him, smelling his pungent odor.

"Is that me?" Rafe asks even though he knows the answer.

"It's your human form."

"Am I dead?"

"No, I wouldn't have done that to you. I need your human form to exist."

"I don't understand what you want from me." Rafe turns and looks at me. His eyes are deep spheres of green set within the semi-translucent body—a shell of his human form. He looks over my shoulder. I let the veil of deception fall on this, his final journey. He now sees the hell that I have brought him to.

"Do you like your new home?" I turn and stand beside him. The train is the same as in his world, as are most things in our alternate realities, but the passengers on my train are quite different from the ones he's used to seeing. My riders never leave. They can't. They are the trapped forms of the men I have captured over the centuries. They hang suspended from the metal handrails of the train's roof, their hands bound above their heads. Their naked semi-bodies sway and rock from the motion of the train that never stops, nor ends. Their cocks remain engorged from the unending pleasure that prevails in my world. Their semi-bodies glisten with sweat. The scent of their sexual exertion permeates the air.

"I don't understand." He looks at me, then back out through the mass of naked men. "Is this my future?"

"It's not only your future, it's your purpose—your destiny. Our individual journeys have become one. You see, my plan for you started out like many of the others. I wanted to take your soul, making you a shadower so that you could join my other boys. But when I found out about your gift, I realized that your purpose was greater than that. I needed your human form to survive."

"My gift?"

"You, like these men around you, are special. You have an extraordinary gift of sexual energy. You are insatiable. You have conditioned your body over the years to refresh and recharge your sexual ability quicker than most men. Shadowers like myself need the souls of men in order to survive. You see, a man's soul is part of his sexual identity. When a man ejaculates, he releases a part of his soul. It's through their orgasms that we feed. The men you see around you have become the vessels from which their souls flow. You are one of those vessels. When your human body has sex, your orgasm will flow through this." I touch his sweat dampened chest. "This body that I've created will allow us to feed." I silence my tongue and give him time to absorb what I've told him.

"Did you do all this?" Rafe looks at me and then back out at the hundreds of naked bodies swaying around us.

"Some might say these men made a pact with the devil, but alas the agreement that led them here had nothing to do with Lucifer. Their agreement, spoken or otherwise, was with me. I allowed them access to my world. In return for sparing their lives, I took a piece of them, an image, if you will, of their body. That is what they are—it's what you are. These semi-bodies will stay suspended in my world, living in a state of constant pleasure. Some men readily agreed to my terms, anything for what they truly desired. The ones that didn't agree, well, they're here as well. I took them by force. Lucky for you, you were one of the more agreeable ones."

"But I didn't agree to any of this."

"Yes, you did. You came to me in the subway. You asked me to take you here again, that you couldn't get me out of you, so here we are. You'll never be without me again." I run my finger down his chest. His cock responds to my touch. "You want me just as much as you did before, maybe even more. Why deny it?"

"What about my body?"

"You will awaken very soon and go about your life, oblivious to what has happened." I grab his arms and bring them between us. "When your body has sex, the orgasm will flow through this altered state I've created and feed us." I pull out a leather strap. I tie his wrists together. "You will live here in my Netherworld in a constant state of pleasure and arousal. Unfortunately, that means we will eventually have to dispose of your body."

"What do you mean?"

"The human mind cannot sustain itself indefinitely once split, nor can it endure the residual pleasures that it will experience here in my Netherworld. It will eventually break down, causing insanity. When your human form reaches that point, and it will, your mirror image will be of no use to us. We will return to your world and remove your life, thus consuming your soul permanently."

He doesn't fight when I pull his arms up and bind him to the metal rails of the car. His armpits are damp. Sweat drips through the thick curls of hair and then runs down the sides of his semi-body. I run my tongue through his left pit, savoring his ripe scent. "Yes, that's desire I taste in your sweat." I grab his engorged cock. "Good, you're already getting acclimated to your new surroundings. Let me show you what you have to look forward to."

The soul next to Rafe begins to shudder. I believe his name is Jeremy. His moans of pleasure are deep, guttural, and animalistic. It will be a good feed. Jeremy's image sways with the motion of the train. I fall to my knees. I open my mouth as the first drop of cum pools at the tip of Jeremy's cock. He ejaculates. My hand fondles Rafe's cock as Jeremy's warm cum sprays like a broken faucet into my waiting mouth. I slip the head of Jeremy's cock between my lips as the last of this orgasm races through his shaft. Jeremy's semi-body shivers and then relaxes. I lick my lips and run my tongue over Jeremy's softening cock before turning my attention back to Rafe.

As I stand mesmerized by Rafe's essence, the door connecting the last two cars opens with a loud rattle. Derrick, one of my favorite boys, is standing at the other end. I can feel his hunger. He comes to me—to Rafe. I took Derrick a little over a year ago in a small town in southern Vermont. It was during one of our carnival days. He's been by my side every night since. He's now the conductor of my train. We ride the rails through my Netherworld searching for those special young men who can give us what we want and need to survive—their unending pleasure followed by their souls. Derrick stands in front of Rafe's semi-body. He smiles at my selection.

"I take it you approve?"

"I never doubt your abilities." Derrick runs his tongue through the sweat-dampened hair that covers Rafe's chest. "He tastes so good."

Rafe's body begins to quiver. His human form has awakened and is going about his business as usual. Rafe closes his eyes as a loud groan escapes his parted lips. The first time as a vessel is always the most powerful. Derrick kneels in front of Rafe's glistening body. My hand is on his shoulder. We wait as Rafe's orgasm builds and races through his body. Rafe gasps and shakes from side to side. His groans turn to screams as his orgasm, his soul rushes out of him. A thick, heavy stream of white cum explodes from Rafe's swollen cock, showering Derrick's face. I lean down and lick a trail of it off Derrick's cheek. We kiss, sharing Rafe's cum between us. Rafe's warm, tart soul stirs my hunger. I kneel down next to Derrick, and together we feed from our newest arrival as my train, the last train, continues its unending ride through my Netherworld.

AFTERWORD

Trains don't run themselves. It takes a great crew working in perfect sync and harmony to get us to our destinations. Books about trains are no different, so kudos must go out to the people who helped keep us on schedule.

First of all, I'd like to thank the wonderful authors—truly creative engines that drove this incredible journey with their time, talent, and imagination. But back at the station house, thanks also go out to Radclyffe and all the wonderful people at Bold Strokes Books who gave us space to lay the track (so to speak) and made the whole thing sparkle like a silver miracle.

My engineer's cap is also tipped in the direction of Bill Holden, Dale Chase, Gavin Atlas, and Steve Berman for their inspiration and support in making whatever weirdness comes to my mind a reality.

And last, but certainly not least, a big thank you to the passengers out there for buying the fares and letting us take you to places you might not have gone otherwise. We hope you've enjoyed the trip and we look forward to traveling with you again.

Even though we're not exactly Amtrak…

CONTRIBUTOR BIOGRAPHIES

JEFF MANN has published three books of poetry, *Bones Washed with Wine*, *On the Tongue*, and *Ash: Poems from Norse Mythology*; two collections of personal essays, *Edge: Travels of an Appalachian Leather Bear* and *Binding the God: Ursine Essays from the Mountain South*; a book of poetry and memoir, *Loving Mountains, Loving Men*; and a volume of short fiction, *A History of Barbed Wire*, which won a Lambda Literary Award. He teaches creative writing at Virginia Tech in Blacksburg, Virginia.

ROB ROSEN (www.therobrosen.com), San Francisco author of the novels *Sparkle: The Queerest Book You'll Ever Love*, the Lambda Literary Award–nominated *Divas Las Vegas*, *Hot Lava*, and *Southern Fried*, has had short stories featured in more than 150 anthologies. He also has his own collection of erotic shorts, *Good & Hot*.

'NATHAN BURGOINE (n8an.livejournal.com) is an expat Brit living in Ottawa, Canada, with his husband, Daniel. His previous works appear in *Fool for Love* (Cleis Press), *I Like It Like That* (Arsenal Pulp Press), *I Do Two* (MLR Press), *Tented* (Lethe Press), and *Blood Sacraments* (Bold Strokes Books), and he has also appeared in issues of *5x5* literary magazine. Riding the Silver-Blue train from Vancouver to Toronto on his honeymoon was grand, except for trying to wedge himself in a bed designed for someone about a foot shorter.

JEFFREY RICKER (jeffreyricker.wordpress.com) is a writer, editor, and graphic designer. His writing has appeared in the literary magazine *Collective Fallout* and the anthologies *Paws and Reflect*, *Fool for Love: New Gay Fiction*, *Blood Sacraments*, *Men of the Mean Streets*, and *Speaking Out*. His first novel, *Detours*, was published in November 2011 by Bold Strokes Books. A magna cum laude graduate of the

University of Missouri School of Journalism, he lives with his partner, Michael, and two dogs, and is working on his second novel.

HANK EDWARDS (www.hankedwardsbooks.com) is the author of the Charlie Heggensford series: *Fluffers, Inc.*, *A Carnal Cruise*, and the Lambda Award Finalist *Vancouver Nights*, all available from Lethe Press. He has also published three books through Loose Id: *Holed Up*, *Destiny's Bastard*, and *Plus Ones*, as well as over three dozen short stories in a variety of magazines and anthologies. A proud member of the Story Orgy group, he posts prompt inspired story chapters every Monday morning on his blog.

ERASTES (www.erastes.com) is the pen name of a female author. She was born in Essex, England, and has lived in more places than she can remember. She started to write in 2003 after discovering that no one seemed to be writing gay historical fiction, but was happy to find out she was wrong. She's got three novels and six novellas in print and ebook, and her second novel, *Transgressions*, was shortlisted for a Lambda Literary Award.

RICK R. REED (www.rickrreed.com) is the author of dozens of published novels, novellas, and short stories. He is a two-time EPIC eBook Award winner. His work has caught the attention of *Unzipped* magazine—"The Stephen King of gay horror"; Lambda Literary—"A writer that doesn't disappoint"; and *Dark Scribe* magazine—"an established brand—perhaps the most reliable contemporary author for thrillers that cross over between the gay fiction market and speculative fiction." He lives in Seattle. Visit his blog at rickrreedreality.blogspot.com.

DALE CHASE (dalechasestrokes.com) has written male erotica for over a decade with numerous stories in magazines and anthologies. She has two story collections in print: *The Company He Keeps: Victorian Gentlemen's Erotica* from Bold Strokes Books and *If The Spirit Moves You: Ghostly Gay Erotica* from Lethe Press. She is currently at work on an erotic Western novel.

DANIEL M. JAFFE (danieljaffe.tripod.com) is author of the novel *The Limits of Pleasure* (Bear Bones Books, 2010), which was a Finalist for a *ForeWord Magazine* Book of the Year Award when initially published in 2001. An excerpt of the novel appeared in *Best Gay Erotica 2003*. Dan is also author of the fiction chapbook *One-Foot Lover* (Seven Kitchens Press, 2009) and compiler/editor of *With Signs and Wonders: An International Anthology of Jewish Fabulist Fiction* (Invisible Cities Press, 2000).

GAVIN ATLAS (GavinAtlas.com) studied creative writing under Faye Moskowitz at George Washington University as well as under Bill Wright at the LGBT Community Center in Manhattan. He was first published in 2007, and his best-selling collection of gay erotic short fiction, *The Boy Can't Help It*, was released in 2010.

JAY NEAL has very romantic notions about train travel that he got honestly from his father, a true train aficionado; he also has some odd and disturbing notions about what goes on inside those trains. He's also been fascinated by possibilities "On The Twentieth Century" ever since he performed in the musical of the same name. Murder and musicals! He's written stories since late in the last century and has published dozens in a number of magazines and anthologies. He and his partner recently celebrated eighteen years of domestic bliss by getting married in the District of Columbia. The adventure continues!

A transplanted Westerner, **J.D. BARTON** has worked as a freelance writer, social worker, and health care professional. Drawn to open spaces, he strives to include as much of the outdoors as he can in his writing, which includes novels and radio plays. When not writing, he spends time with his boyfriend and listens to Motown and all the great '70s singer/songwriters that inspired him to write in the first place.

JOSEPH BANETH ALLEN grew up in Camp Lejeune, North Carolina. An avid reader and writer, his short stories have appeared in *Blood Sacraments* and *Wings*. His nonfiction has been published in *OMNI*, *Popular Science*, *Final Frontier*, *Astronomy*, *Florida Living*, *Dog Fancy*, *Pet Life*, *eBay* magazine, and many others. He now lives with his family amongst an ever-growing collection of Big Little Books, Gold Key Comics, and G.I. Joes in Jacksonville, Florida, where he continues to write fiction and nonfiction.

DUSTY TAYLOR grew up in Los Angeles, near rails of the Santa Fe and Southern Pacific main lines, and has always been enchanted by passing trains. As a child he played on the engines at Travel Town in Griffith Park, where some of the engines in this story still reside today. Now living in San Francisco, Dusty enjoys searching out the many former routes that once carried trains along city streets.

WILLIAM HOLDEN's (www.williamholdenwrites.com) writing career spans more than a decade, with over forty published short stories. He is co-founder and co-editor of Out in Print: Queer Book Reviews at www.outinprint.net. His first collection, *A Twist of Grimm*, is a Lambda Literary Award Finalist. His latest book, *Words to Die By*, will be published by Bold Strokes Books in 2012.

ABOUT THE EDITOR

Co-founder of Out in Print: Queer Book Reviews (www.outinprint.
net), Jerry L. Wheeler's erotica, fiction, and nonfiction has appeared
in a number of anthologies—most recently in *In Plain View* and *Wings*
(Bold Strokes Books) as well as *Melt in Your Mouth* (Lethe Press). His
first effort at editing, *Tented: Gay Erotic Stories from Under the Big
Top*, was a Lambda Literary Award finalist. He is currently preparing
a collection of his short fiction and working on his first novel—which
has been titled, at various times, *Seventy Times Seven*, *The Dead Book*,
and *The Novel from HELL*. Its current working title is *Why Won't This
Damn Thing Write Itself?*

Books Available From Bold Strokes Books

Franky Gets Real by Mel Bossa. A four-day getaway. Five childhood friends. Five shattering confessions...and a forgotten love unearthed. (978-1-60282-585-7)

Riding the Rails: Locomotive Lust and Carnal Cabooses, edited by Jerry Wheeler. Some of the hottest writers of gay erotica spin tales of *Riding the Rails*. (978-1-60282-586-4)

Rescue Me by Julie Cannon. Tyler Logan reluctantly agrees to pose as the girlfriend of her in-the-closet gay BFF at his company's annual retreat, but she didn't count on falling for Kristin, the boss's wife. (978-1-60282-582-6)

Snowbound by Cari Hunter. *"The policewoman got shot and she's bleeding everywhere. Get someone here in one hour or I'm going to put her out of her misery."* It's an ultimatum that will forever change the lives of police officer Sam Lucas and Dr. Kate Myles. (978-1-60282-581 9)

High Impact by Kim Baldwin. Thrill seeker Emery Lawson and Adventure Outfitter Pasha Dunn learn you can never truly appreciate what's important and what you're capable of until faced with a sudden and stark reminder of your own mortality. (978-1-60282-580-2)

Murder in the Irish Channel by Greg Herren. Chanse MacLeod investigates the disappearance of a female activist fighting the Archdiocese of New Orleans and a powerful real estate syndicate. (978-1-60282-584-0)

Sheltering Dunes by Radclyffe. The seventh in the award-winning Provincetown Tales. The pasts, presents, and futures of three women collide in a single moment that will alter all their lives forever. (978-1-60282-573-4)

Holy Rollers by Rob Byrnes. Partners in life and crime Grant Lambert and Chase LaMarca assemble a team of gay and lesbian criminals to steal millions from a right-wing mega-church, but the gang's plans are complicated by an "ex-gay" conference, the FBI, and a corrupt reverend with his own plans for the cash. (978-1-60282-578-9)

History's Passion: Stories of Sex Before Stonewall, edited by Richard Labonté. Four acclaimed erotic authors re-imagine the past…Welcome to the hidden queer history of men loving men not so very long—and centuries—ago. (978-1-60282-576-5)

Lucky Loser by Yolanda Wallace. Top tennis pros Sinjin Smythe and Laure Fortescue reach Wimbledon desperate to claim tennis's crown jewel, but will their feelings for each other get in the way? (978-1-60282-575-8)

Mystery of The Tempest: A Fisher Key Adventure by Sam Cameron. Twin brothers Denny and Steven Anderson love helping people and fighting crime alongside their sheriff dad on sun-drenched Fisher Key, Florida, but Denny doesn't dare tell anyone he's gay, and Steven has secrets of his own to keep. (978-1-60282-579-6)

Better Off Red: Vampire Sorority Sisters Book 1 by Rebekah Weatherspoon. Every sorority has its secrets, and college freshman Ginger Carmichael soon discovers that her pledge is more than a bond of sisterhood—it's a lifelong pact to serve six bloodthirsty demons with a lot more than nutritional needs. (978-1-60282-574-1)

Detours by Jeffrey Ricker. Joel Patterson is heading to Maine for his mother's funeral, and his high school friend Lincoln has invited himself along on the ride—and into Joel's bed—but when the ghost of Joel's mother joins the trip, the route is likely to be anything but straight. (978-1-60282-577-2)

Three Days by L.T. Marie. In a town like Vegas where anything can happen, Shawn and Dakota find that the stakes are love at all costs, and it's a gamble neither can afford to lose. (978-1-60282-569-7)

Swimming to Chicago by David-Matthew Barnes. As the lives of the adults around them unravel, high school students Alex and Robby form an unbreakable bond, vowing to do anything to stay together—even if it means leaving everything behind. (978-1-60282-572-7)

Hostage Moon by AJ Quinn. Hunter Roswell thought she had left her past behind, until a serial killer begins stalking her. Can FBI profiler Sara Wilder help her find her connection to the killer before he strikes on blood moon? (978-1-60282-568-0)

Erotica Exotica: Tales of Sex, Magic, and the Supernatural, edited by Richard Labonté. Today's top gay erotica authors offer sexual thrills and perverse arousal, spooky chills, and magical orgasms in these stories exploring arcane mystery, supernatural seduction, and sex that haunts in a manner both weird and wondrous. (978-1-60282-570-3)

Blue by Russ Gregory. Matt and Thatcher find themselves in the crosshairs of a psychotic killer stalking gay men in the streets of Austin, and only a 103-year-old nursing home resident holds the key to solving the murders—but can she give up her secrets in time to save them? (978-1-60282-571-0)

Balance of Forces: Toujours Ici by Ali Vali. Immortal Kendal Richoux's life began during the reign of Egypt's only female pharaoh, and history has taught her the dangers of getting too close to anyone who hasn't harnessed the power of time, but as she prepares for the most important battle of her long life, can she resist her attraction to Piper Marmande? (978-1-60282-567-3)

Wings: Subversive Gay Angel Erotica, edited by Todd Gregory. A collection of powerfully written tales of passion and desire centered on the aching beauty of angels. (978-1-60282-565-9)

Contemporary Gay Romances by Felice Picano. This collection of short fiction from legendary novelist and memoirist Felice Picano are as different from any standard "romances" as you can get, but they will linger in the mind and memory. (978-1-60282-639-7)

Sex and Skateboards by Ashley Bartlett. Sex and skateboards and surfing on the California coast. What more could anyone want? Alden McKenna thinks that's all she needs, until she meets Weston Duvall. (978-1-60282-562-8)

Waiting in the Wings by Melissa Brayden. Jenna has spent her whole life training for the stage, but the one thing she didn't prepare for was Adrienne. Is she ready to sacrifice what she's worked so hard for in exchange for a shot at something much deeper? (978-1-60282-561-1)

Pirate's Fortune: Supreme Constellations Book Four by Gun Brooke. Set against the backdrop of war, captured mercenary Weiss Kyakh is persuaded to work undercover with bio-android Madisyn Pimm, which foils her plans to escape, but kindles unexpected love. (978-1-60282-563-5)

Suite Nineteen by Mel Bossa. Psychic Ben Lebeau moves into Shilts Manor, where he meets seductive Lennox Van Kemp and his clan of Métis—guardians of a spiritual conspiracy dating back to Christ. But are Ben's psychic abilities strong enough to save him? (978-1-60282-564-2)

Speaking Out: LGBTQ Youth Stand Up, edited by Steve Berman. Inspiring stories written for and about LGBTQ teens of overcoming adversity (against intolerance and homophobia) and experiencing life after "coming out." (978-1-60282-566-6)

Forbidden Passions by MJ Williamz. Passion burns hotter when it's forbidden, and the fire between Katie Prentiss and Corrine Staples in antebellum Louisiana is raging out of control. (978-1-60282-641-0)

Harmony by Karis Walsh. When Brook Stanton meets a beautiful musician who threatens the security of her conventional, predetermined future, will she take a chance on finding the harmony only love creates? (978-1-60282-237-5)

nightrise by Nell Stark and Trinity Tam. In the third book in the everafter series, when Valentine Darrow loses her soul, Alexa must cross continents to find a way to save her. (978-1-60282-238-2)

Men of the Mean Streets, edited by Greg Herren and J.M. Redmann. Dark tales of amorality and criminality by some of the top authors of gay mysteries. (978-1-60282-240-5)

Women of the Mean Streets, edited by J.M. Redmann and Greg Herren. Murder, mayhem, sex, and danger—these are the stories of the women who dare to tackle the mean streets. (978-1-60282-241-2)

Firestorm by Radclyffe. Firefighter paramedic Mallory "Ice" James isn't happy when the undisciplined Jac Russo joins her command, but lust isn't something either can control—and they soon discover ice burns as fiercely as flame. (978-1-60282-232-0)

The Best Defense by Carsen Taite. When socialite Aimee Howard hires former homicide detective Skye Keaton to find her missing niece, she vows not to mix business with pleasure, but she soon finds Skye hard to resist. (978-1-60282-233-7)

After the Fall by Robin Summers. When the plague destroys most of humanity, Taylor Stone thinks there's nothing left to live for, until she meets Kate, a woman who makes her realize love is still alive and makes her dream of a future she thought was no longer possible. (978-1-60282-234-4)

Accidents Never Happen by David-Matthew Barnes. From the moment Albert and Joey meet by chance beneath a train track on a street in Chicago, a domino effect is triggered, setting off a chain reaction of murder and tragedy. (978-1-60282-235-1)

In Plain View, edited by Shane Allison. Best-selling gay erotica authors create the stories of sex and desire modern readers crave. (978-1-60282-236-8)